SKYBORN

BATTLE OF THE HORIZON TRILOGY BOOK I

CAMERON BOLLING

ISBN-13: 978-1-69340-374-3

Published by Realmwrite Publishing

For Diana,
who gifted me the book that sparked a love for fantasy.

CHAPTER ONE

A thick-shafted arrow protruded from the boy's chest. Dark blood pooled below him, picking up swirls of sand as it trickled through cracks in the rust-colored stone ground. The flint head punctured deep between his cracked ribs, and the feathered fletching cast a shadow over his glassy eyes. Stuck vertical in the boy's body, the rough-hewn nock rose nearly five feet off the ground, and the wooden shaft rivaled the thickness of two fingers held side-by-side. No human could possibly shoot an arrow of such proportions; this arrow belonged to the eclipsers.

Oleja stood at a distance alongside the dozen or so others who gathered to behold the scene. None approached the boy, and she knew they wouldn't dare to for a while yet. Finding people dead on the ground never came as much of a surprise, but this one stood apart from the others. The eclipsers killed those who attempted escape—never the innocent, rule-following miners. The boy on the ground fell

1

into the latter category. Before finding an arrow in his back, he hadn't done so much as look up to the strip of sky visible from the canyon floor. But now he lay dead.

Oleja looked up the cliffside to where the arrow came from. No figure stood there—not that it would've mattered if one did. The people of the village never saw more than a dark silhouette of their oppressors, backlit by the sun above. But even if she couldn't see an eclipser looking down, she knew they were watching. They were always watching.

For generations as far back as anyone could remember, the eclipsers had held Oleja's people in that canyon, forcing them to mine in exchange for their supper. The more they dragged up out of the mines, the more food they got in return, lowered down to the canyon floor with the same system of pulleys they used to send the products of the previous day's labor up to the surface.

Living in the canyon under the eclipsers' reign came with two rules: spend the days mining, and don't try to escape. Breaking the first resulted in starvation. Breaking the second resulted in death. Given how few people in the village sought out starvation or death as their goals, they fell in line easily. As long as they followed those two simple rules, they were safe—at least from the eclipsers.

Until now.

Whispers drifted through the crowd. Fear ebbed out in ripples from the boy's body. Oleja set her jaw as she let her eyes fall upon him once more. His death served as a grim reminder; things changed. Safety was never guaranteed.

Though they believed that if they remained docile, the eclipsers would leave them be, it wasn't like such a promise had been agreed upon and punctuated with the signing of a document and a firm handshake. Relations between the two groups could be called many things, but *civil* found no home among those ranks. Safety seemed to dwindle by the day, and if they didn't do something, Oleja's people could soon meet their end—picked off one at a time by an unseen force a thousand feet above their heads. Two rules, but they didn't matter anymore. All bets were off.

Fortunately, Oleja had never been good at following rules—those two in particular.

She ducked her head and made her way out of the crowd. The bag across her shoulder bounced against her hip with each step, the contents rattling and clanking within. She held it with one hand to muffle the noises until more space lay between her and the somber gathering. Though she felt a pang of guilt doing so, she tried to push the image of the boy, dead on the ground, from her mind. Dwelling on hopelessness would lend her no boons. She hadn't known him beyond merely in passing. Death found a comfortable home down in the canyon anyhow—with business as treacherous as mining, Oleja doubted she could count the number of her ancestors who lay buried in cave-ins deep below her feet. Luck shone bright upon those who lived more than fifty years in their conditions. Death had lost its sting long ago.

The ground sloped upwards beneath her feet as she hurried through the village, heading to the northern end of the canyon. She passed others as she went, people going about their morning routines as usual despite the commotion back behind her. They came and went from homes and workshops carrying baskets of goods or armfuls of tools.

Buildings receded into the face of the canyon walls, each only one or two rooms deep beyond the front door, though families or other groups often laid claim to more than one structure, acquiring dwellings that neighbored their own for their children when the previous inhabitants vacated the space. The rooms rose several stories high, set along ledges reached by staircases and ladders, but the people never built more than six or seven stories up. Climbing too high up the sides of the canyon served as the quickest way to find an arrow in one's back, so none were willing to live any higher despite hundreds of feet remaining between their doorways and the surface.

Between the canyon walls stretched streets and meeting places. Open fire pits provided the people of the village with places to cook their supper, lining the central river like guiding lights in the night. Streets ran the length of either bank. Bridges spanned the distance across at intervals, though the flow was neither particularly wide nor deep. Smaller channels branched off from the river, cut with tools to direct the water flow into shallow basins for bathing or doing laundry.

Up ahead loomed the north wall—a great structure of grey stone rising all the way up from the canyon floor to stand flush with the ground. It was a fine, clean-cut thing that had stood as her people's northern barrier for as long as any could remember. Who built it, no one knew, as it looked too fine a thing to be of eclipser make. Their captors were strong, and certainly cunning enough, but they did not seem to be of the fine-craftsman sort.

The south wall seemed more in the vein of what passed as fine eclipser handiwork. It too rose to the height of the ground above, though it was built from enormous boulders of orange-tinted stone to match that of the natural canyon. Piled high—and Oleja could only venture a guess as to how thick—it served its purpose well, keeping the people contained in their small stretch of land within the canyon.

Just before the north wall towered Oleja's objective. Referred to as "The Heap" among the people of the village, it lived up to its name well, as it was, indisputably, a heap. Every morning at daybreak, the eclipsers carted their junk down a walkway of rusted metal supports that hung out over the edge of the canyon just south of the wall. From there, they dumped whatever scraps they had lying around, usually rife with things Oleja didn't know the names for. It provided a supply of materials—wood, rusted bits of metal, and other odds and ends for the people to make use of in the mines. The junk swelled high in a hundred-foot-tall monument to the Old World—the world before the canyon, and before everything fell to ruin.

Oleja's morning routine included stopping by The Heap to sift through it for anything useful hidden among the utterly useless. Most considered The Heap trash, and they were mostly right, but every so often, buried beneath the garbage, a real gem of a find waited to be unearthed. Some others collected metals to melt them down for new tools, while all wooden beams found new homes down in the mines as supports if they retained some strength, or as firewood if not. Oleja sought the other stuff—odds and ends, knickknacks of all sorts, and the strange pieces she could turn into something new. Her bag bulged with stuff of that nature, stuff to tinker with. She kept the bag within reach at all hours. Tinkering let her mind rest and gave her something to do with her hands. Plus, what problem couldn't be solved with a few pieces of scrap? In Oleja's experience, none.

As she passed through the crowds, she kept her ears alert, listening to the comments the other people of the village made to one another. Sometimes she picked up on just the right conversation—any mention of a broken cot or window shutter, rickety chair or other damaged item in need of repair. She liked to take note of who needed what, then find the pieces necessary to fix the problem at The Heap and return to do the work for them. She was skilled with her tools and wanted to use them to make living as slaves at the bottom of a canyon just a smidge more bearable. They were always thrilled to have her help, and she was more than happy to provide. Operating as an undercover repairwoman brought a tinge of excitement and purpose to an otherwise dull and cyclical life.

She followed along the river bank as she covered the final distance up to The Heap. The river came in through a heavy metal grate in the corner and ran along the left wall before settling into its path through the center of the canyon. This way it stayed clear of The Heap, as drinking water and old rusted metal made a bad combination.

Oleja's boots slid in the wet clay as she stepped up to the base of the immense pile. She threw aside a long, bent strip of metal and then a larger square chunk with a hole in the center lodged below it. Shifting things in The Heap came with a heavy dose of danger given how easily things could start sliding, but Oleja had mastered it through years of practice. Determining which pieces bore the weight of countless items above and which moved without consequence came naturally now.

Beneath the pieces she threw aside, Oleja found a large spring, which might have been useful if not so badly crushed. She first thought to toss it aside but ultimately held onto it instead. If she found nothing better, perhaps she could mend it.

"Raseari!"

Oleja paused when she heard her name. She knew the voice. Feigning busyness, she held up the spring again and looked it over.

"Oleja!" the voice called again, louder this time as the owner drew nearer. With an exasperated sigh, Oleja turned to look over her shoulder.

The woman marching towards her stood taller by several inches, and bore muscular arms, though Oleja had her beat there. Otherwise, she and Oleja looked much alike, though most in the village did; same tanned brown skin, same dark hair—though the other woman's was closer to brown and bound in a ponytail as opposed to Oleja's black braid, rarely tended to which left messy strands flying loose around her face.

The woman came within a few paces of Oleja and stopped, thin eyebrows raised as if implying a question she had yet to voice.

"Hi Jisi," said Oleja, waving the spring in halfhearted greeting. "Is there something you need?"

Jisi might have been considered the leader of the village, if anyone had claim to such a title. No one officially reigned over the people—save for the eclipsers. Instead, the people of the village tended to rally around whoever took charge in a way that seemed fair, or who was too strong or intimidating to question. Jisi sat somewhere in the middle.

"Yes, actually, there is something I need from you. A *haul*, Raseari. You haven't come out of the mines with so much as a pebble's-worth of copper—or anything—in a week. Just because food is divvied evenly doesn't mean you don't need to pull your weight around here. You're young and strong, and I see you go down into the mines every day. So, where's the haul?" Jisi looked down at Oleja with a cold and questioning glare. Her jaw clenched and muscles tensed. Behind her, a few people stopped and looked to see the cause of the disturbance.

"I'll have one tonight, don't worry about it," said Oleja as she ducked her head and stepped around Jisi. Jisi grabbed Oleja's arm and spun her around before she could run off.

"I will worry about it, because this isn't only about you,

or me, it's about everyone else down here. Everyone has to eat, so everyone who can lift a pickaxe has to mine. Those are the rules. That's how we survive. And I *know* you'll have a haul tonight, because that's how you play this game. You contribute nothing until someone takes notice, and then you show up toting a bag bursting with more than you could have possibly mined in a day. And then we have a food surplus for a few days, and everyone applauds you as a hero. But that's not enough. You need to bring up a haul every day, and do it so that everyone gets to eat, not just to get me off your back."

Oleja stood frozen to the spot as her heart beat faster. Jisi did not let go of her arm. More people overheard as Jisi's voice grew in power. A crowd began to form around the two of them.

"Jisi is right!" said a man from somewhere in the group. "Oleja has been taking advantage of us. She thinks she's better than everyone else."

"The girl's just lazy," said a woman.

Oleja wrenched her arm free of Jisi's grasp. She dropped the bent spring to the ground.

"These claims are false, I work just like everyone else," she said, raising her eyes to scan the crowd. She did her best to keep her voice calm. If she didn't diffuse the situation as quickly as possible, things could get bad fast.

"It's because she has been hanging around with the old man, Ude. He's Tor's blood," said a new voice. The words rippled through the crowd.

"Make her get double the haul or she gets executed!"

"Execute her now so she stops eating our food—we hardly have enough to go around as it is!"

Everything happened at once. Several people stepped forward and grabbed at Oleja. She yanked her arms away and backpedaled until her feet scrambled across the scrap at the base of The Heap. A voice in her head yelled for her to climb, but she wasn't fast enough. Hands grabbed her and pulled her in different directions. Oleja lashed out with her feet until the mob grappled those as well and held fast. Someone ripped her bag away from her, snapping the single strap.

"Stop! Let me go! Jisi!" Oleja called. Her eyes met Jisi's, but she found no sympathy there. She could expect no aid from her.

Despite her tugging and flailing, Oleja could not free any of her limbs. Each time she knocked a hand away, two more took its place, until they held her so tightly that she could hardly move at all. The mob pulled her down the street, shouting things she no longer paid attention to. Only the pounding of her own heart filled her ears as it drowned out the voices. Desperately, she ran through her options. They were few. Option one: get away. Option two: pacify the mob. Option three: die. Even if she got away from the mob, where would she go? The canyon walls and eclipsers above trapped her within. Losing her pursuers in the mines might work, but only until she needed to resurface for food and water. When she did, she'd be walking right back to her grave.

If she wanted to pacify them, she was on her own there

as well. Certainly no one in the village held strong enough feelings to consider vouching for her and risking their own neck with this mob—save Ude perhaps, but the people of the village would be all too happy to execute him alongside her. They'd been looking for an excuse to off the old man for decades. She was alone in this.

And she wouldn't die. Death was not an option. It never had been, and it never would be.

The mob threw Oleja to the ground, but before she managed to stand, they seized her wrists and ankles again and quickly bound them with rope. She lay in the center of a flat stone dais stained with dried blood. Four metal stakes poked up from the ground, their tips hammered deep into the rock. Her arms stretched out to either side and her legs splayed as the crowd tied each rope to a stake. The coarse rope burned her wrists and ankles as she tugged against the bonds. They didn't budge.

A procession broke through one side of the crowd—a line of people carrying wide stone slabs. The first reached her and placed the slab atop her chest. Not an unbearable amount of weight, but the slab-bearers lugged plenty more.

By the time they laid the third slab on the stack, Oleja struggled to breath, and with the fourth, the panic took over.

Her eyes flicked over the people around her. Some looked angry. Some, confused. Most filled out the crowd as merely passive bystanders, watching the morning's spectacle before heading down into the mines and forgetting about it altogether. And then she met Jisi's eyes again. She stood to the side, watching, her face devoid of any emotion.

A cold determined power swept through Oleja.

"Stop!" she shouted, forcing the air out despite the crushing weight on her chest. Pleading did not drive her voice, imbuing it not with the cry of someone desperate for life. It was a command. She looked to Jisi.

"Jisi. A word." Jisi raised an eyebrow but did not move. The slab-bearers looked between the two of them, uncertainty plain on their faces.

"I'd come to you, but I'm afraid that's not an option at the moment," said Oleja. For a beat, no one moved. Then Jisi looked to the slab-bearers and waved a hand. She stepped away from the crowd and walked to Oleja, crouching by her head.

"What is it?"

Oleja's words struggled to wriggle out from beneath the immense pressure on her chest, but after a labored inhale she managed. "You're right—when you confront me about my lack of a haul, I show up with a big one soon after. So, what does that mean if I die right now?"

Jisi narrowed her eyes. "I cannot be bribed, Raseari."

"No? Look around. Everyone is on edge. Food has been in short supply lately… There's talk of changing the mining grounds since the current ones are running dry. Setting up a new mine requires days of labor before any fruits are possible. You *know* all of this. A food surplus right now could keep up spirits long enough to make the shift. You need it—the *people* need it—and I can provide. But not if I'm dead." It took several breaths to get it all out, but she managed, slowly, relishing in the way Jisi's face changed as she spoke. For a long moment, Jisi only gazed silently out at the mob. Then she stood.

"Show's over... I'll handle it from here," called Jisi. A few groans of protest came forward in response, but everyone dispersed before Jisi had to issue another command. When only the two of them remained, Jisi lifted the slabs from Oleja's chest one by one and cut the ropes binding her to the stakes. Oleja's bag lay on the ground nearby, and she started towards it. Jisi clamped a hand down on her shoulder and held her in place.

"You had best lug a truly *impressive* haul out of those mines by sundown, or I will *personally* see to your execution. Is that understood?" Oleja did not turn to face her. She nodded her response. Jisi released her shoulder.

Oleja scooped up her bag in her arms, tucking the broken strap into her grip to keep it from hanging free, and hastened away towards the mines. She didn't need to turn and look back to know that Jisi's gaze stayed on her until she disappeared through the threshold that would take her deep underground.

CHAPTER TWO

W ith a torch held aloft in her right hand, Oleja wandered through the otherwise dark passageways of the mines. The walls crumbled. The support beams buckled and splintered—if they weren't gone altogether, taken away to be recycled in a newer, active section of the mines. The village abandoned this wing when Oleja still lay in a cradle, and in the dozen and a half years since, few had ventured through the halls. The entire sector had been bled dry of ores and minerals after years of mining, and now lay empty, a husk of its former opulence, useless to the people above. All except for Oleja.

As she rounded a bend, the torchlight illuminated a pile of rubble ahead, giving the impression that the passage ended at a dead-end due to a cave-in. Oleja approached and clambered up the pile. At the top near the ceiling, a thin opening just large enough for a person to squeeze through led into a deeper hollow. Oleja stuck her torch between a few rocks inside. She pushed her bag through the opening first, and it dropped down through a hole just beyond, hitting the floor somewhere out of sight and sending back a muted cacophony as proof. Oleja followed, crawling over the rubble and swinging her legs down the concealed hole.

She dropped and landed beside her bag. Reaching up, she pulled the torch free from where she wedged it, and after scooping up her bag, she started off down the hidden hallway.

The walls seemed more eager to meet in this section of the passageway, creating a space just wide enough for Oleja to pass through without her shoulders brushing the sides. The ceiling dipped lower too, and in a few places she had to stoop to avoid hitting her head. While the passages above had been cut long ago and since abandoned, more freshly carved stone lined the walls of this one. As she neared the end, her torchlight mingled with a similar dim orange light flickering out from the larger chamber beyond.

A wide, oval-shaped cavern with a high ceiling stretched before her. Stalagmites dotted the floor, some joining with stalactites on the ceiling to create columns of stone. Torches burned at intermittent spots around the cave. Light reflected off the various metal items that were scattered throughout but concentrated near a large rectangular block of clean-cut stone that sat near the left wall, leveled to serve as a worktable and decorated on all sides with carvings. A wooden figure made from a few beams assembled into the vague shape of a human stood guard by the workbench, showing off a suit of armor pieced together from various mismatched scraps of metal. At the far end of the cave, a thin sheet of wood leaned against the wall with a target drawn in charcoal on its face.

From where Oleja stood at the entrance, a handful of stairs led down to the main floor. She wedged her torch into a makeshift sconce by the door and then descended the stairs two at a time.

"You're usually down here earlier," came a gruff voice from the shadows.

Oleja shrugged as she made her way to the stone table. "Got caught up. Some people even declared the whole ruckus your fault, so I guess you've only got yourself to blame for the wait."

"My fault? And what have I done this time?"

"Talked to me, and apparently that's enough." Oleja lifted her bag and deposited it onto the surface of the workbench. "'It's the old man, he's Tor's blood,'" she said in a mocking tone.

"Old man? That's quite rude of them indeed. I haven't even reached my seventieth birthday!"

"You're the second-oldest in the village," said Oleja, raising an eyebrow to herself as she opened her bag and began pulling out tools.

"Until I'm the first, I see no reason to point it out."

"Fair enough, old man." Oleja selected the tools she needed and took a look at the broken strap of her bag. The voice from the shadows was quiet for a moment. Oleja turned to where it had come from.

Ude stepped into the torchlight as he approached her, a

gentle smile playing across his lips. The low light exaggerated the wrinkles and stubble on his face, highlighting his features with shadows. His silver hair hung in a short ponytail.

"Anyhow—what an impolite greeting I offered. Where are my manners?"

"Buried beneath the sarcasm, as usual."

"Right alongside yours then, hm?" The reflected light winked in Ude's eyes. "Good morning, Oleja. I hope I didn't cause too much trouble for you."

Oleja shrugged and turned back to her worktable. "Nearly got executed, no big deal."

Ude walked around to the opposite side of the table. Oleja did not meet his eyes.

"That can't be just because you've spoken to me…"

Oleja put the tools down and leaned on her hands. "Jisi noticed that I haven't been mining… again. A mob formed. They accused me of not pulling my weight; didn't want me eating their food anymore if I wasn't going to bring up a haul." When she finished speaking, she grabbed a heavy canvas bag from a hook hammered into the cavern wall and made her way to the corner near the door. A mound of ores and crystals rose up from the floor, piled taller than Oleja. She opened the bag and shoveled ore inside by the fistful.

When she discovered the untouched cavern, hidden below the old section of the mines, she found it rich with ores and minerals. She stockpiled them there and brought portions to the surface periodically. Nothing could come of bringing it all up at once except a food surplus so grand the people wouldn't know what to do with it all. They'd get comfortable with their full bellies, and when the food supply wore thin again, no one would be used to living on half-full stomachs and mining desperately for what they had. It would ruin them. She did the village a favor by keeping the hoard a secret and surfacing with it in portions. That, and it bought her time to do more important work, work she wouldn't have time for if she spent her days with a pick in hand.

That work culminated in a plan—a plan she'd been working on for years. She was going to escape the canyon. And she was going to get everyone else out with her.

"Well, *are* you pulling your weight?" asked Ude. Oleja closed the bag, now full to bursting, and dropped it by the entrance. She turned to face him.

"Yes. I'm doing work that's more important than anyone else's in the entire village," she said, annoyance creeping into her words.

"But you aren't mining, so everyone else has to mine a little more so that you can eat too." Ude leaned against the worktable with his hands clasped in front of him, a thin smile on his face.

"I'm working to get us out of here. *Everyone*. They do a little bit of work for me, and I do everything for them. In the end, I do more than my share. They will owe me more than a few strikes with their picks and a cut of the day's food."

"But you have yet to actually make those contributions. So, in the meantime, you are in debt to them."

Oleja returned to her tinkering bag and withdrew a cloth-wrapped bundle—her lunch—and took a seat with her back to a stalagmite. "Can it," she said with a glare. "Everyone else in the village would happily see you vanish, don't add me to that list too."

Ude held up his hands in mock surrender. His smile had not faded; he didn't pester Oleja to anger her, rather he did so only playfully—that she knew. But it didn't make the jabs any less annoying.

"I thought only to invite you along to see their side of things," he said as he took a seat on the ground near her. He pulled a similarly-wrapped package from a small satchel he wore over a set of dirtied clothes not unlike Oleja's, though while he wore a loose shirt that might once have been white, she had one of tan canvas, torn and tattered, that stopped at her midriff and left her arms equally exposed. Their grey pants and leather boots were almost identical, however—made in the style common throughout the village.

Together, they unwrapped their lunch and began to eat. Hard bread and tough meat made up the bulk of the rations, but they were accustomed to nothing better except on rare occasions. Though hard and tough, they found the bread and meat more edible and considerably less hard or tough than the rocks and metals—the only items they could produce on their own—so they ate without complaint. Some said the food had gotten worse overtime. Ude made such claims often. As one of the oldest in the village, he would certainly be the one to know, though Oleja sometimes suspected not that the eclipsers started sending down worse food, but that the others in the village gave Ude the worst food of the batch when they divided it up. He was not widely liked, that was easy to say. He earned the contempt by no fault of his own, rather from residual hatred for his father, Tor.

Tor was once considered a hero among the people of the village. The plan that led to the greatest escape attempt in their people's history came from his mind. He suggested they mine a tunnel east—far east, as far as they could go—and then head upwards for the surface. The people thought it foolproof—they would surface beyond the borders of the eclipser territory and be long gone before the eclipsers noticed anything was amiss. Tor rallied the village, gave them hope of escape and a better life.

But the plan failed. They didn't mine far enough. Tor led the group from the front when they surfaced, but when they broke ground and saw the blue sky peeking through the cracks in the stone, they found themselves not met with sights of expansive wilderness landscapes, but the heart of the eclipser camp. Many died that day—the eclipsers dragged out nearly everyone mining in the tunnel and killed them, then caved the passage in on the rest.

But Tor managed to get out alive. He ran back through the tunnel and reached the village as the eclipsers collapsed the path at his heels.

If leading so many people to their deaths wasn't enough, Tor being one of only three survivors truly dragged his reputation through the mud. The village pinned the blame for all of the deaths on him. Many of those who lost a loved one believed it should have been Tor who died instead, taking out their anger and grief on him. They said he only escaped because he bailed, left them to suffer for his actions, and got out just to save his own skin. They executed him the same day. His name became something accompanied only with a sneer, something people spat out with disgust.

Ude, as his son, bore Tor's name. *Ude Tor*, the only surviving member of Tor's family. Ude was only twelve when it all happened, and while the people of the village refrained from executing him alongside his father, they had been less than kind to him ever since. The fact that Ude still lived at sixty-eight when most didn't even see their fiftieth birthday only added to the scorn that accompanied him wherever he went. The only one who spoke to him with more than a jeer was Oleja.

Perhaps it was because she found herself among the outcasts as well, or perhaps because she seemed to be the only one beside Ude who still regarded Tor as anything but a villain, but the two had become friends of a sort. He was the closest thing to a friend she had, at least. And she loved to hear stories of his father. Though admitting it to anyone but Ude would surely get her punched in the face—and the punch being merely a warning—she could not help but see Tor as a hero. He did what he believed was right; how could he have known the future held only failure for him? He did his best but inevitably failed, and for that he suffered gravely.

Oleja picked through an assortment of small uncooked vegetables, popping them into her mouth one by one. She gave the orange ones to Ude. In return, he gave her his red ones, whatever they were. He didn't like them because they had too much of a kick. She liked them for the very same reason. When she finished eating, she wrapped up the remainder and placed the bundle in her bag.

Laid out on the workbench rested a hand-carved bow. Oleja ran her hand along its surface before picking it up. It fit snugly in her grip, formed in such a way after years of whittling the wood into perfection. With her right hand, she reached over the worktable and grabbed a cylindrical container propped up against the other side. Constructed from a thin sheet of metal, her quiver looked not unlike those she heard about in stories, though with one addition. A screen of burlap formed a loosely-domed lid, and when she unlatched the copper clasp, the cover fell away and hung to the side, leaving a dozen and a half arrows visible with their fletching poking out the top. Oleja had given the matter careful consideration and deemed the cover a necessary feature. The clasp was easy enough to hook and unhook with her free hand, so her modification to the classic design came with few drawbacks.

Ude watched her as he chewed. "You never do get tired of that thing, do you?"

Oleja grinned and held the bow a little higher. "Not in the slightest."

She made her way over to a line carved in the stone floor and faced the target. The weight of the day's events fell away as she let herself relax. The bow bounced loosely in her hand. One breath in, one breath out, and then she flicked her eyes up to the target.

In one quick motion she raised the bow with her left hand and swung an arrow from her quiver with her right, nocking and firing it with one movement of her arm. The arrow whizzed through the air and struck the target with a *thud*. It stuck in the soft wood, left of the bullseye by the width of no more than two fingers. Oleja studied it for a moment and then cocked her head, disregarding it as her hand leapt for another.

"Easy…" came Ude's voice from behind her. Faint tinges of strain leaked in his voice as he got to his feet. "Don't just go for the next one. What did you do wrong with the first?"

"I missed."

"Well, clearly, but that's not the right answer," he said as he came to stand beside her. "You're going too fast."

"I'm going to have to be fast when I'm fighting eclipsers."

"If you slow down to aim and manage to fell them in one shot, you won't need the speed for a second."

Oleja let the bow fall to her side and turned her head to meet the man's eyes. "I've taught myself this far, I think I can manage."

Ude chuckled. "Do I get no credit for my snarky remarks over your shoulder? Some of them have been quite good."

Oleja ignored him as she drew another arrow. She fired

it with the same speed as the last. This one found its mark at the center.

"I'll stand corrected, I suppose," said Ude with a shrug. "You say you're going to be fighting eclipsers—you're going through with it, then?"

"Yes," replied Oleja as she loosed another arrow, her eyes never drifting from the target.

"When?"

"Soon. A few days at most. I didn't plan for quite so soon, but…" Oleja paused, thinking back on the events of that morning. "They killed someone today. A boy. He didn't make any attempts at escape. Things are dangerous down here, and if I wait too long it'll be too late."

Ude let out a slow breath. "I see. That is soon. Everything is ready?"

Oleja sent another two arrows to find their marks at the center of the target before voicing her response. "I have inspected the gate by the south wall as extensively as has proven useful. I won't know what sort of mechanism opens it until I am outside, but I'll figure it out—it can't be too complex. Once I'm out, I'll go to the gate and open it, releasing everyone. Then, we fight for our freedom. And we win. And we walk away from here to begin our new lives." Though she still did not turn her eyes away from the target, Oleja could hear Ude scratching his stubble. A period of silence settled between them. Oleja drew and nocked another arrow.

"And your plan of escape?"

Thud. "I just have to test one last thing."

"Have you enlisted anyone to aid you?"

Thud. "I can manage it alone."

"Just because you can doesn't mean that you have to." Oleja lowered her bow and met his gaze now. He looked troubled, deep in contemplation.

"Your father made his plans by himself. Why shouldn't I?"

"My father worked alone on the plans, yes, but others helped when it came time to act." Torchlight flickered in his eyes. He watched Oleja carefully, unblinking.

"Others will act once I open the gates and they join me to fight. The first part is merely an escape and a dash to the gate, I don't need others getting in my way." Ude raised an eyebrow at that. Even the small gesture made her grind her teeth. Did he not trust her? Did he think her too incompetent to pull it off? She had been working towards this, training for it for years. He watched her do so on many occasions. What squashed his faith now?

She loosed another arrow. *Thud.* It struck the target, the metal tip imbedding itself in the wood at least a forearm's length away from the center. Ude studied it with a shake of his head. Heat rose into Oleja's face.

"You know, one day you may have only one shot. You cannot let your anger doom you. You need to learn to keep it in check."

Oleja shoved the bow into Ude's hands before stepping out to retrieve her arrows. "Thanks for the life lesson, I'll keep it in mind," she said. There was no hiding the biting sarcasm in her voice.

But Ude only chuckled and shook his head.

With her arrows back in her quiver and the cover fastened shut once again, she returned to the worktable. She put the bow and quiver away. Other things demanded her attention—so little time remained before she put her plan into action.

The image of the boy from that morning came back to her, his body dead on the ground with an eclipser arrow buried in his chest. No one else would meet the same fate. She wouldn't let it happen.

Escaping from the canyon had proven to be nothing short of impossible in difficulty, given the history of the village. Through the years, none had ever succeeded. Some tried climbing to the top—the most obvious route. But no matter when they made their dash for the surface—day, night, under clear skies, or during the rare rainstorms that swept across the land, the results were always the same: an arrow in the back before they even managed to reach the top and behold the world above. If the arrow didn't kill them, the fall finished them off.

Others tried to swim out. The river that ran through the canyon had an entrance and an exit, a gap in the stone walls through which they ran. But fixed within each stretched a metal grate, a lattice of bars as thick around as Oleja's skull and completely unbreakable. Those who tried often drowned before even managing to scratch the metal, leaving the others in the village with the harrowing task of dragging their bodies out of the water to keep them from clogging up the water supply.

Tor's attempt finished off the list as the third method of escape the people had tried. Mining through the ground proved no more successful than climbing or swimming if the slaughter of Tor's team said anything about the viability of such a plan.

None had ever escaped, not by climbing, tunneling, or swimming. But Oleja had a new idea. Something no one had ever tried.

From the end of the table she lifted a wooden box. It was tall and rectangular, no thicker than the length of her palm. Four straps of heavy rope hung from it, two at the base that she stepped into and pulled up to the top of her thighs, and two more that fit over her shoulders like a backpack. The top of the box rose to the nape of her neck, while the bottom extended just past the base of her back. As broad as her shoulders and thin enough that she could wear her quiver over it, the compact contraption fit easily against her frame. Aside from the four straps, the only other external feature was a small cord dangling from the center of the bottom, nearly invisible to those who did not know to look for it. Stepping into the center of the space, Oleja reached behind her and grabbed the cord between her thumb and forefinger, and with one quick tug, yanked it downwards.

From either side of the box, the side panels sprung outwards, hinged at the top so they rose to become level with her shoulders. As they reached the top of their arc, the *click* of another release sounded as a second set of limbs, attached to the first but hinged at the far ends, swung around and out to extend the wingspan farther.

As they went, they pulled along with them two triangles of grey fabric, and when the limbs snapped into their final position, two great wings splayed from Oleja's shoulders.

It was not enough to climb. It was not enough to swim. It was not enough to tunnel. But Oleja had a glider, and she was going to get out of the canyon by flying.

CHAPTER THREE

Oleja dropped the canvas bag on the ground, letting the mouth fall open to reveal the glittering contents. A few fist-sized chunks of copper ore slipped out and rolled across the ground. They shimmered in the orange light of sunset as they came to rest at Jisi's feet. Oleja spun on her heels and headed the other way without a word. Being the largest haul she'd ever surfaced with, she figured it should keep Jisi satisfied for a few days.

And a few days was all she needed. If all went accordingly, she would free the whole village within that span of time, and no one would be forced to mine ever again.

She didn't look back at Jisi's face, though she longed to see the shock that surely twisted her features. Leaving without a word seemed better. More mysterious. More *dramatic*. She spun her pickaxe in her hand as she went, an added show as she walked away.

With Jisi and the morning's conflict behind her, she made her way south down the street through the canyon. Miners shambled along with their hauls, a thick coating of dirt smeared across their faces, arms, and legs that turned to mud as it mixed with their sweat. Young children ran about, leaping into the arms of their exhausted parents returning home for the evening. With the crowd came the sounds of life. Evenings marked a small moment of transition—a shift from the quiet of day, when few milled about above the ground, to the quiet of night, when everyone slept. The village only seemed so alive at sunup and sundown, the two brief times when all were both out of the mines and awake. The moments served as times to gather, eat together, and hold meetings.

"... and as you go about your daily work, remember that you do so for the good of our saviors. Sky eclipsers, the deliverers of life and death, are the bringers of our salvation and protection."

Oleja looked towards the voice. It came from a young, angular man. His long dark hair rushed for the back of his skull in an oily cascade, leaving his wide eyes unobscured. His pinched lips quivered between words, and he wore clothes that looked too fine to belong to a miner, though still spattered with a collection of dirt smudges and other stains. He perched on the walkway ledge leading to the second-story homes, arms splayed, gaze directed tenderly down to the crowd gathered below him. Some looked up thoughtfully, while others kept their eyes closed and heads tilted to the ground. Though several such individuals stood below, the majority looked up to him with scowls. Booing calls and other obscenities rang out. A few rocks sailed through the air, though none struck the man. The calls did not seem to deter him.

"These walls keep us swaddled from the harsh outside world, and our guards stand ever vigilant in our protection," he continued. "In their great benevolence, they send us their food and water as payment for our service to them, though what more could we humbly request than their sanctum in which we are so blessed to reside?"

Oleja kept her head down as she passed. The man was delusional, and she would soon show him that, but for now she did not want to get involved. She'd had enough dealings with angry mobs for the day.

She found an unclaimed fire pit downriver. A fire already burned in the center of the stone ring, though the circle of benches and chairs all remained vacant. Oleja lifted the newly-repaired strap of her bag over her head and threw it down onto a bench, leaned her pick against the end, and flopped onto the empty seat. An assembly of scrap metal comprised the bench, clearly with little regard for aesthetics. Fine craftsmanship seemed equally out of the question. Oleja could certainly do better in both aspects if she cared to spend her time on seating instead of weaponry. Perhaps if she got dragged into the execution circle again, she could make an offer of rebuilding the benches as community service to get herself off the hook. Otherwise, it wasn't her issue.

As she shifted positions, the bench creaked and

squealed under her weight. Cringing at the harsh sound, she shifted again, and once more the grating of metal on metal filled the air. Resigning herself to ignore it, she let herself relax, but even that shift created another round of shrieks. With a sigh, she stood, moved her bag and pick, then grabbed the underside of the bench with one hand and flipped it upside-down.

From her bag she withdrew a few tools and set to work. The back right corner seemed to have come loose from the nail holding it in place. Rusted and bent, it came as no surprise the nail failed in its role and left the bench a shrieking mess. She pulled the nail out and fished around for a replacement in her bag. Once fixed in place, she checked the other nails for good measure, then righted the bench. Seated back in her spot, she found, with relief, the bench made exactly as much noise as a good bench should —none.

She tilted her head back and looked up to the sky. A river of dark blue arced overhead, framed by the peaks of the canyon cliffs. A few stars emerged, mere pinpricks of light amidst the dark and cloudless expanse above. She would be up there soon—up on the surface where nothing could obstruct her view of it. The whole sky would be hers.

A stampede of approaching footfalls found her ears. The footsteps coupled with giggling as they grew nearer. Oleja brought her eyes back down to the earth and looked across the fire to see a cluster of around eight children running across the ground, making a beeline for her spot. The oldest could be no more than seven years old, and the youngest no fewer than four. When they saw her take notice of their approach, they slowed, and some took a new interest in the ground or their shoes or something behind them. They came to a halt on the other side of the fire. A few of the kids eyed Oleja curiously while others exchanged whispers. Oleja watched them with an amused smile.

After a moment of conferral, one of the kids stepped forward—eyes on the fire, hands behind his back, shy smile creasing his face.

"Um... could you make something for us?" he asked, flicking his eyes up to meet hers to punctuate his question. The rest of the group looked on expectantly.

Oleja grinned and tugged open her tinkering bag. "What would you like me to make?"

"Something cool!" said one girl from the group.

"A snake!" said another.

"Fire!" offered a third.

Oleja twisted her face into mock contemplation. "Hmm. So... a fire snake?" she asked. One boy's mouth fell open.

"Can you really do that?" he asked. Oleja pulled a hammer from her bag and spun it in her hand.

"Hate to break it to you, but I can only make lightning snakes. Haven't managed to make a fire snake just yet." A couple of the kids giggled.

"Of course she can't make a fire snake," said one girl to the others. "She can't make things that are alive. Live things have to be *born*." She looked to Oleja with an expression as if asking for confirmation on her facts.

Oleja raised an eyebrow. "I can't? Says who? I might have to sneak a lightning snake into their blankets."

From her bag, she withdrew a rectangular-cut sheet of copper about four inches in one direction and shorter in the other. She flicked it between her fingers, letting the firelight glint off the polished surface. Its prior fate had been to find a home fixed to her armor, but she had plenty more. She could spare this one.

With two pairs of pliers, she held the copper on either side and stood from the bench, crossing the few feet to the fire. She held the metal in the flame—low, close to the charcoal lining the ground. The copper glowed hotter and hotter as the minutes ticked by. It transferred heat up the pliers, which grew hot in Oleja's hands. She ignored it—her tolerance for heat had grown since she started working with metal and flame.

Children clustered around her, looking over her shoulders and peering at the work from where they sat cross-legged on the ground. One picked up a stick and poked at the logs, causing them to shift and expel clouds of glowing orange embers into the air.

After a cautionary warning to the young ones, Oleja backed up a few steps away from the fire. The copper glowed red-hot. She twisted the pliers inwards to bring the edges together until she held a perfect cylinder with a diameter similar to that of one of her fingers.

"There. A fire snake," she said. One of the kids reached out to poke it. "Easy there," she said as she moved it away from his curious finger. "It's not done yet. I said I couldn't make a fire snake, remember? But I can make something cooler—at least to the touch." Taking the metal tube—which still glowed hot, pinched within a single pair of pliers now—and after picking up a clay pot from where it lay on its side beside a chair, Oleja shuffled over to the river where it cut through the stone ground not far from the fire circle. At the bank, she filled the pot with water, then went back to the fire and set it nearby. Water sloshed from the rim and dripped down the sides. With a quick look to each of the children in turn, she dunked the metal into the water. Steam rose from the surface as the metal hissed in protest.

"Hear that?" Oleja asked.

"The snake!" cried one boy before Oleja could reach the punchline herself. She winked at him in response.

With the tube removed from the water, she returned it to the fire and rummaged around in her bag for the hammer she had stowed back within. Hammer in hand, she waited patiently for the metal to heat.

"Are you going to put it in the water again?" asked one child.

"Can I do it?" asked another. The girl bounced excitedly at her proposal.

"Yes..." said Oleja, pointing with her hammer to the one who asked the first question, "... and no," she finished, pointing now to the bouncing girl. "This is dangerous work. I don't want any of you getting burned." At that, a few of the children scooted away from where Oleja worked, perhaps realizing for the first time that molten metal was indeed hot.

When the copper grew hot enough, she withdrew it from the flames and placed one end down on a rock by the fire. Maintaining her grip on the tube with the pliers, she tapped the end a few times with the hammer, flipped it over, and did the same on the other side—not exerting enough force to close the opening, but flattening it into a narrower slit. Then into the water it went, and then back to the flames.

After she heated the metal a third time, she removed it again and set it on the rock. This time she grabbed a sharp pointed tool and began carefully puncturing the tube with calculated precision.

"She must be so good at this because she's skyborn," said one child to another. Oleja glanced up and then back down.

"Talents are learned through practice, not given as gifts at birth," she said, speaking down to her work.

"Lavhi is a skyborn too," said one boy, pointing to another. The other boy—Lavhi—nodded with a grin.

"My father is named Soln, so I am Lavhi Solnri," said the boy. He put emphasis on the extra letters of his surname, beaming as he formed the sounds.

Tsss. Wisps of steam curled into the air as Oleja cooled the copper a final time. The children turned away from their conversation to watch.

From the water, Oleja removed the final product of her efforts. Water dripped from the surface as she released it from the pliers into her palm. With a rag, she wiped away the droplets and bits of soot that clung to the shining surface, and then held it out in her hand for the kids to see.

"What is it?" asked a few voices in turn. In response, Oleja brought the pinched end to her mouth and blew. A shrill whistle pierced the night air.

Several of the kids grabbed for it at once, each wanting a turn with the trinket. One of the younger girls got ahold of it first. She sprinted off at top speed, whistles and laughter filling the air, the other children hot on her heels. The whistle changed hands several times as the group ran off together, the calls of their new toy echoing through the canyon.

Only one girl remained by the fire—one of the older ones, around seven in Oleja's estimation. Her hands hid behind her back as she watched Oleja sheepishly.

"Hi... is there something I can help you with?" asked Oleja.

The girl shuffled forwards a few paces. "My name is Palila. I thought—*hoped*... well, my dad..." she grappled for words for a few moments, but when none came, she brought her hands in front of her. Clutched in her grip, pressed tightly to her chest, she held a pickaxe head. No handle protruded from it, save for the nub of splintered wood no longer than her thumb that still jutted out where the handle once attached. The head itself was bent into uselessness. The tip hooked sideways at an angle that would serve no miner well as anything but a back scratcher.

"I see," said Oleja, taking it in her hands and flipping it over once, twice, three times to get the full picture.

"It's my dad's. But it broke. He wanted to get it fixed or get a new one, but he hasn't had a good haul in ages, so he has nothing good to trade, and they said there are no spares available right now. And now he has no hauls at all because he has no pick, so he has been moving rubble and tailings down in the mines but it's not enough. I was just hoping that maybe... you could fix it for him." She looked up to Oleja with pleading eyes.

In the canyon, "prosperous times" never came; no one could be considered "well-off," but some fared worse than others. The rationing and dividing of food kept everyone fed, but beyond that, individuals bartered on their own for the things they needed. It sounded like Palila and her family had fallen on difficult times—or rather, more difficult than usual.

Oleja looked at the pickaxe head in her hands, and then to her bag where it sat on the bench. Tough, durable metal constituted the pickaxes—meant for breaking apart solid rock day after day for as long as they could possibly hold up. She had tried to use the metal before in her work, but it proved too difficult to manipulate. Fixing a bent pickaxe was no simple trick to perform as entertainment for group of kids. She'd have to expend hours of labor—a day, likely, with her makeshift facilities. She didn't have the time. Her plan called her to action.

Her eyes drifted to her pick where it leaned against the

bench. She no longer needed it. None would need pickaxes soon, but she couldn't tell Palila that. The village couldn't know what she planned, or they might try to stop her or get in her way, and seven-year-olds weren't exactly renowned for their tight-lipped secret keeping.

"Here," said Oleja, hefting her pickaxe into her hand and holding it out to Palila. "This is mine. Give it to your father, it's his now. I'll take this one here and fix it up for myself."

Palila took the pick in both hands, looking up to Oleja with wide eyes. The weight of the tool made her wobble, but she held her balance.

"Are you sure?" she asked, but the relief already rose in her voice. Oleja nodded. Palila rushed forward and hugged her, an awkward embrace given the pick pressed between them. She spoke a muffled thanks into Oleja's shirt, then hurried away, vanishing into the darkness.

Oleja retook her seat on the bench. She looked over the pickaxe head again. She had no intention of repairing it, and if all went well, she would never need to. Gathering her tools, she repacked her bag, placing the bent pickaxe head at the bottom.

She must be so good at this because she's skyborn. She smiled, thinking back on the child's words. No secrecy shrouded who in the village held the skyborn name—the title was not particularly rare, though certainly not common either. It indicated someone born outside the canyon walls —a peculiar phenomenon indeed.

Only newborns arrived in the village—never adults or even toddlers—and so they brought with them no news of the world above. In fact, the oldest person to ever arrive in the village had been no more than a week old. The people of the village called these individuals "skyborn," babies who arrived in the village in shaky parachute-topped bundles.

Some believed the skyborn possessed some special essence after being created in the clouds. Others considered this a myth and believed the skyborn to be nothing but regular babies. It seemed the latter won out as time went on, because these days the only special badge bestowed to skyborn children were the two extra letters tacked onto their adopted parent's name when they acquired it as their surname: "ri."

But even still, the skyborn carried an air of mystery. Even if the eclipsers sent them down as some assumed, where did they come by children never more than a few days old? Human blood ran through their veins, certainly—not eclipser blood. That much Oleja knew.

Because, just as the children said, she was one of them.

After she arrived in the village, she was adopted by her father Uwei and mother Rasea. They named her Oleja, and as her mother's daughter, she became Oleja Raseari. They raised her for the first eight years of her life until a cave-in took both of their lives, among a dozen others. For the eleven years that followed, she'd cared for herself. And as far as she was concerned, she could continue doing so for the rest of her life.

Leaning back, she cast her gaze upwards again. The stars had exploded in number, now set against a backdrop of black in place of the deep blue. Someone told her once that in the Old World people made pictures with the stars. She smiled at the thought. Soon she would behold the masterpiece in its entirety.

CHAPTER FOUR

Of all the things to do first thing in the morning, climbing up a hundred-foot high pile of scrap metal and junk took the award for the best and certainly the safest. The Heap stood like a sentinel at the north end of the canyon, shrouded by the grey light that pooled across the landscape before dawn. The sun had not yet emerged for the day, lingering somewhere beyond the canyon walls, but the sky lightened just a bit in anticipation, from black to a shade lighter, approaching something that eventually could be called blue.

Oleja had slept a few hours, but nothing more. Grogginess clouded her mind; it would make scaling The Heap even more of an event. She preferred not to rise so early, as there was never any danger of others beating her to the best of the morning's scrap. Today, though, more pressing aims than twisted metal drove her. Her plan to free the village hinged on her ability to get herself out of the canyon first. The glider would keep her from plummeting to her death—an indispensable service, truly—but before it could be of any use, she needed elevation. A glider could only prove so useful from the ground.

At the base of The Heap she let out a long breath, shook the sleep from her mind, rubbed her hands together, and began her ascent.

She had climbed the slopes on several occasions. Sometimes the pieces she needed were higher up in the pile, or sometimes, if she couldn't find them near the base, she wanted to believe she would find them with a bit of climbing. Sometimes the sentiment rang true, sometimes it did not. Apparently, her wants did not influence the whereabouts of scrap metal.

Higher and higher she climbed. Sometimes the structure shifted under her weight and she slid, but always she managed to keep her balance. One wrong step could land her with deadly consequences, but death was not an option. At intervals she stopped to turn and look down at the canyon below. Only once did she see someone moving around through the village, and that lone figure quickly disappeared through a doorway, making no indication that they saw her in her escapades. Everyone else still slept, though not for much longer. She could feel the village beginning to stir.

No rules dictated that she *couldn't* climb The Heap, but if they spotted her, people might flock over to see what business propelled her to the top of the mass of junk. Prying questions put the truth at risk, and Oleja would not risk jeopardizing all of her work. Therefore, she decided it best to go unseen.

But as she reached the top and surveyed the ground below again, that didn't seem to be an issue. Nothing moved in the village.

Oleja set to work. She located a wooden beam, wider in surface than it was thick and so long that moving it was a tricky task. Dragging the beam through the scrap dislodged bits and pieces and sent them skittering down the slopes, letting out a new *clang* with each bounce. If she aimed to keep her business quiet, she did a poor job of it. Sounds from The Heap would only get louder though; they did every morning. Daybreak marked the time when the eclipsers threw down the day's hoard of junk.

Jutting up from the top of the immense pile poked the end of some contraption. It was large—too wide to fit through a doorway in all directions and too heavy to move. There were many of them in The Heap, all in various states of disrepair and each differing in exact size and shape. Oleja had never been able to discern quite what they were beyond large box-like things, some of which still had a number of opening hatches which only revealed more complex—and terribly rusted—contraptions inside. She gave up trying to find a use for them long ago, but this one could serve a purpose. The end that stuck out rose just high enough above the surrounding scrap for her plan. Shifting the wood onto the peak, she gave it a quick test. The beam teetered back and forth when she put weight on the near end.

A short distance down the slope lay a chunk of splintered wood and grey stone approximately the same size as her. Heaving it up in front of her, she managed to push it to the top and get it on the surface of the far end of the wooden beam. After a moment to check that everything was positioned the way she wanted it, she started her descent.

Descending The Heap was no less precarious than ascending, and she slipped a few times on her way down as well. Relief came only when at last her feet hit the solid stone ground. From there, she hurried off south a ways. Up ahead she spotted a section along the street lined with tables for making baskets or preparing food. All lay empty at the moment. Oleja ducked behind them and seated herself at an angle from which she could see The Heap. Then she waited.

The sky continued to get lighter, and the air warmer. A few people emerged from their homes, though the majority of the village remained asleep. Then, just as day broke, something moved on the metal walkway above The Heap.

The structure stuck a few hundred feet out from the edge of the canyon, leaning heavily on supports of rusted metal. The jagged end scraped at the sky, indicating that the structure might once have been longer but had since broken. The supports formed the beginnings of an arch, but those, too, stopped abruptly in a mangled and bent salute to their former glory. The eclipsers used the ledge to dump their scrap during the one regularly-recurring instance at which the people below could catch a glimpse of their masters, albeit from a great distance.

A pair of two figures walked along the ledge, each silhouetted against the grey-blue sky. Their forms were a darker grey—tall, hulking, but beyond that, impossible to make out. Between them rolled a wide, flat cart laden with a heaping mound of discarded odds and ends that towered over their heads at least twice their height. Slow and straining, they proceeded down the metal walkway as they guided their heavy cargo.

The eclipsers possessed impressive strength. Though the two loomed larger than humans in stature, the cart surely weighed an immense amount, and Oleja doubted even she could exert the force needed to move a proportionally large and heavy burden with the ease they did. She was certainly strong—her thickly-muscled arms were quick to betray that fact, a side-effect of her work mining and training and forging contraband armor and weaponry in the depths of the mines—but the strength of the eclipsers exceeded beyond that of a human. They could not be bested by brute strength alone; Oleja relied on her ability to outwit them during the first stage of her plan and outnumber during the second. That was how she would play her cards.

At the end of the walkway, the eclipsers stopped and moved to the back of the cart. With one great heave they lifted the end in unison, spilling the contents down the sloped surface and over the edge. They raced towards the top of The Heap. Oleja held her breath, her eyes wide as she absorbed every detail.

Something big hit first as the smaller debris rained down. At the moment of collision, the wooden beam whipped upwards, catapulting the wood and stone dummy with the force of the scrap thrown from hundreds of feet in the air.

Oleja tracked the dummy in its ascent. One of the eclipsers pointed, and though the pair stood too far off to tell, it looked as if they laughed as they watched the object fly through the air.

As the dummy reached the top of its arc, Oleja tried to estimate the height. One hundred feet above the top of the canyon? More? She grinned. That should be enough.

The dummy hovered in the air for a moment as the momentum carried it to its zenith, and then it raced back for the ground at the bottom of the canyon.

Oleja flicked her eyes across the projected impact zone in an instant. Few had emerged from their houses, and most of the ground remained clear of bleary-eyed miners. No one looked to be in danger of an unpleasant wakeup call.

When the chunk of wood and stone landed, it crashed into the river. The splash sent a wave across an impressive radius, raining droplets down in something reminiscent of the rare rainfalls, though with twice the excitement and none of the relief, as it stopped a split second later. A few drops pelted Oleja, one hitting her just above her eye. She wiped away the water and moved from her hiding spot. The few conscious villagers looked around in shock, still processing the events that had just unfolded before them. More emerged upon hearing the commotion, hovering in their doorways, looking about in confusion and trying to discern what, exactly, they missed. Oleja paid them no mind. She had the information she needed. Her plan was set, and she knew it would work. All that remained were the final preparations. Tomorrow morning, she would be on the end of that catapult, and by midday, when the bloodshed ceased, the people of the village would be free.

Oleja left the street behind as she slipped down into the mines. It was time to get ready for a war.

She didn't surface until late in the evening when most people in the village slept—equal parts due to her desire to avoid Jisi during her final evening of being expected to drag up a haul from the mines, and from her desire to conceal what she carried. Thrown over one shoulder, wrapped carefully in burlap and placed within a dirtied sack, was the suit of armor she had spent so many months perfecting. No one would be able to tell what the sack contained from how Oleja packed it, nor would anyone suspect she carried a suit of armor any faster than they'd guess a bag of live snakes or a baby eclipser—if the wretched things had babies, that was. Still, the bag could be mistaken for a mining haul, and if someone called upon her to add it to the trough with the rest by the lifting site, the ensuing conversation would be awkward at the very least.

Few others walked the street, creating an atmosphere reminiscent of the quietness of the morning. By the time she reached The Heap, no one ambled about to witness her climb. She stowed the armor by a stone outcropping beside the river and then began her ascent for the second time that day.

No matter how often Oleja climbed the slopes of The Heap, it never got any easier. It was a constantly shifting terrain of junk, never the same from one day to the next as pieces moved and slid. When she came to the top, she found it more or less the same as it had been that morning, though with the wooden beam pinned below the immense carcass of whatever metal contraption had landed on it.

A good deal of heaving and huffing ensued as she pulled it free while also keeping the large boxy object from careening down the slopes, waking the entire village as it went, but eventually she managed and got it back into the proper position. With the site set, she made her way back down and retrieved her armor.

Her second errand of the night drew her to the opposite end of the canyon. She planned to stow her armor just inside the gate by the southern wall. Wearing it during her flight would add too much weight, and she carried a lot of that already. When she launched, she would take her quiver and bow, plus her tinkering bag in case she needed to throw something together on the fly when she got to the gate, or in case she needed the tools. Besides, the idea of parting with it was one she couldn't bear, so she elected to bring it despite the added weight to her flight. And then, of course, there was the weight of her own body. That was not something she could cut down on in any easy manner save amputation, and she preferred to avoid that if possible. She was quite fond of her limbs.

With any luck, she could avoid the need for the armor until she got the gate open. Once she landed, her goal was to alert as few eclipsers to her presence as possible while she went to the gate and opened it. She couldn't avoid the ones who carted the scrap, that she knew, but beyond them she hoped to keep the number of eyes that spotted her to the barest minimum manageable. After she opened the gate, she could grab her armor, don it, and lead the people in a charge against the eclipsers. With stealth as her objective, the armor wouldn't be necessary. Hopefully.

The walk from the north wall to the south took up the better part of an hour, and when at last she turned the final bend and came before the wall, a good twenty minutes had passed since last she saw someone else walking the streets.

Few dared approach the south wall. The gate loomed in the eastern side of the canyon not far from it, a feature that by nature the people of the village opted to avoid. Carved from what looked to be one massive slab of stone, the gate towered at least a hundred feet tall, set part of the way up the cliff and reachable by a staircase of wide, steep stairs. Above the gate, the stone of the canyon side continued, maintaining the height of the wall. Oleja had spent a night investigating the colossal doorway several years back after first hearing of Tor and becoming obsessed with the idea of escaping and heroism. As far as she could tell, the slab looked to be on some sort of track and would slide southwards into the stone of the cliff.

The gate had not been opened in Oleja's lifetime, or in the lifetime of anyone currently living in the village, but the story of the last time it opened was still quite alive. The tale was a bloody one. Some said that one morning the people awoke to find it just... open. Many feared what it meant and went about their business, but others rushed the doorway. Eclipsers killed those who tried to flee—shot them dead before they even crossed the threshold. The gate didn't close immediately, however. It stayed ajar for the remainder of the day. Occasionally throughout those hours, a lone individual attempted to sneak through, or sprint as fast as they could, or try some other tactic. All were killed.

Though it almost always stood unused, the gate drew fear about it in the minds of the people. No one wanted to risk being nearest to it in the event that it open and a wave of bloodthirsty eclipsers rush in.

Oleja climbed the steps. The gate did not strike fear into her, only curiosity. Well, curiosity and determination.

At the top, she searched for a concealed place to stow her armor. She found what she searched for in the form of a pile of boulders, behind which hid a crevice just wide enough for her to slide the burlap bag into and where shadows and outcroppings of stone kept the bundle out of sight. Not that she expected anyone from the village to be poking around at the base of the gate—most feared even rounding the last bend into the southern end of the canyon. Her armor would be safe there.

"Hiding things?"

Oleja whirled around, but even before she saw who spoke, she recognized the voice.

"It's late, Ude."

"I could say the same to you," said the old man. He sat on one of the steps halfway down the staircase. Oleja descended to where he waited and took a seat beside him.

"Tomorrow is the day," she said. She fixed her eyes straight ahead as she formed the words.

"I know. The whole village is talking about it."

Oleja turned to face him with a start. "What? They are? How..."

"No. They are not. It was a joke."

Oleja sighed. "A bad one."

Ude pursed his lips. "Don't you think perhaps they should be? I mean, they are the ones expected to fight. Shouldn't they be ready?"

"They'll be ready," Oleja assured him quickly. "They'll be armed with picks, ready to go down to the mines for the day. As soon as the gate is open, they'll take up arms."

Ude studied her for a long moment. At last he turned away.

"I hope you're right."

"I am."

"I believe you."

Silence settled between them for several long minutes.

"I take flight at daybreak."

"I will be there," said Ude.

Another silence.

"Oleja?"

"Yeah?"

Ude cleared his throat. "In case the message got lost... I am incredibly proud of all the work you have done. You have proven that you can do anything you set your mind to with sheer determination alone. If anyone can pull this off, it's you. You will take us home. My father would be proud; you remind me so much of him."

Oleja sat there for a moment, unsure of what to say. Eventually, Ude got to his feet.

"Get some rest. You have a big day tomorrow," he said. He picked his way down the stairs and walked off with an unsteady gait, never taking so much as a backwards glance. Oleja watched him go: the closest thing to a friend and a parent that she had in the world. Everything that happened at dawn and afterwards, she did it for him, and for everyone else down in the canyon.

CHAPTER FIVE

When dawn broke, Oleja was ready.

Just as the morning prior, she rose early and readied her things. Her glider straps hugged her body, winding over her shoulders and around her thighs. She double and tripled checked that each of the straps would hold—there was nothing like falling out of the sky to end a perfectly good escape plan.

Her tinkering bag hung at her hip. She wore her quiver across her back where it fit snugly atop the glider, cover latched, locking the arrows within—she had added the feature for this very moment. Losing all of her arrows mid-flight would be disastrous, leaving her with only the knife sheathed at her side for defense. Her bow, which she carried in her left hand, would be useless with nothing to fire from it.

She stood at the base of The Heap, preparing to climb the slopes for the final time. With a deep breath and one last look back to the village behind her, she began her ascent.

This time, it didn't matter if anyone saw her. In fact, if she was going to be the first in history to escape, she wanted others to see her do it. She wanted to be a legend and a hero, like Tor, but finding success in the end. Let them watch.

Oleja crested the pile of metal and did a round of final checks. The straps still held her glider secure. The wings deployed as designed. The quiver latch was fastened tight, and everything else was bound tightly to her body. With her checks done, she settled into place on her end of the catapult and waited.

Time moved slowly. Her heart did not. She waited with eyes skyward as she watched the walkway far above. Her fingers drummed on the surface of the wood beneath her or plucked at her bowstring. She wanted to open her bag and pull out her tools to busy her hands and calm her nerves, but that struck her as a bad idea. She would only have so much notice before being launched into the air, and having her tools scattered around her at the moment of takeoff was be a surefire way to lose them.

Relief filled her when distant noises came at last from the walkway above. Relief, and a flare of anxiety. Mere moments remained of her final chance to turn back, and after they ticked away, she would be launched—literally— into a new world from which there could be no return.

She did not move from the catapult. This was it.

Down in the village below, a few figures moved about,

unaware of the events about to unfold. Among them, she could pick out the unmistakable form of Ude. He was the only figure not moving, the only one with something to watch. In the middle of the street he stood, eyes turned upwards to the pinnacle of The Heap, or perhaps the walkway far above. He was too far away to tell.

Oleja looked back up. The edge of the cart stuck out over the lip of the walkway.

And then things were falling. Scrap metal raced down towards her, among it the monstrous silhouette of something big, framed by the sky, plummeting towards her. As it neared, she tracked the trajectory to the opposite end of the catapult—exactly what she needed to send her airborne. Smaller pieces of debris rained down around her. At the last second, she spotted a twisted piece of a metal frame falling towards her. She held up her arm on instinct. Pain shrieked through her as the metal tore her skin, the frame missing the rest of her by an inch and clattering off down the side of The Heap.

Blood poured from the wound on her left forearm, but she had no time to examine it. Her limbs and head snapped back with a paralyzing force as her end of the catapult flung upwards. Up she went, the speed dizzying her. The walls of the canyon flew past until they were gone. For the first time in her life, Oleja looked out past the canyon walls. Before her, stretching beyond her in distances she had never even imagined, lay the rest of the world.

Hills dotted the horizon, farther away than Oleja could even fathom. Flat, red landscapes reached out in all

SKYBORN

directions below her, and behind her—beyond the grey stone of the north wall—stretched more water than Oleja thought could exist in the whole world. It looked like the ground itself was made of water for miles across, waves glittering in the morning sunlight. It stole the breath from her lungs. Or perhaps that was due to the fact that her body hurtled through the open air.

But what she saw off to her left, to the east of the canyon, seized her attention and refused to relinquish it. Spread across an immense swath of land below lay the eclipser camp. It was big—bigger than expected.

Much of the area housed crumbling structures of stone —or what might once have been structures, but now looked like no more than the discarded husks of old buildings. A wall of stone and metal surrounded the nearest section, encircling a squashed cluster of towers and huts—enough to contain hundreds of eclipsers.

Shouting on the walkway below caught her attention just as her ascent began to slow. Oleja reached her right hand behind her and found the cord dangling from the base of her glider. Foolish as it seemed, the functionality of her glider was the one thing she had never tested—after all, how could she have? For all she knew, the wings were too feeble to bear her weight, or too small to keep her aloft, or improperly balanced. It was a gamble she was forced to take, since she lacked other options. She couldn't simply take a test flight. Either the glider worked, or she died. And dying was not an option.

With one quick tug of the cord, the wings unfolded. For

57

a brief second, Oleja started to fall, but then the wings snapped to their full positions and carried her forward. The glider worked.

A quick glance down to her village showed many figures running about and pointing to the sky, but her gaze snapped back upwards as something sailed by just beneath her.

She turned to see a tall tower standing upon wooden stilts below her and to the left. Beneath the cover of the roof, she could just make out the shape of an eclipser drawing back another arrow, readying to fire.

In a panic, Oleja tried to make the glider go faster by leaning forward. Her face tilted towards the ground and she began speeding towards it at a dangerous pace.

A whistle rang out as the arrow sailed by. Oleja didn't know how closely it flew past her, but judging by the lack of fresh stabbing pain she could be relatively sure it missed. The ground—which she still hurtled towards—would be harder to dodge, however.

With some awkward squirming, she managed to get her descent back under some semblance of control. She leaned left and right, causing her to swoop back and forth in a zigzagging pattern. More arrows flew by. Up ahead lay the gate—she just had to make it a little farther.

As she neared it, she could see that a smaller canyon led to the gate, the bottom sloping down from ground level to create a winding ramp that led to where the doorway into the village stood. She took note of the details as she flew overhead. Cursing, she tried to hasten her descent, missing her target once but now making attempts at circling back.

She leaned forward to speed up her descent, but once again began to plummet at a rate that would result in an unhealthy collision between her body and the hard stone ground. Hastily trying to rectify her mistakes, she tried to lean back, but given that she was already leaning left in an attempt to turn around and fly over the gate again, she only managed to flip her glider over.

The world spun as she went upside-down. When she righted herself again, the ground was coming at her fast. Quickly she tried again to pull up. She managed to slow herself slightly, but not enough—she was going too fast.

Oleja threw her legs out beneath her as she tried to land running. She took one bounding step, and then two, but her legs couldn't keep up with her and she tripped, landing on her right shoulder and rolling over in the dirt, a cloud of sand rising up behind her in an orange haze. Snapping and splintering echoed in her ears. Her bag clattered and quiver rattled as everything she carried with her jostled together, thrown about in her crash landing. Soon she came to a halt, lying on her back in the dirt. Her ears rang. Her head spun. It took her several seconds to figure out which direction was up, though she never questioned which way was down. Down was the direction of pain.

Scrapes covered most of her body, though nothing worse than the cut she got just before takeoff. She had no doubt that time would reveal a whole host of bruises as well. It seemed nothing was broken—the only relief she received.

As she got to her feet, her previous reassurances were proven wrong. Something *had* broken, just not her bones. Her glider still clung to her body by the straps around each of her limbs, but little more remained intact. A large crack ran down the side of the main casing, and the left wing hung by nothing but the fabric. The right wing was in worse shape, however, evidenced by the moments it took for her to locate the piece. It had snapped clean off and lay in a crumpled mess a few feet away. Fortunately, her other belongings seemed fine; no harm had befallen her bow, and for that she was beyond grateful. If her flight gave her any taste of the fight to come, she would need her primary weapon functional. Her quiver was mostly fine as well—a dent marked the side of the metal cylinder, but nothing she couldn't fix.

Shaking off the haze of her crash, Oleja drew her knife—a blade the length of her hand and curved until it came to a honed point—and cut the straps of the glider, freeing it from her body. It fell to the ground in a heap. She hated to leave it behind, but it served no purpose in its current state, and she couldn't afford to drag it around with her. Haste was her best asset now, as stealth appeared to be off the table. She spun the knife in her hand and slid it back into its sheath.

A large building with a sagging roof sat to her left. It was not a fine structure, pieced together from scraps of wood of various sizes. Beyond it stretched a large fence-rimmed field of dry yellow grass. A few creatures she could not name roamed around, ripping up mouthfuls of grass and chewing mindlessly, unconcerned with the girl who had just crash-landed nearby.

Over the animals peeked the sun in its early-morning debut—east. She turned her back on the building. The gate lay just to the west, if she remembered correctly. With her bearings returned, she started off in that direction.

"Hey!"

Oleja paused and looked back over her shoulder to the building. A boy shimmied through an opening between two sections of the wooden wall. He waved to her with one arm, trying to get her attention.

He looked about her age, with the same dark, tanned skin, though his was a bit lighter. A mess of loose dark brown curls framed his face, bouncing around as they fell in front of his eyes and over his ears down to the top of his neck. Patchy facial hair dotted his chin. He ran towards her.

She had no time to babysit this boy, wherever he had come from, so she turned away and resumed her course west.

Another tower of wood loomed up ahead, raised on a set of stilts just like the one before—guard towers. A fair distance remained between herself and the structure, but Oleja wouldn't risk being spotted. She went left, making her way around. As the smaller canyon leading down to the gate came into view, she ducked behind a boulder and poked her head around, surveying the path ahead.

Another set of footsteps just behind her caught her

attention. When she turned, she saw the boy running to join her in her hiding place.

"Hey! Who are you? What are you doing?" asked the boy in a whisper, breathing hard as his lungs tried to catch up with him, though that didn't slow his rapid-fire questions. Oleja looked him up and down. Muscular arms hung at his sides, just as her own—another slave, most likely. Even still, he was thin and looked underfed, a state she had become used to seeing. He stood taller than her by a few inches, but now that she could see him up close, she guessed he was younger by two years at least; seventeen, perhaps? He was unarmed and carried with him nothing but a small bag. He could offer little help to her here.

"Oleja Raseari; escaping and freeing the people in the canyon," she said, answering his questions in one breath and then turning away in dismissal. She had to focus.

The guard tower before her seemed to have heard the alarm. Bellowing boomed from the top floor, though no eclipsers came into her line of sight from the ground. After a few moments, a hatch in the floor opened with a loud *thud* and an eclipser emerged, clambering down a short ladder and then rushing down the staircase that led to the ground.

Oleja had never seen one up close. Its skin was light grey, with an appearance like it had once been bone-white but then stained with soot. Pinkish-red scars marred its body and made it look like the skin was scraped raw in patches. Frizzy, unkempt hair of silver matted its head, though cut too close to the scalp to be tied up. It was somewhere between eight and nine feet tall, with arms of thick muscle partially obscured by armor crafted from glinting metal and thick leather. Sheathed at its side bounced a sword too big for any human to wield.

On the other side of the tower, the small canyon sloped downwards. The uneven ground created a rough path—a ramp in some places dotted with a handful of stairs in others. Abruptly ending at the bottom, the base of the gate cut off the path from continuing unimpeded into the village. On the wall just beside the door, a few features stuck out from the stone, the grey of metal contrasting the orange of the stone so that they showed in plain detail. First was a lever, its thick, arm-sized handle pointing upwards. Next to it was a crank attached to a wheel. A few gears— some bigger than Oleja's head in diameter—dotted the wall higher up, and cables ran up, down, and around, crossing in various directions Oleja could not follow. Regardless of how odd the mess looked from a distance, the purpose was clear: the machinery opened the gate. All she had to do was throw the lever.

"What's your plan?" The words snapped her out of her concentration. She had nearly forgotten about the boy.

"See that lever?" she asked, pointing down to the gate. The boy peeked around the boulder to where she indicated, then nodded. "I need to pull it to open the gate and free everyone in the canyon. That's my plan."

"I'll help," said the boy, a steely look of determination crossing his face.

Oleja rummaged in her tinkering bag for a moment,

eyes flicking between the gate and the eclipser running down the stairs of the tower. She let touch guide her hand until her fingers found a cool, flat object, slightly chalky to the touch—a safety net, hopefully unnecessary, but she had come too far to take any chances. Alarm swept through the eclipser camp, and the search for her would only intensify —she couldn't afford to wait any longer, even if it meant a mad dash for the gate. As long as she prepared herself for anything, she'd be fine.

"Thanks, but I'm all set," she said, and then slipped the object from her bag into her mouth, tucking it along the inside of her cheek.

She ran from the hiding spot, sprinting as fast as her legs would go. It took only a moment for the eclipser to see her. He sped down the stairs and vaulted the railing, falling the final ten feet. As soon as his feet hit the ground, he charged towards her, sword drawn, gaining on her with every step. Oleja already knew she wouldn't make it to the lever.

She spun in an instant and raised her bow, throwing her right hand back. With her thumb she unlatched the cover to her quiver, and then plucked an arrow from within. She nocked it, drew back, and fired just before the eclipser got within range to skewer her on his sword.

And she missed.

Pain ebbed through her wounded arm, the intensity hitting her as she released. She winced but pushed it down. The arrow sailed to the left of his head and imbedded itself in the stilt of the guard tower. As Oleja followed it with her eyes, she saw the hatch in the tower floor open once more and a second eclipser dropped onto the staircase.

Her focus returned to the fight as her attacker swung. Oleja dodged right and danced around to the eclipser's left. He turned again to face her, giving her the moment she needed to nock another arrow.

She loosed the second, and this time her aim was true. It slammed into his chest, the metal tip striking his armor. A loud *clang* reverberated through the air as the arrow bounced off his breastplate and landed in the dirt.

Oleja backpedaled, assessing the weaknesses of the eclipser's armor. Leather comprised the majority of the suit, not metal, which cloaked only the upper torso. Piercing the leather would not be a problem, though she had hoped her arrows were strong enough to punch through metal as well —they worked perfectly against her test-armor down in her workshop. Clearly the eclipser's armor was of a finer make or of thicker metal.

The eclipser continued advancing, swinging wildly with the sword. Either the brutes knew little in terms of fighting forms, or this one just sucked. Or, perhaps her self-taught form was just too advanced for these lowly abominations. Facing two at once would still present a challenge, however. She had to take care of this one before the second reached the ground.

He swung again and she barely jumped out of the way. Oleja went left and tried to put distance between her and the eclipser. She had the advantage of being able to attack from a range, while his reach was limited by the length of his sword. But while he remained close to her, she did not have the opportunity to load and loose another arrow.

Oleja stopped backing up and stood her ground.

The eclipser grabbed his sword in both hands and raised it over his head. He swung downwards, poised to cleave her in two. Just as the blade was about to strike her, Oleja ducked out of the way. She dashed past his right side and drew her knife as she went. Using the speed of her movements, she raked the blade across the side of his upper thigh, cutting a gash that leaked dark blood. It was darker than her own, a deep brown bordering on black with only the faintest tinges of red. The eclipser snarled at her as he pivoted, slowly due to his wound, but Oleja already sprinted away behind him.

He pursued her slower now, limping each time his full weight fell on his injured leg. Soon, a few dozen feet lay between the two of them, and then she turned, bow at the ready. When she loosed the arrow, it sailed through the air and struck its mark in the eclipser's neck. He took several wheezing, whistling gasps for air as he fell, first to his knees, hands grabbing at the arrow buried to the fletching in the soft flesh of his neck. Eyes wide, he fell forward into the dirt, and after a moment of writhing, lay still.

Oleja had only half a second to congratulate herself on the victory before a strong hand grabbed her by the throat and threw her backwards. Stars danced in her vision as her back struck something hard. She slumped against its surface, and only after shaking the dizziness from her head did she realize she had her back against one stilt of the guard tower. The second eclipser stood before her, a woman, just as tall and intimidating as the first one. She, too, wielded a sword, and made quite sure Oleja saw it as she held it below her chin, the tip only a hair's breadth from her neck.

Movement behind the eclipser caught Oleja's attention. It was the boy again. He sprinted down the incline towards the lever.

If anyone was going to pull that lever and free the people in the canyon, it was going to be *her*.

He reached the lever and grabbed it with both hands.

"Wait!" shouted Oleja as loud as she could muster.

The boy turned, confusion plain on his face even from a distance. He hesitated, hands still on the lever.

A rock flew through the air, hurtling towards the boy. With a yelp, he ducked as it flew just over his head and slammed into the wall behind him. On impact, the lever, crank, and several gears crumpled, reduced to broken hunks of metal adorning the wall. Oleja looked to where the rock came from.

Approaching the tower were two more eclipsers, one toting a spear, while the other carried a war hammer gripped in both hands—the head so large it might have seemed comical in any situation where Oleja was not pinned against a post with a blade to her throat and reinforcements approaching. Under such circumstances, the mere idea that the eclipser possessed strength enough to wield something so large filled her ears with the pounding sounds of her heartbeat. The one with the spear approached the boy, who had nowhere to run at the end of the canyon and thus no option but to stare down the approaching eclipser. He did so with surprising boldness, though there was no hiding the fear that clutched him tightly. The eclipser grabbed him by the shirt and hauled him up to the tower.

"This is the one from the mining camp," said the eclipser with her sword to Oleja's throat, speaking to the others though keeping her eyes on Oleja. "The boy is just a stable hand." Surprise filled Oleja as she heard the eclipsers speak, and in her language no less. Though it seemed silly now, she had always thought them too barbaric to communicate in such ways—she had imagined something more along the lines of grunts and howls. But that was hardly the most pressing thing about the situation.

The eclipser with the war hammer stepped up behind the one at Oleja's throat. "That glider thing... you make that yourself?" she asked, dropping the hammer to the ground with a thunderous boom that shook the ground and made the guard tower at her back rattle and creak. Oleja kept her mouth shut, eyes locked on the eclipser's.

"Should I pry the words out of her myself?" asked the one with the sword. Oleja's pulse quickened.

"No, The Earthtremor may have other plans," said the second, who seemed to be in some position of authority. "Reurl and I will go to seek council and then return. Remain here and guard the prisoners." She grabbed a coil of rope from where it hung at her belt. The eclipser with the spear—Reurl—pushed the boy to stand against the post beside Oleja. Their captors stripped away all belongings from the two of them and piled them a few feet away, then quickly bound them, wrapping them tightly with rope—first across their shoulders, then their arms and wrists, and then down to their thighs. The boy struggled when they started to tie them up, but his rebellious efforts were quickly suppressed. Oleja let them do it. She could escape from this.

When the taut rope scraped against the gash in her forearm, Oleja winced. The eclipser who held it only sneered. Oleja kicked herself for showing any weakness. She clenched her teeth and forced through the stinging as the rope chafed against her raw and bleeding wound.

With the knots pulled tight, the two eclipsers hurried off in the direction of the walled fortress. The third stood guard, pacing around them. This was the time for escape—when there were two of them and only one eclipser. They had to make themselves scarce before the others returned.

"Oleja… Oleja what do we do," asked the boy in a hushed tone. She shot him a glance in response but said nothing. He furrowed his brow. "What… come on, we need a plan." She tugged against her bonds to nudge him. Still she said nothing. He turned away, blinking in confusion.

Oleja looked down to the gate and the obliterated machinery. There was no way they could get the gate open without it—the only other way would be to push the gate ajar with brute force, and given that the slab rose up taller than her at least three times over, the odds of her managing to do so seemed—at best—zero. Even an eclipser would struggle with such a task.

She could fix the mechanisms, sure, but for that she needed time—far more than she had. As ashamed as she was to admit defeat, her best course of action at the moment was to free herself so she could return and finish what she started on another day.

Freeing herself from the bonds was the easy part—the question of where to go next posed the dilemma. She could not fight all of the eclipsers herself. She had been counting on having an army for that part. She had to go somewhere, and it seemed only two options sat before her.

She could find a way to get back down into her village in the canyon. If she could scale down the wall, she might be safe inside. She could hide in the maze of mine tunnels underground. At least, until the eclipsers dug her out by whatever means necessary.

Or, she could keep running. Head out into the world beyond. She knew nothing of it—in the canyon, food was handed to her. Where would she find it for herself? And what other dangers lay waiting for her to encounter? She didn't know the first thing about surviving out there—she had spent her whole life in that hole in the ground, and everyone she had ever known lived the same way.

But if she went back into the canyon, she'd have no glider and need a new plan. The eclipsers would learn from their mistakes; they were smarter than she expected. Getting out again would likely require several more years of planning, if she could figure out a new plan at all.

If she ran off into the wilds, at least she retained her newly-acquired freedom. At least she could return on her own terms to free the people of her village and kill the eclipsers.

Off into the wilderness it was, then.

She turned to see the boy looking at her, still lost but seeming to get more panicked as time passed. The other eclipsers would return soon, perhaps with an even larger force, or an order to kill the two of them. Oleja watched their lone captor as she paced. She walked several paces away and surveyed the way down to the gate and metal carnage on the wall that once comprised the opening mechanism.

With her tongue, Oleja dislodged the item in her mouth from where she held it inside her cheek. She clamped it between her teeth and parted her lips. The boy, still watching her, contorted his face into a look of surprise and realization. Clenched between her teeth she held a sharp piece of flint.

Oleja bowed her head and scraped the sharpest edge along the rope. It was an awkward angle, but she moved her head back and forth, sawing into the rope. Her braid fell into her face multiple times as she worked. Loose strands of hair caught in her mouth. Several long moments passed as the boy looked back and forth from her to the guard with a pleading gaze. At last, the final coarse threads snapped, and the rope started to unravel. With some help from the two of them as they pushed away from the stilt of the tower, it fell to the ground in a heap. Oleja scooped up her bow and quiver just as the guard turned around.

"Hey, sto—" was all she managed to get out before an arrow sailed through her open mouth and she fell twitching into the dirt.

"What now?" asked the boy, following Oleja in scooping up his belongings.

"I can't remain here. I'm leaving until I can figure out a plan to get everyone else free. You..." She paused and looked to him. He couldn't remain any more than she could. He made a choice to aid her, whether she wanted it or not, and now they would be after him just the same. She sighed. "You should come too. It won't be safe for you here."

He met her gaze and his lips curled into a smile. "I'll make sure I don't slow you down, but unfortunately *I* can't fly. I'm Pahlo, by the way. Where to?"

"Considering east will lead us straight into the heart of their camp, I'd say west—the more distance between us and them, the better."

Pahlo cast a wary glance east. "No need to convince me."

Oleja spun and looked west. The canyon crossed their path, but the south wall could serve as a bridge. She looked back to Pahlo.

"Best make ourselves scarce before the guards return," she said. And then she took off running.

CHAPTER SIX

A low fire burned between the two of them, built from scattered twigs and part of a shrub Oleja pulled from the sandy soil. It had put up a fight, something Pahlo explained was due to "roots"—parts of the plant under the ground. Oleja refused to give up. She could best even the toughest plant, no matter how much of it thought it could hide underground.

The fire popped and sent a spray of embers into the air. Skewered on a stick, Oleja roasted two small rodents over the flame, the only animals she had managed to catch all day. Foolishly, she left the village with no food and only a small supply of water, which was now almost gone. Pahlo carried little more in his own supplies. While lacking in food and water, he did have a small strip of clean bandage, which Oleja used to dress the wound on her forearm. But bandaging her wound offered no favors to her empty belly. By this point in the evening, she had expected to have free access to all the resources of her village, plus any stockpiles looted from the eclipser camp. She did not foresee a trek out into the desert, all alone save for the company of a strange boy she hardly knew. Perhaps she could have better prepared for failure, though in honesty, the only failure she could have anticipated was the death of herself and all of her people.

The desert proved more difficult than Oleja expected. Nothing she couldn't handle, but harsher than she imagined the world beyond the canyon walls would be. For one thing, the sun was one of her least favorite celestial bodies at the moment. In the canyon, its light illuminated the ground throughout the day, but the sun itself was only visible—and shining directly down on them—for a period around midday, a time when most worked down in the mines. The canyon floor spent the rest of the day in the relatively cool shade offered to them by the immense cliffs all around.

Up on the surface, there was no escaping the sun. It shone down in full force throughout the entire day, and nothing stood tall enough to cast significant shade for her to seek refuge. In fact, the only real features of the dry, sandy landscape were the low shrubs and scraggly trees, the only spots of green amongst a great expanse of rolling red hills and flat plains that went on for ages. Oleja found herself aching to return to the enormous expanse of water she saw during her flight—the lake, Pahlo called it. There, perhaps she could immerse herself in the cool water, a break from the heat of the sun that made them burn and sweat and drink their water all too quickly.

During their walk they had reached the edge of a smaller canyon. It looked quite unlike the one Oleja had lived in all her life, as this one bore steep sloping sides that one could feasibly walk up or down, and descended not nearly so deep. Disappointingly, it also lacked a river running through the bottom. They decided not to cross it immediately, and instead follow the rim in hopes that they could go around without making the possibly treacherous descent and then grueling climb back up the other side. The canyon ran northwest, and so it did not deter them from their path too severely.

In truth, Oleja did not know what her path should be. Straying far from the canyon and her village would make for a difficult return. But what was she waiting for? Time to pass so the eclipsers could fix the gate mechanism? How long until that happened? The gate opened so rarely that there was no telling whether or not they even intended to fix it. She could do it herself, but to do so required reaching it first, and the guards from the tower would spot her before she got her tools out—if she could even get to the gate without raising the alarm.

"Careful not to burn them," said Pahlo. Oleja looked down at the rodents. They grew crispy on one side, a result of her having not turned them in several minutes while lost in her own thoughts.

"I know what I'm doing. I like them that way."

Weariness weighed down her voice, a result of the long day of travel. It made the lie sound even less convincing.

Clearly, Pahlo picked up on it as well. He gave a single beat of laughter and then leaned back, stretching out in the sand. Over the course of the day's walk they had exchanged stories of their captivity. Pahlo was also a slave of the eclipsers, though that much was clear upon meeting him. He worked aboveground, tending to the animals that the eclipsers kept for food and for other uses. Apparently, many slaves worked aboveground, but nowhere near the numbers from Oleja's village. It seemed the mines were where the eclipsers concentrated their slave labor.

"They're probably about done," said Pahlo without even looking up to check on their supper.

"Yeah I was about to say that," said Oleja. "Uh... hang on, I can probably..." She looked around for a second stick.

"Here, let me see it," said Pahlo, holding out his hand. Oleja handed it to him after a moment of hesitation. He took the stick and poked one of the rodents, testing the temperature. Then, in haste to avoid a burn, he pushed the one lower on the stick down to the opposite end. After snapping the stick in the middle, he handed one half back to Oleja.

"Oh, yeah that works. Thanks."

Pahlo ripped off a bite and chewed for a moment. "So, Oleja Raseari, what's the plan?" He spoke through his food. The tone with which he said her name rang of playful mockery, a jab at her initial introduction. He reminded her of Ude—Ude, who probably thought she died in her attempt to free them all. She had to get back.

She swallowed a bite, then spoke. "The guard tower by the gate poses a problem. I can't fix the opening mechanism without being seen, so I have to take the guards out first. It seems like they post two guards per tower; I can kill them both and then go to the gate, but I'll have to surprise them and keep them from calling out or raising the alarm in any way, otherwise reinforcements will be close behind. I'll also have to make sure I go unseen as I approach, otherwise they'll raise the alarm and... well, you know. But that's tricky because there's no natural cover. So, I'd have to get there unseen, kill them before they can call out, and then fix the mechanism and open the gate before the guards change shifts. I don't know when that is, so I might have to scope it out for a few days first. But, again, there's no natural cover, so I'm not sure where I'd hide out." Pahlo looked on with an increasingly skeptical expression. Normally, she would be angry at receiving such a look, but the tiredness staved off irritation. Her shoulders slumped. Pahlo mirrored her own concerns. "In other words... I'm working on it."

"Hey, no worries, we'll figure it out. Maybe we can find some other people who will help or something."

We. She could do this on her own, he only tagged along because he had nowhere else to go. If she enacted a stealthy plan, the fewer bodies she had to keep hidden the better. It would be best if she went alone. And she especially didn't need to get even more people involved—more people who would get in the way, people who could falter and leave the whole plan in shambles if given too much responsibility. It only expanded the possibilities for failure, multiplied the weak links. No, she had to do this alone.

Pahlo chewed, deep in thought, then perked up after a moment and turned his eyes upwards to hers.

"Why did you tell me to wait when I grabbed the lever?"

Oleja's heart caught in her chest. What could she tell him? That she wanted to be the one to pull it so that she could be the hero? That sounded too selfish. Her heart thudded in her chest. She slowed her chewing, using it as an excuse to put off her answer. A moment passed. She swallowed.

"I saw the other two eclipsers approaching. I thought if you opened the gate, they would kill you for it."

The lie sounded weak—she knew it did. Pahlo did not look convinced. He started to open his mouth to say more, but he was cut off by a sound in the dark—footsteps, and many of them. The flurry of footfalls sounded too soft to indicate eclipsers, but they were accompanied by something else: a dragging, scraping noise.

Oleja scanned the dark landscape until she saw the source—a shape, indistinguishable, but moving towards them.

"Grab your things..." Oleja said in a cautionary tone. She shoved the last of her supper into her mouth and rose to her feet, nocking an arrow.

Closer and closer the form drew as details presented themselves. It was not one thing, but many. Eight animals in two rows bound by harnesses and tethers, together pulling something large behind them. Oleja squinted, trying to make out the shape of their cargo. As they got closer still, the firelight helped to reveal what approached.

The creatures ran on four legs. Sand-colored fur covered their bodies, from their pointed ears and snouts to their bushy tails. They howled and snarled and gnashed their teeth at Oleja and Pahlo, but their harnesses held them back. The tethers ran down the line to a structure of metal and wood. A platform of wooden slats rested upon two long, flat beams of metal which slid across the sand. On the platform, steering the sled, stood an eclipser shrouded from head to toe in gleaming silver armor.

Oleja backed up and took aim with her bow. She did not fire, but instead waited for the moment when a weakness presented itself. She now knew she could not puncture the metal armor that the eclipsers wore, and with the other guards it was easy enough to aim for the spots not covered by metal. This figure showed no such weaknesses—at least none that she could see while it remained in the shadows.

The eclipser lifted one foot and pressed down on a downward-pointing spike at the front of the sled. It plunged into the sand, bringing the whole thing to a jerking stop as the creatures that pulled it struggled against the stake. The eclipser stepped off the sled and flicked a visor on his helmet, revealing his face.

Oleja fired her arrow. The eclipser put one gauntlet-clad hand up and deflected it. The arrow disappeared into the darkness.

"There will be none of that," said the eclipser, stepping into the firelight and revealing his features. His skin was the same white-grey color patterned with scrape-like streaks of raw pink. His hair, silver and white like that of an older human, stuck out from his visor, and looked to be around the length of Pahlo's, though pulled back. Black eyes like two deep holes punctured his face. Firelight glinted in them, casting shadows across his face that enhanced his menacing appearance. He loomed taller than the guards by about half a foot. Two swords hung at his hips, and he carried a rectangular shield slung across his back. In his hand he held a crossbow, pointed at the ground quite fortunately, though loaded. Still, it was better than having it aimed at her head. She figured it would not be long before she lost the courtesy of such a pleasantry.

Oleja took another slow step back as he stepped forward. Her fingers itched for another arrow, but she didn't know where she should aim it.

"Your attempt to kill me was cute," said the eclipser, stopping his advance. "It won't be that easy. Word back at the camp says you killed two of our guards. Impressive. Few of your kind have ever managed even a fraction of that feat." He stooped so his head was level with hers. "But I'm not some guard. They are trained to watch, not fight. My name is Honn, I am a soldier, one of the best under The Earthtremor. You, a lowly miner girl, could never best me in a fight no matter how many decades you spend training. So, I advise you not to try." He straightened back to full height. "Make my life easy, and I will bring you back alive. This is your only opportunity for mercy."

Oleja stood her ground despite her mind screaming at her to run. Give up? Not a chance. Honn did not move his eyes from hers. Oleja gestured to Pahlo standing beside her.

"What of him?"

Honn cracked a grin. "Him? He is a stable boy. Next to you, I don't care about his fate. If it was about him, perhaps in my place you'd have one of those lowly guards you are so good at besting. I'm here for *you*."

"What makes her so special?" asked Pahlo, his voice a strange mixture of relief and hurt.

"For one thing, she's proven herself to be deadly. But she also gave the miners hope, something we have been trying to breed out of them for generations. They'll get unruly. Start trying to follow in her footsteps. And that's something we just can't have." He turned his focus back to Oleja. "Now, what will it be?"

Oleja paused for a moment. "Yeah, I'll go with you."

"Wise cho—"

"Straight to hell." Oleja swung an arrow from her quiver. Honn flicked his visor down. It made no difference. Oleja fired. Honn's crossbow flew from his hand as the arrow collided with it.

And then they ran.

Oleja took the lead. They sprinted around shrubs and zigzagged across the terrain until they reached the lip of the canyon. Oleja took hardly a moment's pause before she jumped. It was a drop of no more than six or seven feet down onto the slope of sand and rubble that led to the base. Just as Pahlo landed beside her, the whistle of a bolt sped by overhead. They raced down the slope, struggling to keep their balance on the loose terrain as they descended to the canyon floor.

It didn't take a backwards glance to know that Honn was close behind. The sounds of his heavy footfalls in the rubble could have reached Oleja's ears from miles off.

At the bottom of the slope, they took off running northwest. They could not outrun Honn—his legs were longer, his muscles stronger, and he'd likely been trained in this sort of endurance. If he caught them, a fight would be no better skewed in their favor. Oleja needed a plan.

"Up there!" called Pahlo. Oleja looked to where he pointed. Up the opposite slope a short distance was the entrance to a dark crevice. It looked barely wide enough for them to squeeze through—if they got to it and the opening was too small, they would be cornered. But Oleja had no better suggestions.

They took the upwards slope in bounding leaps, but the ascent was harder than the descent. Rubble shifted under their feet, causing them to slide with each step. A crossbow bolt flew between them and ricocheted off a stone. When they reached the crevice, Pahlo slipped inside first, turning sideways to squeeze through the narrow opening in the rock. Oleja followed. Her bag crashed against every outcropping of the stone, and she had to hold her bow vertically, but she managed to disappear into the darkness just as Honn reached the opening.

The path ahead slanted down several paces and twisted this way and that so the low light from the moon outside could not find them. Honn tried to fight his way into the passage. His metal armor scraped and clanged on the rock. Oleja followed Pahlo deeper, and soon she waded through thick, muddy water that rose up to her shins. The sounds of Honn's anger quieted for a few moments, and then came the echoing *ca-thung, tck tck tck* of one crossbow bolt after another sailing through the opening, only to bounce along the twisting rock walls and land on the ground somewhere behind them.

Following the attempts with his crossbow, it sounded as though Honn opted for trying to dig them out. His boots and gauntlets crashed against the stone, but it was clear he made little progress by the increasingly aggressive shouts of frustration that echoed off the walls.

Again, the air fell to stillness for a moment. Then came his voice.

"You had best hurry through this hole and hope I don't send my coyotes through after you. Whether I have them drag you out or I find you myself, know that you will see me again. My blades are sharp. You will know them well."

And then the night fell to silence.

CHAPTER SEVEN

By the time they reached the other end of the passage, the sun was rising. They had slept for a few hours at a wide point in the crevice where they could lie down and where the floor remained relatively dry, but nevertheless, they emerged from the dark looking exhausted, caked in mud and sand.

Oleja's stomach groaned impatiently. All she'd eaten in the past twenty-four hours was the rodent—hardly enough to constitute a meal, and not nearly enough to sate her. Water still posed a bigger problem. Though initially reluctant to do so, they had each taken a gulp from the silty water they trudged through in the crevice. Thick and muddy, it tasted like metal and dirt, and left a coating of sand in Oleja's mouth so that every time she brought her teeth together, they crunched in the grit.

The crevice opening deposited them back on the surface

after a tricky steep ascent in the dark. Back aboveground, they turned their course west once more and began the new day's trek, redoubling their speed now knowing Honn pursued them.

When Oleja untied her bandage, she found her wound looking better—the only good news of the morning. After washing it the day before with water she wished now she hadn't wasted, she discovered it was not nearly as bad as expected, and that the blood leaking out made it look much worse. Mud saturated the bandage, and sand clung to the surface, so she discarded it. The wound beneath was scabbed and raw, but ultimately healing, so keeping a bandage around it no longer seemed crucial.

A few times throughout the morning, Oleja tried her hand at hunting. Her efforts proved useless with each attempt. The first step in hunting—at least as far as Oleja knew—was to find an animal, and she couldn't even manage that. Without something to shoot at, hunting got an awful lot harder. A few birds, gliding through the air high above, continued to taunt her throughout the day. Too high to shoot, they stayed out of her reach, and though she watched them carefully they never seemed to land, instead soaring off into distant hills where they disappeared.

It was not until the sun rose high above that at last Oleja caught her first glimpse of ground-based wildlife. She picked her way across the arid landscape, weaving around shrubs and boulders. A shrill rattling piped up from somewhere unseen and filled the air. Oleja jumped and halted her pace. Her eyes darted across the ground until she saw it. The snake lay only another pace and a half ahead of her, stretched across her path where she hadn't noticed it previously. Beady black eyes watched her.

Occasionally, rattlesnakes turned up in the village, though how they got down the cliff Oleja could never tell. Every now and then someone fell victim to their venom, so Oleja knew how dangerous they could be. She took a few steps back to put a safe distance between herself and the creature.

Only when her arrow pierced the head and pinned it to the ground did she relax. She severed the body from the head with her knife, retrieved the arrow, and showed the catch to Pahlo. It was no feast, but it was something edible to put in their mouths, and they welcomed anything of the sort given how little filled their stomachs.

Oleja cooked the snake over a small fire, but they took their meal along for the walk. Though she wouldn't voice the feeling, she feared Honn, and felt no desire to give him the opportunity to catch up with them again. When Pahlo suggested turning their course south to loop back and meet up with the river that ran through Oleja's village farther downstream, she rejected the plan. Their dehydration might have been killing them, but Honn would kill them faster. Once she knew what to do about the hunter, she would go back—she would have to sooner or later in order to rescue her people. For now, the more distance between her and the eclipser, the better, even if that meant traveling farther away from her village.

As they walked, the groups of scraggly plants gradually grew denser and denser, the shrubs turning from low bushes around Oleja's height into taller trees. But the deeper into this expansive landscape of trees they got, the deader everything became. In most places the trees were little more than pillars of grey wood. The trunks cast some shade upon the ground, which brought the temperature down slightly—not enough to be of any great relief, but a noticeable degree nonetheless. All too soon, they reached the other end of the strange landscape, returning to the flat desert land. As she passed through, however, Oleja gathered a few sticks to fashion into arrows. She had lost six so far in her fights with the eclipser guards and Honn, leaving her with only a dozen.

As the sun set ahead of them, casting the world in a deep orange light, something emerged on the horizon. Framed in the evening light rose structures that stood out against the natural wilds they had been traveling through for the past two days. Boxy things, they clustered together like huddled creatures, all built from grey stone, wood, metal, and other materials—buildings, most likely, though only holding such titles long ago while still in their prime. Now they crumbled to piles of rubble. Ruins, Oleja determined, not unlike those that comprised much of the eclipser camp. Remnants of the Old World.

Warily, they approached. The ruins bore an eerie resemblance to the ones inhabited by the eclipsers. But when a brook of clear water came into view, glittering in the low sunlight as it fed a wider pool on the outskirts of the ruins, all hesitations evaporated and they both broke into a run.

The water was cool on Oleja's skin and cooler on her tongue. She drank her fill and then waded into the water—clothes, boots, and all—washing off days' worth of dirt and sweat. Dark brown mud, orange sand, and red blood stained the water around her as it all washed away. She remained in the water until it ran clear around her. With her need for water sated, she turned to the needs of her stomach. Where there was water, animals likely dwelled nearby—that she knew. She made her errand clear to Pahlo, who decided to stay behind to start a fire, and set off following the river through the ruins.

The land to either side of the small river stood out as a strip of green amidst the rusty sand and dirt of the landscape beyond. The air smelled of damp earth, and somehow held a scent she could only describe as "clean," which contrasted the dusty hot air she was used to breathing. Lush trees and bushes rose up on either bank. In the dwindling light of dusk, insects buzzed, calling out to one another. Even in the dark, the plants displayed a more vibrant green than anything Oleja had ever imagined. This strip of land was alive, more so than she thought possible.

Scattered buildings—or what once could have been referred to as such—clustered together more closely the farther along Oleja went. The water ran through a gully that grew deeper as she walked upstream, and when the sides became too high to see over, she climbed up from her path beside the riverbed and walked along the ridge.

The ruins showed no signs of life—or rather, no signs of hostile life. Eclipsers were big, and therefore would struggle to hide an entire camp's worth of soldiers amidst such meager cover. Few of the buildings had much more than a wall or two left standing, or in some cases even as little as a few metal supports, stripped of whatever material comprised the rest. They looked to have been untouched for ages by eclipsers and humans alike.

Whether or not humans existed beyond the border of the eclipser camp, Oleja still didn't know. Pahlo's knowledge on the matter was equally thin, though he said sometimes he heard conflicts unfolding on the borders of the camp. Whether those noises came from humans, other eclipsers, or wild animals always remained unclear to him.

A rustle in the brush down by the river caught Oleja's attention. She stopped walking and crouched low, peering through the darkness, praying whatever moved was more interested in being eaten than in eating her.

She saw its ears first, standing tall atop its head. It took a few hops on all fours out into the open, looking up and down several times and then standing still, watching. Oleja drew an arrow with the utmost level of slow, nonaggressive movement one can achieve while drawing a weapon. She took aim, then released. The creature fell with the arrow stuck through its neck.

Two identical animals bounded from the underbrush, panicked after the death of their companion. Surprise held Oleja immobile for a moment. Then she snapped to her senses and drew another arrow. The creatures moved with impressive speed, but she hit a second before it disappeared. The third vanished into the shadows and was lost to her. She shrugged off the loss. Two would be plenty; they had enough meat on them to provide a few meals each.

With her catch in tow, she returned to where Pahlo waited, triumph carrying her all the way back. She had food, water, and a relatively safe place to sleep. If not for the eclipser soldier and eight angry coyotes after her, she couldn't have been more successful in her detour expedition into the wilderness—or whatever she should call it.

Pahlo looked up from where he sat tending a fire as Oleja approached. "Jackrabbits, fantastic! I'm starving."

Oleja held the two animals up by their hind legs. "If that's what you call these things, then yes."

"Last I checked, we definitely call jackrabbits 'jackrabbits.'"

Oleja dropped them on the ground and drew her knife. "Seems sensible."

Pahlo took the knife and set to work skinning the animals and cutting the meat from the bones. Oleja would have preferred to do it herself, but she was entirely unfamiliar with the work. Pahlo, on the other hand, had worked with animals all his life, and done his fair share of preparing them to be cooked. She looked on as he worked, trying to learn from observing. It didn't look all that hard.

"Speaking of what you call things," said Pahlo after a moment, "why do you call them 'eclipsers'?"

Oleja looked at him, confused. "What do you call them?"

"We call them what they call themselves—the earthborn. But I suppose they don't interact with you or your people the same way they do with us."

Oleja shook her head. "I didn't even know they spoke the same language as us until I met the ones at the guard tower. Well, 'met' might not be the right word, since I killed both of them shortly after. So no, not quite." Oleja lifted her bag off her shoulder and pulled out a few odds and ends, fiddling with them mindlessly as she spoke. "Technically we call them 'sky eclipsers,' but that's long so usually people just shorten it to 'eclipsers.' I'm not sure why it started, probably because when they stand at the edge of the canyon they sort of 'eclipse the sky' or something. But they aren't *that* big. It almost seems like more than they deserve. Why do they call themselves the earthborn?"

Pahlo shrugged. "I didn't have casual conversations with them. It wasn't like we all sat around to chat, the humans and the earthborn. Just because we had more contact with them than you, doesn't mean we wanted to interact with them any more than was absolutely necessary. They told us what to do, we did it, and that was it."

"Did any of your people ever run away? I imagine it would have been easier for you, since you didn't have walls hundreds of feet high keeping you in."

"Some tried," responded Pahlo. "But nearly every time, the earthborn caught them. A few hours after an escape, they always threw the person's corpse back into the slave quarters. The bodies were horribly broken and mangled. The earthborn said they caught the escapee, brought them before the leader of the earthborn camp, and beat them. Then they showed the rest of us the body as a lesson."

Oleja let that sink in for several long minutes. Something about it seemed off to her—besides the horrifying maltreatment—but she couldn't quite pinpoint what it was. She kept thinking of Honn, chasing her into the desert, dragging her corpse back to the village. At least so far, she was doing pretty well—sure she'd had a rough couple of days, but things were looking up now. It was a far cry from "dying in the wilderness."

And then it dawned on her.

"What happened to the ones that escaped?" she asked. "You said '*nearly* every time.' What happened when someone succeeded?"

Pahlo looked up from the jackrabbit he worked on. "They beat everyone else. Not to the point of death, but someone had to serve the punishment."

"That's it?"

Pahlo looked taken aback. "Uh, yes. Why?"

"Well, because Honn said he is after me and cares less about you. He wants to bring my body back to keep my people from getting unruly or thinking they can also succeed in escaping, but your fate is less important to him. Shouldn't he bring your body back too and display it to your people?"

Pahlo slowed his work as his mind worked around the

question. After a moment of consideration, he spoke again. "I don't know. Maybe they just aren't as concerned about keeping us in line. The labor we provide isn't as valuable I suppose."

"So, the cost of going out to retrieve one of your people isn't worth it to them," said Oleja, starting to piece it together. "It's easier for your people to escape, so as long as they catch *most*, they figure it's as good of a deterrent as they can get. Keeping us in line is easier—it's rare that anyone escapes, so when it happens, they are willing to maintain a record of catching *all*. Because there are more of us. And we are armed."

Pahlo shrugged. It was all a theory, of course. The only one who could explain it to them fully was Honn, and in all honesty Oleja hoped she never got the opportunity to ask him. It was clear why he wanted to capture Oleja and bring her back to the village, dead or alive. She couldn't lie—part of her liked that she carried so much importance, even if it came with a personal hunter set on catching or killing her. Still, if ever she got the chance, perhaps she would pry a more satisfactory answer from the lips of one of those monsters just before she killed them.

Another question sat on her tongue. "Why are you traveling with me?" she asked Pahlo. "I mean, I'm being hunted, you aren't. Even still, Honn would kill you just the same as me, or drag you back as a bonus. You could have your freedom simply by turning your path away from mine."

Pahlo laughed—not exactly the response Oleja expected. She watched him, puzzled.

"Well, first of all, you have the bow, and therefore you can get the food. I may be able to skin the animals, but I can't catch them. I'd probably die of starvation." His grin faltered for a second as he looked like he debated saying more. A moment passed, and then he continued. "I've also always had this idea... I guess it might be kind of stupid or optimistic or something... I just want to help one person. Or, at least one. Because if everyone helps just one person, then everyone gets help in the end, right? You said there are what, *hundreds* down in the canyon? Plus my people, that's definitely more than one. I want to help them... put some good into the world, I guess. I don't know. But I think sticking with you is the way to do it. I certainly couldn't do it on my own."

Oleja listened intently. Pahlo was only the second person ever to open up to her about anything, she didn't want to ruin it. Now didn't seem like a good time to tell him she didn't want his help and that she preferred to do this by herself.

"I see," was all she said in response. She finished it with a smile, unsure of what else to say. She'd have to break the news to him eventually, but not now. He nodded and refocused his attention on the jackrabbits.

When Pahlo finished with the carcasses, they cooked the meat over the fire—enough for their evening meal, breakfast the next morning, and then more still to take with them as rations. They set up the surplus to be smoked and dried so it would last longer on the road ahead.

By the time their supper finished cooking, Oleja was ready to snatch it from the flames if it took even a minute longer. The meat was tough, but she couldn't bring herself to care in the slightest. It was food, and far better than the rodent from the night before or the rattlesnake from their afternoon meal—not to mention much more filling. Even better was the endless supply of water with which to wash it down.

Satisfied for the first time since before she left the canyon, Oleja sat by the fire and tinkered with pieces from her bag. She built nothing in particular—it was the action of creating, of using her hands, that she did it for. It grounded her. Brought some familiarity into this world that felt so far beyond everything her mind had ever conjured up about it. Sounds filled the night—insects, the call of some unknown bird. She let herself feel alive with the world as it breathed around her.

But one sound in the night pulled her back into the reality of her situation. A shrill howl echoed off the hills. Oleja and Pahlo looked to each other.

After some deliberation, they agreed to remain at their current campsite for the night but continue west at first light. For one thing, they couldn't be sure that the coyote they heard belonged to Honn. It was only a single howl, and despite the images it conjured up, it sounded almost peaceful. Honn's coyotes were angry, their calls guttural and full of malice. Even if the howl came from Honn's team, it was distant. No amount of running would change the fact that they needed sleep sometime. They decided it best to at least attempt to remain near their source of water.

Oleja agreed to take the first watch. She kept her bow close so that if anything appeared in the darkness, she would be ready to put up a fight. Soon, Pahlo drifted off, leaving Oleja alone in the night.

CHAPTER EIGHT

Miraculously, they did not die in the night.

When Pahlo woke Oleja after his watch shift, she still had all her limbs, as did he, and they were both still alive as far as she could tell. Not being coyote food was as good a way to start the day as any, and so they readied to be off.

The sun came up as they ate. After their breakfast, Pahlo set to work wrapping the dried jackrabbit meat in the meager scraps of material they had. Oleja paced about, unsure of what she should do to help. The longer they spent without moving, the more agitated she became, and eventually she grew too eager to move that she could not stand around any longer. It felt as though a pressure built up inside her body, threatening to make her burst.

"I'm going to go out and hunt for a bit," she said.

Pahlo nodded, more to himself than to her it seemed. "Yeah, good idea. We'll stock up on food while we can."

"Exactly. I'll meet you back here in a bit," she said, and then set off at a jog. Moving her muscles quickly pared away her agitation.

She followed the stream north for a while. It wound around the outskirts of the ruins, zigzagging back and forth along the bottom the gully carved through the rocky land. She passed the spot where she shot the jackrabbits the night before and continued on, divorcing her path from the riverbank and heading deeper into the field of broken carcasses of long-abandoned buildings. They nestled more tightly together the further she went, right up to the base of a steep, flat-topped hill beyond. After winding through the buildings and arriving at the edge of the ruins, she was confronted by the slope. She looked up to the ledge at the top. Seeing the ruins from above would give her a fresh vantage point that could direct her to the best hunting grounds or give her a better view of the course of the river below. The elevation could be a useful tool for planning the day's course. And in honesty, she just wanted to move.

Climbing the first half of the hill was easy enough. The slopes were steep, but nothing she couldn't manage. Halfway up, the slope turned to a sheer vertical cliff, which then leveled off into another steep slope, and then yet another cliff. Walking up and down along the base allowed her to find a place where the cliff rose up only as high as the top of her head. The pocked stone provided plenty of hand and footholds, and she climbed it easily.

At the top, Oleja looked out over the ruins below. The sun rose to her left, now fully emerged over the horizon, casting the world in warm light. For a moment, a feeling struck Oleja, something new to her that she had never in her life experienced. It washed over her and lifted her up. A weightlessness flowed through her limbs. Several moments of staring out at the expanses of rolling hills and cliffs of various reds and oranges passed before she managed to put a name to the sensation: freedom. She was free. She could go anywhere and do anything she pleased.

Except, an eclipser soldier hunted her.

Just as quickly as the feeling came, it evaporated, slipping away like the sand at the edge of the hill that she toed with her boot, sending it in tiny avalanches over the edge. She had to get going, and the sooner the better. No more wasting time.

Movement in the ruins below drew her eye. For a second her heart froze, and then came back to life in full force. She scanned the ruins. Nothing moved. Did she imagine it? A trick of the light?

There it was again—a white blur moving between stone walls and heaps of rubble. Humanoid in shape, but from her distance she had no scale for size. Another followed the first. Likely not Honn in that case—he seemed the type to prefer traveling alone.

More shapes emerged, though not all of them stuck together in one cluster. Oleja counted seven in total, split into loose groups of two or three. They swept through the ruins in haste, stopping occasionally, though Oleja could not see for what. One thing was clear: they moved with a purpose. They were looking for something.

Her immediate instinct told her to turn and leave. Even if they spotted her, watching them from her perch above the ruins, they couldn't get to her with any great degree of haste. They'd have to cross through a large part of the ruins and climb the hill. By then she could be far away or have found herself a hiding spot. She could pick them all off with her bow as they struggled up the cliff. Relatively speaking, she was in little danger. Whatever went on below, she didn't need to take part in it, and could be off without a single arrow fired. But while she might not have been in danger, Pahlo was.

She could leave him. She meant to part ways with him eventually to return to her people anyway. Why not now? It would be easy enough. Chances were high that if she left in that moment, she'd never see him again. Cutting ties could be as clean and simple as turning the other way.

But returning to save him would be the right thing to do. He carried no weapons; she held the role of fighter among the pair. Equally, he had skills that she did not, including knowledge of the world beyond the canyon that she had been confined to for nineteen years. She could use that expertise as she planned her next move against the eclipsers. But was it worth putting her life at risk to run back through the ruins to save him?

Her feet made the decision for her as she dropped over the edge and picked her way down the steep hill, bounding down the low cliffs as she reached them. Seven of the figures roamed the ruins. She knew their numbers and had the element of surprise. Twelve arrows still rattled in her quiver. She had to pull this off. She couldn't die—someone had to return to free her people from the canyon. Death was not an option.

Back on even ground, she set off at a run. She drew an arrow from her quiver and nocked it, ready should she encounter one of the figures, though still she clung to the hope of evading them. Twisting through the ruins, she vaulted low walls of rubble and debris, sticking to what she hoped was the most concealed path—though she prioritized speed even above stealth. The figures were divided. If it came to a fight, she could take three at once as long as surprise remained on her side.

She rounded a bend and came skidding to a stop. Just ahead, two of the figures looked over something with their backs to her. Her feet ground in the dirt as she scrambled to reverse her course. The figures turned in unison.

Oleja drew back her arrow and took aim at one of the two. The opposing figures drew their own weapons with blinding speed. One grabbed a spear from their back; the other unsheathed a sword. But no one moved to make the first attack.

The spear could be thrown. The sword less-so; or rather, it could be, but the gesture would be ineffective. Throwing a spear took more time than loosing an arrow. As long as Oleja shot the spear-wielder first, the one with the sword would be too far off to attack, giving her plenty of time to fire a second arrow. The balance of the fight leaned in her favor. Hopefully her opponents knew that as well. Either way, she could use the moment of pause to figure out exactly what she was about to shoot.

Both figures wore robe-like garments of white with loose, rounded hoods and veils that shrouded their faces from view. Gloves of white wrapped their hands. Not even the slightest speck of skin remained visible anywhere on their bodies. Now that she saw them closer, she could tell that neither stood much taller than her. Humans, most likely—or at least not eclipsers.

The standoff dragged on as neither party lowered their weapons, nor moved to attack. It was her opponents who eventually broke the trance, as both seemed almost to relax after a moment. Odd, considering Oleja kept her bow aimed at the one with the spear, but if they preferred to die without the tension in their bodies that was none of her business. The one with the spear pulled back their hood, revealing their face.

The head of black hair made Oleja guess "human," but the resemblances stopped there. It looked like a man, but with skin drained of all color—ghastly white with only a dash of pink. The second figure removed their own hood as well, revealing similarly drained skin. But this one, another man, had no color in his hair either. No longer black or dark brown, nor the silver or white of age or akin to that of the eclipsers, his hair was yellow like gold—both that atop his head, pulled into a ponytail, and that of his beard. The yellow-haired man's face showed a tint more color than his companion's, though it came from a redness that stained his nose and plump cheeks. Oleja still could not wrap her mind around the colorlessness of their faces. She glanced back to their hands. Now that she saw their skin, she knew she was mistaken in her assumption that they wore gloves—rather, their skin was the same shade of white all across their bodies.

"Easy there, girl. Mind lowering that before you skewer one of us? We won't hurt you," said the yellow-haired man. His voice was softer than expected, higher and light. No anger fueled his words, nor fear.

He sheathed his sword and held his hands up, palms out. An elbow in his companion's side prompted him to do the same, and soon both were unarmed. Oleja did not lower her bow.

"Are you alone?" asked the yellow-haired man.

"No."

"How many are in your party?"

Oleja paused before answering. "Depends. What number would you like that to be?"

The man chuckled. "Well, I supposed a great number, so long as you all are friendly and looking to join with a group of others. We always like to add new faces to our family."

Oleja stared at him blankly. She expected the man to hope for a smaller group, one that could be easily bested by his own. But now he talked recruitment, and seemed to do so in earnest.

Oleja lowered her bow and eased her draw, but kept the arrow nocked. "I travel with one other."

"No great host, but new faces nonetheless," said the man with a smile and a shrug. "Unless you still wish to put that arrow through me. I wouldn't blame you. Onet here often wants to put an arrow through me as well, but he hasn't gotten his hands on any yet." He gestured to the man by his side as he spoke. "Come on then, where is your friend?"

The dark-haired man—Onet—interrupted before she could answer.

"When have I ever said I wanted to put an arrow through you?"

The first man batted him aside. "You don't need to say it; I can read it on your face every day." He looked back to Oleja as if to restate his question, taking a step towards her.

Oleja stepped back. "First… what is wrong with your skin?"

Both men looked at her in confusion.

"Our…?" started Onet.

"What *is* wrong with our skin?" asked the other man.

Oleja gestured to her own face. "It's all… there's no color left."

Confusion deepened on both of their faces, but then the yellow-haired man's expression snapped into understanding. He burst into laughter.

"What is so funny?" asked Oleja, growing agitated with whatever game was unfolding before her. The man's laughs petered out after a few seconds. He looked to her in amusement.

"Have you never seen a white man before?"

Oleja inched away another step. "What is a whiteman?"

The man looked her up and down, peering at her

though eyes narrowed in thought. "Looks like you have some in you yourself, though nothing is so clean-cut anymore. Everyone has a lot of everything mixed up in them—this isn't the Old World. But don't worry about that right now. Casmia will be wondering after our whereabouts. Would you care to walk with us?"

Oleja didn't know what the man was talking about, but neither of the two looked to be entertaining any lasting threats towards her. If they expected her to trust them, however, they either had too high perceptions of themselves or thought her too weak to bother maintaining her guard. Nevertheless, she fell in step with them after a moment's hesitation.

Each of the men carried a backpack, both equally large and bulging into misshapen dimensions, bearing an odd resemblance to Oleja's own bag in the way in the way the contents shifted and clanked within as the pair moved. She eyed them curiously as she followed along.

"My name is Wulshe, Wulshe Gleathon," said the yellow-haired man. "Do you have a name, or is that a foreign concept to you as well?"

Oleja raised an eyebrow. "Of course I have a name. Oleja Raseari." She straightened her shoulders and held her head high. Wulshe extended a hand in greeting. Oleja paused, again eyeing the strangeness of his skin, but then clasped it in her own.

Wulshe clapped a hand on Onet's shoulder, a full hand's length above his own. "Onet, perhaps offer an introduction to Oleja?"

"Quinje Onet," he said, and held out his hand to her. He was younger than Wulshe by perhaps twenty years, but still at least a decade older than Oleja. After he released her hand, he combed his fingers through his black hair, shaking sand from the dark tangles, and drew his hood back up.

Wulshe shrugged. "You'll have to excuse him. He doesn't take kindly to having weapons pointed at him. But then, few of us do. Ah, there they are."

Oleja followed his gaze. Up ahead gathered a group of people amidst a circle of ruins. For a moment Oleja thought to turn around. Walking into a larger gathering took the option of fighting her way through them in groups off the table, and she still didn't know if she should trust these people. But when she looked closer at the figures, she noticed Pahlo among them, speaking animatedly with a woman who smiled as she listened. He turned as they approached.

"Oleja! Look!" he called out with a wave and a gesture to the others who stood with him. A wide grin split his face.

Around Pahlo stood three others, each one clad in the same white outfit as Wulshe and Onet. A large cart sat just behind them. Wood comprised the body of it, set with four large spoked wheels of wood and metal. An arched canvas tent covered the top, and a wooden gate and dingy curtain at the back allowed access to the interior while concealing whatever lay within. How the group managed to pull such a thing was impressive.

"This must be your companion," said one woman from the group to Pahlo. She was older, though not as old as

Wulshe. Her skin was darker than either man's, though still a few shades lighter than Oleja's or Pahlo's. Brown curls streaked with grey fell around her face, barely brushing her neck and jawline. She held a hand out to clasp Oleja's. "I am Casmia Lashinel. I'm the leader of this party of raiders. I see you found Gleathon and Onet."

"This is Oleja Raseani, she's a feisty one—quick on her weapons," said Wulshe to the group.

"It's 'Rasea*ri*,'" said Oleja with a glare. Nevertheless, she took Casmia's hand. The woman's grasp was firm. Oleja's was more so.

Behind her, Pahlo approached Wulshe and Onet. "I'm Pahlo Dirin, nice to meet you." Oleja could only assume he shook their hands and got their names as well, but she didn't turn to look. She kept her attention on Casmia, sizing up the self-described "leader."

Casmia released first and gestured to the others behind her. "And these are two other members of my crew." The pair came forward. The first was a woman around Casmia's age, while the second was much younger. Aside from age, the pair looked incredibly similar, with the same light brown hair and pale colorless skin. The older woman's hair was cut short, while the girl's fell in waves down to her upper back. Both had the same narrow jaw, high cheekbones, and noses identical in shape. Most startling, however, were their eyes—not a dark shade like every other pair Oleja had ever seen, but a pale and shining blue like that of the sky. She could not help but stare.

"I'm Hylde," said the older woman, "and this is my

daughter, Kella." She put an arm around the girl's shoulders and squeezed. Kella looked at Oleja with eyes and smile alike stretched wide.

"We don't often run into younger travelers," said Kella. "I'm eleven, the youngest of the raiders by…" she scrunched up her face as she counted in her mind, "fifteen years."

"Your eyes…" was all Oleja said in response.

"My—"

"Seems she had never seen light skin until Onet and I," said Wulshe. "The same probably goes for your eyes."

Kella looked back at Oleja. "Oh! Yes, they're blue, like my mom's."

Oleja smiled. "They're nice."

Wulshe let out a huff behind her. "She was scared of our skin—how come you get the compliments?"

"I wasn't scared," she said, turning to face him. Wulshe cracked a toothy grin.

"Ah, I jest! No harm, no harm."

Casmia took him by the shoulder and steered him away. "Leave her alone, Gleathon. Go see if you can find Jeth and Trayde, I don't know what's taking them so long."

Wulshe shuffled away, muttering to himself. Casmia approached Oleja and Pahlo.

"So, you two—will you be joining us, or do you travel alone? We always welcome new recruits. The more hands we have, the more loot we can gather to trade. That's our business, of course—we travel through ruins searching for useful items among them." She looked the two of them up and down. "You're both young and strong. But it's your choice. We leave soon." With a nod to each of them in turn, she took her leave and went to check on something in the cart. Pahlo pulled Oleja aside.

"We could get their help fighting the earthborn!" he said excitedly, though he kept his voice low. "They all have weapons, and probably at least some idea of how to fight. They aren't an army, but they could fight with us."

Oleja shook her head immediately. "No, I won't drag them into this. I don't even know if I can trust them."

Pahlo frowned. "They seem nice enough."

"Maybe. It doesn't matter. I don't need their help, I just need more time to think and to deal with Honn. I don't need soldiers, I need time."

Pahlo considered this for a minute, looking back to the group. "In the meantime, we could still travel with them," he said with a small, hopeful smile. Oleja looked back over her shoulder. At the very least, they'd find safety in numbers—assuming the dangers didn't come from within. But Pahlo was right—they seemed like well-meaning people. They had food and water as well. And if Oleja was honest, the prospect of going to other ruins and searching for useful loot excited her; perhaps she could find what she needed for a new glider.

For the moment, it couldn't hurt to travel with the raiders. But only until the time came to go back and rescue her people.

"Fine," she said. "But I don't think we should tell them about Honn just yet. Might be best to disclose that later. If they know we are being hunted, they may not want anything to do with us."

Pahlo pursed his lips. "All right."

The pair rejoined the group. Casmia watched them approach.

"You will join us then?" she asked, her head poking out through the curtain in the back of the cart.

"We will, at least for a time, if that is acceptable," responded Oleja.

"Splendid." Casmia ducked inside and reemerged a moment later with two folded bundles of white cloth. She tossed one to each of them. "Here, put these on. They will keep you cool in the harsh desert sun. Do you each have enough water?"

Oleja withdrew from her bag the clay canteen she carried from her village. "I have this. I filled it just this morning from the stream." Pahlo held up his waterskin.

"Here, take these," said Casmia and tossed them each another waterskin, both full. "Drinking plenty of water is the best way to fight the heat. We have more in the wagon for refills." She pulled aside the curtain to reveal a wide metal drum with a spigot on the side. "Ah, there's Jeth and Trayde, finally."

Wulshe returned, and with him walked two others. They wore the same white robes as the rest of the group and toted full backpacks that matched the ones Wulshe and Onet carried, which they had since unloaded into the wagon. The trio approached Oleja and Pahlo.

"We have some newbies here," said Wulshe, gesturing

to the two of them. Oleja stepped up to greet the two new faces. Both looked young, somewhere in their twenties. One was a man with skin so dark he looked to have absorbed all the color the others had lost. He was taller than her by a few inches, and just as muscled. His dark brown hair bounced as he swung his pack off and put out a hand.

"Nice to meet you. I'm Jethilan Nodo."

"Oleja Raseari," she said. He shook Pahlo's hand and got his name next.

The girl beside Jethilan wore a complexion like Oleja's own. Her dark hair was shaved close to her scalp. Though she and Oleja were nearly matched in height, the other girl looked taller from a distance due to her wiry frame, all muscle and bone. Her greeting came in the form of a sneer-like smile and a wave. Oleja gladly accepted the odd welcome—if she had to shake one more hand, she'd lose her mind. Nothing would save her from having to remember the whole chorus of new names and their corresponding faces, however, though it helped that, for some reason, everyone in the group looked startlingly different—more so than Oleja knew possible.

"Fressa Trayde," said the girl. "But just call me Trayde. You don't look all that old—how old are you, kid?"

"Nineteen."

"I'm seventeen... uh, in case you wanted to know that too," said Pahlo. "How old are you?"

Trayde looked him up and down with a smirk. "Too old for you, cattleboy."

Pahlo's face reddened. "Oh, no, I didn't mean... I

wasn't, like, flirting. Just trying to be polite. Wait, how do you know I've worked with cattle?"

"You reek of it. You seen the horses yet? They're mine, had 'em since before I joined the raiders."

Pahlo looked around. "You have horses?"

Trayde rolled her eyes. "How else are we hauling that thing around?" She stuck her thumb at the wagon. Oleja kept quiet—not only because she thought they pulled it, but also because she didn't know what a horse was. If she had to guess, she'd definitely venture to say it was some type of animal.

Trayde went to the wagon and tossed her backpack inside, then returned. "I actually have to go fetch the horses now. I left 'em to graze in a field just that way near the river." She pointed southwest and looked to Pahlo. "If you can ride, you can come."

Pahlo beamed. "I can ride! Well, mostly. I've done it a few times."

Trayde shrugged. "Eh, good enough for me. Come on." She headed off with Pahlo at her heels.

Oleja put on her new clothes. They were surprisingly light and cool. She stuffed her old tattered shirt and pants into her bag—even if she didn't wear them again, the fabric could be useful for other things.

A short while later, Trayde and Pahlo returned. Oleja jumped in fright when they rushed in atop a pair of the largest animals Oleja had ever seen. One was brown, and the other was grey. Each had a long neck with hair in neat little braids. Their feet seemed to be hard like bone, as each step on the stone ground resulted in a loud *clop*. Oleja backed away and gave the animals plenty of space. Wulshe eyed her from the side.

"Horses!" he called out to her, as if answering a question before she asked it.

"I *know* that!" she shouted back. She didn't like being treated like a fool.

When the horses were hitched to the wagon, Casmia surveyed everything and counted the group.

"Right then. Shall we head out?" From a pocket in her clothes she withdrew a folded piece of paper, opened it up, and looked over whatever was depicted on the other side. "Southwest will take us around this plateau to the next ruins," she said. She looked back up at the group and smiled. "Let's go."

CHAPTER NINE

The wagon was strictly for carrying supplies and not to ease the burden of walking, as it turned out. If Casmia had not explained that they walked alongside the wagon rather than seated inside, Oleja would likely have urged them all to do so anyway in order to lessen the weight for the horses and increase their speed. Even without the burden of bodies, the wagon was not fast by any means, and the group set their pace by the slowness of it. Oleja felt as though they moved forward by the inch. The cart bumped along, catching and creaking and sliding over the uneven terrain. The sandier patches gave no reprieve— the wheels sank into the soft sand, putting additional strain on the horses just to keep it going. Oleja could hardly imagine how much slower their travel would progress if they all rode aboard—if, under such circumstances, the horses could even move at all. Just because she joined the group did not mean she no longer prioritized speed.

Anxiety burrowed deeper and deeper into her mind as the day wore on.

Multiple times she approached Casmia, who led the party in front of the wagon, to ask about their route and destination. Casmia showed her the paper she carried—a map of the area—but only briefly. It seemed to be of great importance to her, and she kept it close. She said the ruins they aimed for lay due west of the ones they had left, but their path cut around in a wide semicircle in order to stick to the lower, flat terrain where the wagon could pass with relatively little trouble. Her best estimate was that they'd arrive the following day. Oleja's requests to see the map in more detail were politely declined. While she walked with the woman, Casmia took several curious glances at Oleja's bag, which clattered against her hip as she walked.

"What do you carry in the bag?" she asked at last.

Oleja lifted the flap and exposed the contents. She took a few pieces in her hands, along with some of her tools. "Odds and ends mostly. Food and water too."

Casmia surveyed the collection. "That's not too unlike the stuff we gather from the ruins, though often we look for things more intact, or old artifacts. Why do you collect it?"

"I like to tinker," said Oleja. "I make things—sometimes for a purpose, other times just for something to do."

"That's impressive. We don't typically use the scraps we gather, but trade them for items more useful to us. If you are versed in your skill, you could find an important role here among the team."

"I'd like to think I am," said Oleja with a smile.

"Although, typically I need more specialized parts to make anything worthwhile. What I carry is mostly generic additional components."

"Come with me," said Casmia, and started off on a path that led them around behind the wagon. She opened the gate and hoisted herself up through the curtains, then extended a hand to Oleja to aid her. Oleja managed without the help. She pushed through the curtains and into the dimly lit bed of the wagon.

Shelves lined the sides, each holding rows of crates and boxes. More piles of stuff filled the center, creating two aisles down the length of the wagon. Casmia went to a few boxes and began pulling them from the shelves. Each sang with the familiar shrill sound of metal clanking against metal.

"We have a wide variety of things in here," said Casmia, sifting through the contents. "Feel free to take a look. If anything catches your eye, let me know. It's all property of the raider party, but if you have a worthy design that will benefit us or perhaps that we could sell, run it by me and I may let you use it." Casmia smiled to Oleja. "It's good to have you on board; with your skillset, I'm sure you'll fit right in."

"Thank you," said Oleja, but she didn't have time to say more—such as voice her question asking what she meant by selling things—before Casmia ducked back out of the wagon to retake her position at the front.

Oleja left the wagon soon after, knowing her added weight would only slow the horses more, and though excitement beckoned her to see what sort of tinkering materials the raiders carried, Honn still lurked in the shadows of her mind.

She returned to walk beside Pahlo. He kept pace where the two had taken up a position at the back of the group between Oleja's trips up to ask Casmia about their route. Not long after Oleja rejoined him, the younger girl, Kella, fell back and walked alongside them.

"Hey," she said, a note of shyness in her voice. "Uh, what do you think of your new clothes?"

"Surprisingly cool," said Oleja.

"And really soft," added Pahlo, running his hands over them.

"Yeah, they are," said Kella, looking down at her own. "We got them from a merchant in a town back northeast a ways. She said we would want them if we planned to travel south because it would get hot. And it certainly has. We traded for a few extras to keep as spares, so you two got pretty lucky."

"A town?" asked Oleja. "Like, other people?"

Kella gave her a funny look that Oleja could only partially see beneath the girl's veil. "Yes, that's what a town is. Have you never been to one?"

"We haven't," said Pahlo. "Up until a few days ago, we both lived as slaves, and no one from our villages knew anything about the world. Oleja escaped and brought me with her." He beamed. Oleja ground her teeth. That was not information she wanted to disclose—it carried too much shame.

Kella's eyes widened. "Oh! That explains a lot! So how much do you know about the world outside of... uh... where you were?"

"Nothing really," said Pahlo.

"We know a good deal," said Oleja.

Kella looked between the two of them. "Well, I can help try to fill in any gaps."

"That would be great!" said Pahlo. "What's the story with the ruins? Where did they come from? What were they?"

Kella's face lit up. "Aren't they cool? They used to be towns a long time ago, back in the Old World. Now you're lucky to find any structures in them that can still be considered buildings, but they used to have *thousands* of people living in them. Most of the useful stuff has been looted or decomposed long ago, but we collect materials and stuff too, then bring them to towns to trade."

The idea of looting the ruins excited Oleja more and more as people talked about it in greater detail. It sounded a lot like what she did at The Heap, but on a larger and more adventurous scale. Perhaps after she freed her people she would return and join the raiders again or start her own group.

Pahlo looked around in wonder. "Thousands of people... I've heard about the Old World—there are a few stories that mention it floating around amongst the people I've spoken to, but I never knew so many people lived back then. What happened to them all?"

"I don't know," said Kella with a sigh. "I've asked

after that information, and so have my moms and the raiders and others we've met. A lot of information and history about the Old World was lost, that bit included. From what I've gathered, the world went through a period of incredible suffering and darkness for generations after whatever brought about the end. A lot of people died. But eventually, those who survived created new civilizations. Some say they don't come anywhere close to rivaling what we used to be, but I can't even imagine what a town of thousands would look like. It just seems too big."

"Less than a hundred live in the camp of slaves I come from," said Pahlo. "Oleja says hers has several hundred, but I never saw it. I can't even imagine that, let alone thousands."

Kella kicked a rock, which skipped away through the dirt. "I've been to towns of several hundred before. The biggest might have reached a thousand, I'm not sure. But never multiple thousands."

"Where's the nearest town?" asked Oleja, jumping into the conversation again.

"Ruined or inhabited?"

"Inhabited."

Kella thought for a second, then shrugged. "Not sure. It's been weeks since the one we visited northeast of here, but there could be one closer, somewhere on the edge of the desert. Casmia will know."

"So, there are edges of the desert," began Pahlo, bringing the topic back to his questions of the world beyond. "We had stories about places with lots of trees and water and colder air. Are they true?"

"Oh, definitely. This heat is the worst, I don't know how you've put up with it all your life." Reaching under her veil, Kella wiped her brow. "Actually, in the town where we got these clothes, I heard a story about the desert. Apparently in the Old World it was smaller and cooler, at least by a bit, but after whatever happened, it expanded and the temperatures changed. So, it wasn't always this big or hot."

Pahlo laughed. "I'm used to the heat at this point. When we get to a colder place, I'll probably freeze to death!" He wrapped his arms around himself and pretended to shiver.

"It got cold in some places underground," said Oleja. "It's not that bad. Kind of refreshing, actually."

Kella danced around so she stood in front of Oleja, facing her and walking backwards. She hiked up her veil with one hand and studied Oleja with amazement. Oleja couldn't help but focus her gaze on the other girl's eyes, blue as the sky.

"You've been underground?" Kella asked, her face alight. "That's so cool!"

"Yeah, it was… it was neat," she said with a weak smile. In honesty, the mines lost all their charm before she ever set foot in them. "That's where I did all my training."

"With your bow?" asked Kella, looking to the weapon in Oleja's hand.

"Yeah, actually. And learning to build. I taught myself

some sword fighting too, but I never made myself a proper sword."

"I have a bow too! And a spear. I haven't gotten super good with either yet, but I'm practicing. Will you teach me some of what you know?"

Oleja blinked at her for a moment. "Oh, okay, sure. Yes, I'd love to." She had never taught someone else before.

"Swear on it?" Kella held out her hand. Another handshake—as if Oleja hadn't had enough of those for the day.

"Sure." Oleja moved to shake the girl's hand. Kella moved her hand away.

"No, you're doing that wrong."

Oleja looked down at her hand. "What?"

"Here," said Kella. She extended her arm out towards Oleja's, but instead of gripping her hand, she clasped Oleja's wrist. "Now you do it too."

Oleja shifted her hand and grabbed Kella's wrist.

"Now at the same time. Ready?" This time they swung their arms in towards each other in unison, clasping with a warrior's force. Much better than a handshake.

"Good. You better not break that deal, or I'll have to hunt you down," said Kella.

Oleja grinned. "You can try, Sky-eyes." Kella gave her a funny look that morphed into a smile after a few seconds.

Casmia called a pause for a water break a short while later. She and Trayde filled bowls of water from the drum in the wagon and brought them around to the horses. The rest of the group sat on rocks or in the dirt beneath the striking blue sky above, dotted by no more than a thin wisp of a cloud here and there. They drank and laughed and looked about at the land ahead. While the horses drank, Casmia stood to the side, looking first down at her map, then up at the horizon ahead, then back again.

What drew Oleja's attention was the horizon at their backs. For the moment, no signs of Honn presented themselves, but even if she couldn't see him, she knew that somewhere behind her, he followed her trail. Tracking her, biding his time, planning the perfect moment to strike; she could only stay ahead of him for so long. Could she trust the other raiders to keep watch through the nights, or should she and Pahlo keep their own watch?

Their slow pace troubled her, but she couldn't tell Casmia why in a bid to move faster. Admitting that she was followed, hunted by an eclipser, would be an admittance of failure. Failure to escape cleanly, failure to free her people, and failure to kill Honn. She had not yet figured out a way to kill him, to penetrate his thick armor and deadly skill. Turning to face him or allowing him to catch up was to face her own death. She hated that hopelessness, the feeling of defeat. She would kill Honn, she just needed to figure out how, and that required time. To gain that time, she had to stay one step ahead of him. She had to keep moving.

Why bother trying to convince Casmia of the urgency to move? She had the map, sure, which gave her knowledge of the land, but she was getting older, and by no means took the prize for strongest of the group. Jeth should be the leader out of the seven, but he deferred to Casmia—a sign of some other weakness, no doubt. Oleja estimated that she matched Jeth in strength, and therefore tied for strongest. With her physical strength and superiority in fighting, the raiders would listen to her. She just needed to win over their loyalty.

"All right!" she called, pulling the attention of the raider party away from their conversations. "Break's over, get ready to move!"

Several of the raiders exchanged confused looks. None of them got to their feet. Casmia marched over.

"What are you doing?" she asked in a flat tone, one eyebrow raised.

"Trying to get the group moving so we can cover more ground," said Oleja.

Casmia shook her head, her curls bouncing with the movement. "You don't call the orders around here. I do. I'll give you a pass this time because you're new and don't know how we run things, but I won't have you coming in here thinking you can usurp me from my position, understood?" She did not wait for a response—merely turned on her heels and walked away. Oleja scowled after her. She wasn't trying to usurp Casmia, because Casmia had no honest claim to the title of leader. It didn't make sense that all of the other raiders treated her as if she did. Nothing held her in that role, minus the map, which the real leader could demand she hand over, stripping her of that as well. It just didn't make sense.

Back in the village, leadership was—in most cases— never requested, it just sort of established itself. Everyone acted as they felt they should, and those of lesser wills fell in behind whoever they naturally gravitated towards. Once a majority made a choice, the remainder fell in by intimidation, not wanting to clash with the larger force. If a more reasonable leader presented themself, the process repeated. In no way did Casmia seem to represent the strength or will of the group.

Casmia called the party to move on shortly after, which they did with no hesitation, much to Oleja's annoyance. The day wore on beneath their feet, and by nightfall they found a stretch of scrubland in which to make camp. The raiders unloaded tents and blankets and cooking utensils from the wagon and then set to work fulfilling their evening duties.

The camp rose up in a whir of motion, and in what felt like hardly more than a minute, the group had a fire burning and their supper cooking, all situated in the center of a semicircle of tents. The party sat around the fire as they waited for the food to cook, the rich smells rising into the air amidst the smoke.

Oleja found herself sitting between Onet and Pahlo. Onet drew spirals in the dirt with a stick; Pahlo chatted with Kella and Hylde, who sat on his right.

"Good first day?" asked Onet without looking up.

"What? Oh, yeah, I guess so," she said.

"Word going around says you two are escaped slaves."

Oleja took a long breath. "Yeah."

For a few moments, Onet only nodded and shared a sad smile.

"I was too, several years ago," he said, but just as quick

as he said it his head snapped up at attention. He raised a hand as a signal. The group went quiet.

Sounds echoed in the darkness: scratching, gnashing, sniffing. They grew closer. Oleja grabbed her bow from where it rested on the ground behind her and nocked an arrow. If it was Honn, she just prayed the group collectively contained enough fighting skill to kill him before he killed her. She wouldn't die by his hand, or any other.

What emerged from behind the scraggly bush was not Honn and his coyotes. The creature crawled on all fours, hunched and rigid as it crouched, with a long body and tail stretching ten feet long from end to end and an arched back that rose to the height of Oleja's chest. Scales covered its form, black with jagged lines and blobs of yellow. A wide jaw split its face, showing a forked tongue that flicked at them as the beast hissed. A collection of sharp claws lined each foot. They clicked on the hard ground as the beast padded towards them. Set behind the nostrils on the rounded snout were two black eyes that gleamed in the firelight. It cocked its head and snarled, letting its tongue dance on its lips before disappearing back within its maw. It looked past the ring of people to the food where it cooked in the center.

Trayde moved first as she dashed to the horses. They whinnied and stamped as they tried to escape their tethers and flee from the beast. The rest of the raiders seized their weapons. As they did, a second beast appeared behind the first, this one less inclined to wait and size up its opponents before rushing into a fight.

Jeth led the charge, blocking the lead monster from Oleja's view as he moved to slash at it with his swords.

"Jeth, look out!" Oleja called. She loosed an arrow without waiting, hoping he'd get out of the way in time.

"Wha— whoa!" shouted Jeth as he leapt out of the way of Oleja's arrow just in time. The arrow struck the first of the beasts in the snout, causing it to rear up in pain. Jeth lost his balance and fell onto his backside, dropping one sword.

Oleja dashed past the fire and moved around, trying to get a better angle. She loaded her bow and drew, ready to strike.

Onet plunged his spear into the neck of the same one Oleja shot, and it bucked twice before going still save for the occasional twitch.

Casmia swiped at the second with her sword but it backed up out of her reach. Hylde helped Jeth to his feet. Pahlo and Kella stood back, watching the fight unfold.

Wulshe sprinted towards the second beast to flank it with Casmia just as she scored a hit, causing the beast to roll its head towards her and bite at her legs. She staggered back and out of range as Wulshe lifted his sword, but Casmia's absence opened Oleja's shot.

"Hang on Wulshe, I've got this one!" called Oleja.

Wulshe glanced to Oleja as she called his name. As he did so, the beast whipped its head back around and it collided with his legs, sending him crashing to the ground. Oleja fired her arrow and it found a chink in the scales behind the jaw bone, sinking deep into the thing's flesh. It snapped its mouth, and with a choked hiss, it fell.

Casmia sheathed her sword. "You're a fantastic shot, Raseari."

Oleja twirled an arrow in her hand. "Thank you. I actually tau—"

"But you got two of your own knocked on their butts." Oleja looked over to Jeth, who dusted himself off and retrieved his sword, and Wulshe, who nursed a nasty scrape on his chin from his fall. Blood dripped through his beard.

"Oh."

Casmia gave Oleja a stern look. "Looking out for your allies in battle is more important than landing a few blows. We are a team."

"Ah, she's new to this," said Wulshe, hobbling over in an exaggeration of pain. He grinned at her. "Not to worry, we'll get you fighting these nasties like a true raider in no time."

Oleja was somewhat taken aback by his implication that she fought with anything but years of honed skill. She had no time to protest before Pahlo spoke up.

"What *were* those 'nasties' exactly?"

Onet wrenched his spear from one of the carcasses. "They're mutants. Some byproduct of whatever catastrophe ended the Old World. These were mutated versions of the black and yellow lizards you see around here sometimes—Gila monsters. But there are mutated versions of most creatures."

"The mutant bears in the north are fierce," said Hylde. "The rattlesnakes around here aren't too bad—they're bigger, but their venom gives you intense hallucinations instead of outright death, so they have their pros and cons. There are mutant humans too."

Casmia nodded. "They're awful things. Most packs of them call themselves the 'earthborn.' We try not to have dealings with them whenever possible, as they tend to be violent and territorial. There's a group due east from here— we avoided them at a wide range on our way through."

"That's where Oleja and I escaped from," said Pahlo, nodding. Oleja cast her eyes to the ground. Yet another fact she had hoped to keep to herself. What honor was there in sharing the details of their captivity?

A number of the raiders exchanged glances. Trayde sucked in a quick breath through her teeth.

"If you are honest in your assertions," said Jeth, "I pity you both. The earthborn are not kind to their slaves."

No one spoke again for a long while.

CHAPTER TEN

O leja slept better knowing that things just as dangerous as Honn lurked outside her tent.

It was a strange reassurance, but it meant that the raiders knew to be diligent in their watch even if they didn't know how likely it was that an eclipser—or earthborn—would track them to that very location, ready to put up a fight. Knowing the raiders had no love for the mutant humans provided an added bonus—if Honn showed up, the raiders would kill him whether they knew his motives or not. Together, all of the new knowledge helped her sleep like a rock.

In the same manner of speed that they put it together, the raiders broke down the camp and packed up the wagon. They ate, refilled their waterskins from the tank, then set out, walking northwest now after rounding the tip of the plateau the day before.

Oleja was pleased to find the cut on her forearm healing

129

nicely. Scabs and bruises still painted her skin in a myriad of reds and blues and blacks, but pain no longer flowed through the wound unless she coaxed it out with less-than-gentle prodding. Other smaller aches and bruises from her rough landing had since made themselves known as well. She barely gave them a second thought. Minor aches were none of her concern when she had so much else to worry about.

Their pace carried them no faster than the previous day's, but none of the raiders seemed concerned with their traveling speed. They were all too happy to break at intervals, while Oleja waited impatiently to continue. Pahlo seemed to have forgotten his fears of Honn, finding some false sense of safety among the trained, well-armed group. He hung around near the back of the group again with Kella and Hylde. Oleja took up a position on the left side of the wagon. Carved into the wooden side ran a ledge just wide enough for her to prop her tools on, allowing her to tinker as she walked without stowing everything back inside her bag whenever a task required both hands. She used the time to assemble a set of hinges from the scraps in her bag—pieces she needed for a new glider.

It wasn't that she needed a new glider. Her old one served its purpose—she made it out of the canyon and hadn't died from falling back down to the ground, so that leg of the plan had been a success at least. She didn't *need* a new glider, but that didn't stop her from wanting one. Her glider, now a splintered heap of garbage in the heart of the eclipser camp, was one of her most complicated and unique inventions. Being up in the sky... it felt freeing. If the opportunity arose to use a glider again, she would take it. Perhaps she could even figure out a means by which to take off from the ground, removing the need for bulky, rudimentary, and potentially dangerous catapults to get her airborne. But something like that would be tricky, and she had a long way to go before she could defeat gravity altogether. In the meantime, she'd settle for the deadlock she could achieve with a glider.

One problem existed with her new mobile tinkering setup: every significant bump of the wagon pitched her tools and components to the ground. Numerous times she paused to collect her things. On perhaps the fourteenth time that her hammer became acquainted with the ground, Oleja turned to find Trayde holding it out.

"You lost this. Again."

"Thanks," said Oleja, taking it and placing it right back on the same little ledge so it could fall off a fifteenth time.

Trayde jumped up onto the cart, grabbing onto the frame of the roof and bracing herself against the side with her foot.

"Think it's going to stay there this time?" she asked with a note of sarcasm.

"Absolutely not. But it's more productive than doing nothing while I walk, so I'll manage."

Trayde hummed in thought, and then swung herself up and over the rear wheel and into the back of the wagon, never letting her feet hit the ground. Muffled bumping and clattering came from inside, and then she reemerged, a stack of wooden boards under one arm. She dropped to the ground next to Oleja.

"What if you make a little tray? You could cut holes here and here," she pointed to the side of the wagon, "and add pegs to the tray so it'll slide right on and then detach when you're done with it." She held out one of the boards. The wagon hit a bump, causing Oleja's hammer to wobble, then fall. Trayde caught it on the end of the board. She looked back up at Oleja with a wide, open-mouthed smile, clearly impressed with her own reflexes.

Oleja took the board and looked it over, assessing Trayde's plan in her mind. It sounded perfect.

"That will work," said Oleja. "Uh, thank you." She went to take the boards from Trayde, then realized she'd have no free hands to assemble them, nor a stationary surface to set them. "Wait, actually—"

"Yes, I'll hold them."

Oleja laughed. "Thanks." She set to work cutting the holes in the side of the wagon—nothing major, and hardly noticeable to eyes that weren't looking for them.

"What are you working on?" asked Trayde, falling in step alongside her with the boards in her arms.

"The tray design you suggested."

Trayde glared at her. "Don't make me hit you with these boards. I meant the hinges you're making." Oleja smirked.

"Oh, those? Well, I had some wings once, but I don't anymore, so I'm building new ones."

Trayde rolled her eyes. "Fine, don't tell me."

Oleja completed her minor modifications to the body of the wagon and then assembled the tray from the boards. When she finished, it held nicely, giving her the perfect place to put tools and other odds and ends: a wider surface, with sides three inches high all around to keep everything from tumbling off with every bump of the wagon. When Trayde's job was done, she vanished just as quickly as she appeared.

With the sun just past the height of its arc, they caught their first glimpses of ruins ahead, and by mid-afternoon they arrived at the edges of the old town. Oleja tried to imagine it in its prime. Thousands of people bustling about, going about their lives. Kella was right—Oleja struggled to picture so many people and a town that could house them all.

Casmia brought them to a halt just outside the ruins. "We will divide up and sweep the ruins. Raseari, Dirin, you will each go with someone more experienced. Raseari, you're with Trayde. Dirin, with Hylde and Kella. Onet and Gleathon, you'll be together. Jeth, you're with me." She tossed empty backpacks to each person as she called their name. "We will meet back here when the sun touches the horizon."

"Wagon modifier team, back together," said Trayde, clapping a hand on Oleja's shoulder. Oleja shrugged her off. She had no quarrels with Trayde, but she preferred to explore the ruins alone. It would give her time to gather pieces for a new glider and any other fun new contraptions she could build—preferably of the eclipser-killing variety.

She picked a direction and hurried off, joining the rest of the raiders in dispersing.

"What gives?" asked Trayde, hurrying after her. "I held your stuff; what more can a girl do?"

Oleja looked back at her over her shoulder. "Sorry, I was just hoping I'd be able to work alone here."

"No can do, Casmia keeps us in groups. Less dangerous that way."

Oleja sighed. "Why? I'm perfectly capable of collecting scrap and hauling it back on my own. Been doing it all my life."

"And what if you round a corner and walk straight into a pack of those Gila monster mutants? Or a camp of earthborn? None of us can take that stuff on alone."

"Yeah, well, you haven't seen me yet. That fight last night—I could have brought the mutants down in seconds if I hadn't been trying not to put an arrow in any of you. I work best alone."

Trayde shrugged and put her hands up in mock surrender. "Suit yourself, but I'm not going to get chewed out over it. So, until that sun is sitting pretty on the horizon, you're stuck with me."

Oleja trudged on through a lane between two lines of crumbling stone columns. Piled up at the base of one lay a mound of old rusted shards. Parts poked up from beneath the sand. Oleja moved to investigate, kicking up the sand to reveal the treasures hidden below.

The purpose of the contraption now faded to a mystery, but Oleja was more interested in the pieces anyhow. Rust ate away at the parts on top, but as Oleja dug deeper, pushing aside heavily corroded plates that may once have formed the exterior of the thing, she found scrap in better condition. At first, nothing caught her eye. Then, tucked deep below the pile and nestled in a protective layer of sand, she spotted a couple of springs—perfect for her glider.

"None of the stuff is useful anymore. Loads of junk, and not the good kind," said Trayde, kicking a rock into the pile.

"Not to you, maybe," said Oleja as she knelt and pulled up the springs. She brushed the surrounding sand aside as she checked for any more.

Trayde shrugged. "If you need those things, be my guest. I'm going to go check out that stuff over there." She pointed a few dozen feet away to a clearing in a long rectangular pit where scrap metal and other items scattered the ground.

Oleja checked for anything else of use but ended her search with only the springs. She stowed them in her own bag. Trayde said herself that they were useless, so Casmia could not confront her and demand she hand them over, claiming they belonged to the group. They were her hard-earned scraps, and she could make better use of them.

When she joined Trayde in the clearing, she found the other girl lifting the rusted beams and large rectangular cases to search beneath them. Trayde piled the useless scrap in the far corner, the most heavily destroyed section of whatever building once stood on the foundation. Oleja went to the corner opposite, which remained in surprisingly good shape. A piece of the roof still clung to the walls, and below it, a slightly-less rusted case leaned against the wall. Oleja threw it aside. Below it, shards of floor tiles remained intact, scattered with broken bits of glass bottles and another, lighter material that crumbled to dust when she touched it. But her attention quickly turned to a heap of fabric—some sort of banner, fine material despite its tears and stains. It was an old, musty brown in color, with streaks of yellow and light grey. Oleja felt it with one hand, gingerly at first, but the fair condition surprised her. It retained its strength.

"Got anything good over there?" called Trayde over her shoulder. Oleja jumped an inch, startled. In her focus she had forgotten about the other girl.

"A few bottles, mostly broken," Oleja called back, wadding up the fabric and stuffing it into her bag as quickly and inconspicuously as she could manage. Trayde came over to join her.

"Aw, nice," she said, lifting a bottle to her eyes and peering through it. "These are still in great condition. Good find!"

In total there were three unbroken bottles. A bit of metal clamped onto the top stoppered each. Rust had eaten a hole straight through one, the contents now long gone, but the other two retained whatever liquid sloshed around inside— barely. When Trayde tested one of the two intact caps, it split easily, spilling the liquid down her arm.

"Save that one, and try to keep the cap from coming off," she said, indicating the one Oleja held. "Some freak in the next town might want whatever's in 'em." She took a whiff from the open bottle in her hand and choked back a gag. "Now *that*... that's fermentation." She swirled the liquid around in the bottle, then crouched down to pour a small puddle out onto the ground. It was a deep, rich brown color. She looked to Oleja with a strange gleam in her eye.

"If I die, it was in some glorious combat with a nasty mutant vulture. Stab me a few times so I look the part," she said. And then she took a swig from the bottle.

The following fit of interminable coughing echoed through the ruins with a leveling force. After the initial moments of gagging and spluttering, Trayde burst into laughter. She held the bottle out to Oleja from where she lay sprawled out on the ground.

"Give it a try. This stuff's... absolutely fantastic." She punctuated the statement with another fit of coughing.

"Not a chance," said Oleja as she dumped the remainder into the dirt and stowed the bottle in her looting backpack.

They made their way around for the next few hours, collecting a wide variety of scraps and relics. It was as the sun approached the horizon that Oleja found a pile of long metal beams tucked between the lone standing wall of a ruined building and the cliff face of the hill it bordered.

Some of the beams were thick—supports for something immense that could withstand excessive pressure, no doubt. Others were slim, less than an inch thick but just as long as their larger counterparts at somewhere around twelve feet long. All of them were in fair condition, with minimal rust save for those on the very top of the pile.

"Anything good back there?" asked Trayde between coughs, which had faded considerably since she first drank from the bottle, but still forced their way up now and again. Her voice had gone hoarse at least an hour ago and showed no signs of getting better anytime soon.

Oleja hefted one of the thinner beams and slid it out past the wall—still incredibly heavy, but nowhere near the weight that she expected of the larger ones. Trayde ran her eyes along the length of it, coughed, and then spoke.

"Good condition, but too heavy for what they're worth. Probably best to leave 'em."

Oleja flipped it around, looked it over, and then slid it back onto the pile. It glided back into place easily. A spark ignited in her mind, and she slid it back out again.

"I have an idea. We need two of these—help me carry them."

"What? No, are you crazy or something? How do we carry them from the ruins? They won't fit in the wagon, and you'd be lucky to find someone else who wants to bear them with you for the next, I don't know, few weeks?"

Oleja shook her head. "We won't be carrying them. We can use them to turn the wagon into a sled—"

She caught herself before she said "like Honn's."

"So it'll go faster in the sand," finished Trayde, looking over the beam with renewed interest. "I like it. But no one else is going to buy it. 'Cause then we'll all have to walk faster, and no one'll be happy about that."

"Could be nice to get where we are going sooner," suggested Oleja. "We could get out of the desert heat."

Trayde shrugged. "Sure, whatever. Hand me a beam. We can carry them together over our shoulders."

They grabbed two of the thinner beams and each took an end. They were heavy for sure, but Oleja managed fine. They took a few breaks on their way back to the wagon so Trayde could rest and switch shoulders, as she wasn't as strong as Oleja, but they made it back just after the sun reached the horizon. They dropped the beams alongside the wagon while the others stood clustered up off to the side discussing something.

"All right," said Oleja to Trayde. "I'll start unloading the wagon. We can pile stuff over there. You can unhitch the horses; I'll need to flip the wagon up on its side, and that sounds like a very unfriendly position for horses. I'm also going to need your help getting the water drum out of the back, that thing probably weighs a ton."

"Sounds good," said Trayde, and went to the horses. Oleja moved around to the back of the wagon and climbed inside.

Dim light filtered in through the canvas covering, even less than usual under the dying light of day. She surveyed the cargo. Shelves lined with boxes, their tents and other supplies piled up down the middle—Oleja took to moving the supplies from the center first. She emerged with armful after armful, piling the wagon's contents on a flat spot of ground off to the side. When she emerged with her third or fourth trip of stuff, Casmia stomped over.

"Raseari! What is this? Did I tell you to make camp?"

Trayde came around the side when she heard Casmia. Oleja paused at the back of the wagon, a tall stack of blankets in hand.

"I'm not setting up camp, I'm making some modifications to the wagon," said Oleja.

"And when did I tell you to do *that*?"

"You didn't, it was my idea."

Casmia put her hands on her hips and tried to stare Oleja down, but any attempts at intimidation were lost to the fact that Oleja, standing in the wagon, loomed several feet taller than Casmia. When she saw the futility of her efforts, she tried a different approach.

"What sort of 'modifications' are we making here?"

Oleja pointed down to the metal beams. "I'm going to remove the wheels and use those to turn it into a sled. It will increase our speed in the sand and also keep the wagon sturdier so it bounces less."

"There is no need to dismantle my wagon for the sake of a slight speed boost. We are ahead of schedule as it is."

"But we could be going faster," countered Oleja. "You could get out of the desert heat."

"Everyone will have to walk faster to keep up. It will exhaust us all. My answer is no."

"But it will ease the burden on the horses. You're sacrificing the increase in speed for an easier day. You can walk faster, or you can walk longer. They cancel out."

Casmia narrowed her eyes. "Don't talk down to me like I don't understand the specifics of our travel. You have an awful lot of nerve coming in here and speaking to me that way, you know that? What makes our speed so important?"

That was an answer Oleja did not wish to disclose.

"I have your best interest in mind," said Oleja. It could be considered true in some regard—if Honn caught up with them, he could very well decide to kill them all.

"Get out of my wagon," hissed Casmia, and grabbed Oleja by the wrist. Her tug contained nowhere near enough force to bring Oleja down to the ground. Oleja took her wrist back and hopped to the ground of her own volition.

"We need these modifications," said Oleja, her voice lower now that she stood closer to Casmia. She was getting tired of arguing. Her goal was to save time, not waste it. Every minute lost brought Honn a minute closer.

"We do not, and you will not make them," said Casmia, her voice lowering to match Oleja's. A stern calmness resonated through her words.

"Listen to me," started Oleja, regretting the words on her tongue before she said them. "An ecli—. An earthborn soldier hunts Pahlo and me. He is following our trail and will attack if he catches up. Speed is our best measure to counter his advance."

Casmia retained her composure for a moment, but it slipped, slowly, until anger and fear mingled on her face. "And why are you giving me this information *now*?"

Oleja paused. What could she say? She wouldn't admit that she had kept it to herself in order to hide what was undoubtedly a failure—so many failures, all wrapped up into one problem: Honn, pursuing her as far as she could go. She said nothing.

Casmia pinched the bridge of her nose and closed her eyes. "All right. Do what you must. But we leave at dawn, and we will have words about this incident." She stormed off. Oleja turned to where Trayde still stood, watching the conflict unfold.

"I don't know what you said to convince her," she said, "but just for the record, this is *my* wagon, just like they're *my* horses. And I say go ahead with these changes—especially after that tantrum."

Oleja rolled her eyes. "Unnecessary, truly. I'm only trying to help. But thanks."

With Trayde's help, Oleja unloaded the wagon and got it up on its side. The other raiders and Pahlo cycled over in waves, directing curious questions at the pair. After some quick explanation from Oleja, they all seemed to be on board, contrary to the expectations of Trayde and Casmia. Wulshe and Jeth offered some help holding the beams up while Oleja fastened them into place, and Kella and Pahlo sat for a while and kept her company while she worked.

Eventually, the raiders filed off to their tents. Oleja continued her work long into the night. She offered to take the first watch shift, seeing as she had no choice but to stay awake anyway, but even after the time came to wake Onet for his shift she continued working, letting him sleep while he could.

The time she wasted trying to convince Casmia that the sled modifications would be worthwhile replayed in her mind as she worked. As long as she completed the work by morning, the time it took didn't matter—they made camp there for the night and had no intentions of going any further that evening regardless of Oleja's plans. Still, she should not have had to waste the precious minutes. She knew what she was doing; she was plenty capable of making things more efficient. If she had to convince Casmia of her plans every time she formed one, she would soon waste away her years on arguments. The bickering reminded her of precisely why she couldn't bring the raiders—or anyone else—when she went to save her people. Other people got in the way.

She worked alone.

CHAPTER ELEVEN

As it turned out, Oleja knew exactly what she was doing; she was right, and Casmia was wrong.

The new wagon-sled glided over the sandy terrain with ease. On rockier parts it slowed a bit, but overall their speed increased by an impressive degree. The horses no longer seemed to struggle so terribly each time they hit a bump or rut in which the wagon wheels would have stuck. Their hooves easily found purchase on the ground and never hit a patch where they slipped in the sand, trying to pull their cargo along behind them. Using their conserved energy, Trayde guided the horses to a trot, and then it became a matter of matching the horses' speed to the capabilities of those on foot, no longer the other way around. To Oleja, it felt well worth the exhaustion she faced after getting so little sleep the night before.

The raiders—minus Casmia—admired the new wagon and commended Oleja for her work, impressed at how much faster it moved. Oleja made sure to thank them loud enough that Casmia could hear.

They turned their course southwest again as they set out for the day's walk. Casmia told the party that their next destination was something unlike anything any of them had ever seen, but gave no further details. Excited mutterings aplenty flowed through the group during their morning walk as they theorized what this could mean, but even more rousing news commanded the discussion. Beyond their mystery destination, further west amongst some "mountains," there was a town—a living town— which, in time, they would visit. Casmia gave no estimate of *when* they'd reach it, just that it would be after they combed the desert and looted it dry. As far as Oleja was concerned, the other raiders should just make for the town if they wanted to. No need to follow Casmia's orders if they had their own, preferred objective.

Personally, Oleja had other plans—and she would see them through, regardless of what Casmia told her to do. Her people needed a hero—needed their freedom—and she was going to be the one to deliver it. She'd follow in Tor's footsteps to finish what he started. Plans for how to do so dominated her thoughts as she spent the day walking.

Doubling back was not yet an option. Though she so badly wanted to, turning around meant facing Honn. He nearly bested her once and admitted to showing mercy in the encounter. He promised to be less courteous the next time they met. That was a promise Oleja bet he intended to keep. An outright brawl did not lay the grounds on which she wanted to contest him—not unless she caught him by surprise or sprung some other great advantage. Though she had experience, she was a self-taught fighter who learned the ways of combat by torchlight in a cave. He was a warrior, a trained soldier of the eclipser camp. He wore armor tempered in a true forge and wielded blades sharpened on grinding wheels meant for such a purpose. As much as she hated it, he had the upper hand in a fight.

She could double back in a wide loop, leading him in a circle around behind her and then sprinting back for her village with him in tow. They'd play the same game that they played now but going back in the other direction. Sure, it was possible, but it also relied on her knowing how far behind her Honn was, which she did not. He could be five miles back, or he could be fifty. If she didn't loop wide enough and ran straight into him—well, that promised no better an ending than opting to face him in combat directly, except the advantage of surprise could very well fall to him.

Getting through or around Honn in her return was one thing, but even if she managed it, she had no way to tell what surprises waited to greet her upon return. The eclipsers knew she remained at large—after all, they sent Honn after her, and until he returned with her head in a bag, they could only draw so many conclusions. Running full-speed for the lever at the gate—and then Pahlo following in her footsteps—made her ambitions clear, and as a result the eclipsers would be foolish not to guess at her broader plans. If Honn hadn't yet captured her, they had to assume she planned to—and could—return and finish what she started. They'd be sensible to increase security at the gate. Posting more guards in the tower, and perhaps even some down by the lever, seemed like realistic precautions. Or they could even leave the opening mechanism shattered from the rock strike. No human, or even an eclipser, stood a chance of opening the gate with pure strength; if they feared she may try to open it, what better way to deter her than make it impossible?

Pahlo still wanted to help. Not only that, but he still insisted Oleja enlist help from the raiders or others from places beyond. In fact, as soon as Casmia mentioned the town in the mountains to the west, Pahlo had suggested to Oleja that she seek out help there. She didn't know how to explain to him her aversions to turning the rescue into a collaborative project, especially if it included turning him away as well. After all, he had some stock in the liberation of the people as well—he knew other slaves who worked aboveground in the eclipser camp. It would be difficult to convince him that he should stay behind and not partake in their rescue, but she had to. She worked alone.

Including the raiders would become disastrous in minutes. Just as fast as she could lay out a plan, Casmia would cast her doubts over every bit of it. They'd spend time arguing just as they had the night before when Oleja tried to improve the wagon. It would be a catastrophic waste of time, during which the eclipsers could close in and kill them all before Oleja even convinced the raiders to follow her. And that only afforded worry to the dissent of Casmia—what if the others she brought along proposed

147

their own conflicting plans, or refused to follow? What if she gave one of them a significant role—say, identifying the schedules of the guards in the tower—and they failed? The whole plan would collapse, leaving Oleja's people to remain in the canyon. She'd never throw the lever, seeing only failure come of her plans, and all because she counted on someone who failed or who thought they could do better by altering the plan. Everything hinged on the competence of everyone included. The more people there, the more room for failures or for clashing ideas. It could be fatal. She knew she could count on herself to see tasks done and would not have to waste time convincing herself.

That was not to say she had entirely ruled out bringing others along in any capacity. They could not play pivotal roles in the main part of her plan, nor try to influence it—that would lead to all of the challenges she did not have time to deal with—but Pahlo's insistence got her thinking. It might be plausible to bring a small force of fighters along. She could send them to wreak havoc elsewhere in the camp, drawing attention away from the gate. Or she could use them as a strike force, attacking the guard tower while she went for the lever. Even if they failed in such duties and only slowed the guards, she'd have the opening she needed. The risks of including others for such purposes were far lower, and thus worth consideration—just so long as she left them out of the planning process, which could prove tricky.

As long as she pulled the lever—as long as she got to be

the hero—there might be room for others to play more minor roles.

But from where she stood, walking through the wilderness alongside the raiders, she still saw too many hurdles. Taking care of Honn, getting back to the village, ensuring that she could get the gate open, and then actually executing it all. It was a lot to deal with. She had to start by accumulating assets; making a new glider would be a good start. Then she could determine who—if anyone—she wanted to use as a distraction or strike force in her plan. Once all of that was done, she needed to figure out how to kill Honn. In the meantime, she'd travel with the raiders. Their path was the same that she'd place her feet upon whether they walked it or not, as it carried her away from Honn, which bought her time to plot and tinker. Food and water were never scarce in the group, which helped stave off starvation and dehydration, which both became quite lethal in high doses. She hated to keep moving farther and farther from her village, but she had few other options. She'd make a faster return, at least, as she wouldn't take detours through ruins or long breaks. And with any luck, she could make that return soon.

Thoughts of Ude came to her again, accompanied by a pang of guilt. Every minute that she spent away from the village marked another minute he thought she was dead. Only her return could show him otherwise.

That evening, as the group sat around the fire, Oleja found a spot of clear ground off to the side and laid out a collection of wooden boards she had found in the last town of ruins. They were rough and splintering, but she could turn them into the perfect frame for a new glider.

She cut them down and laid them out: two large rectangular slats for the main body of the case, smaller ones for the top and bottom, and a set of four long appendages to serve as the frame for the wings. When she got them all cut to size and sanded down, she began assembling the bones of the device.

A shadow drifting over her work pulled her eyes up. Kella approached. She waved when Oleja saw her.

"Hi. Mind if I sit?"

Oleja waved to the spot across from her. "Feel free. Just doing some work."

Kella settled in sitting cross-legged and surveyed the mess of parts strewn about the ground between them. "What are you building?"

Oleja glanced up from where she hammered a nail through the corner of the frame, and then back down, resuming her concentration.

"It's… well, it's something I made up, actually. I've built one before, but it got a little banged up in landing and I had to leave it behind."

"In landing? So, it's something that flies?" asked Kella, hints of incredulousness leaking into her voice.

Oleja gave her a mischievous smile. "Better—it's something that makes a *person* fly."

"No way."

"Yep."

"How?"

Oleja picked up the body of the glider, now loosely held together, and one piece of the wing frame. "These are attached here and here, and they swing out like this." She demonstrated the motions using her hands in place of the springs and hinges that had yet to be attached. "Then there's a fabric wing along here that catches the wind and makes you glide."

"That's amazing," said Kella, looking down at the other limbs of the wing frames as if they had taken on fantastical new properties, no longer just cut pieces of discarded wood. She met Oleja's eyes again. "Could you teach me? How to build, I mean. I know I already asked you to teach me to shoot—and you better still do that." She gave Oleja a jokingly stern look. "I want to know how to do this too. It's... amazing."

Oleja laughed. "Thanks. I've heard it's because I'm skyborn, but most think that's just superstition. I can teach you."

Kella's face lit up in excitement. "Thank you! What do I do?"

Oleja pulled her bag over and emptied the contents of the largest pocket onto the ground. A heap of scraps and other miscellaneous objects crashed together in the dirt. The fine cloth that would become her glider wings, now folded neatly, remained tucked inside a separate pocket. She handed a fistful of tools to Kella.

"Find things that can be put together to do something," she said. "Manipulate them in your hands until they serve a purpose. Let your hands guide you." Kella took the tools gingerly in her hands. She looked over the pile of stuff with wide eyes. She chewed at her lip.

"I'll do my best."

"That's where you have to start," said Oleja with a shrug. She returned to her work as Kella picked through the pile of scrap.

"What does 'skyborn' mean?"

Oleja paused. "What?"

"Skyborn. You said some people think you're so good at building because you're skyborn. What is that?"

"Oh," said Oleja, realizing that she had indeed made such a statement. "It's something from my village—an old myth about babies who come down from above. Born 'from the sky,' at least according to some, though no one knows for sure how it all happens."

"Well, did you come from the sky?"

"I guess I did. That's what I'm told, at least. I was a baby."

"A baby who came from the sky? How does that work?" It was not disbelief in Kella's voice, but curiosity. Oleja couldn't help but feel compelled to explain.

"They just arrive sometimes swaddled in bundles—not fine blankets or anything, they're usually pretty rough—with little parachutes to keep them from plummeting to the ground and dying. That's where I got the fabric for my first glider. I know it sounds pretty mythical and silly. None of my people understand it either, so some believe those babies are born from the sky—'skyborn'—and that it makes them special in some way."

"Do you believe it?"

"I—"

The question caught Oleja off guard. She'd been ready to chalk it up to superstition as so many did. After all, no one treated skyborn as anything special anymore. Once, generations before, they were regarded as more purified humans, but over time it seemed everyone just realized they were no better than anyone else. Just as capable of stealing, or lying, or slacking off in the mines. They didn't live longer or speak softer or sing any more beautifully than the rest of the people. As time went on, they lost all special treatment. Now they got two letters added to their name, and that was it.

But part of Oleja—a part she had been pushing away for years—bubbled right back to the surface as Kella spoke those four words. A part that wanted to believe something innately special resided within her. She wanted to be better, and to prove that she was worth more than the village seemed to think of her: an orphaned girl who contributed nothing and hung around with a dirty old traitor's son. Maybe she was those things, but she was skyborn too. Her one claim to grandiosity, to heroism, even if her exceptional birth came a few hundred years too late for anyone to believe it.

"Maybe. I haven't decided yet," she said, finally answering the question. Kella nodded.

"Well, I see something in you. I think you could be born from the sky," she said. Oleja pushed her dark hair from her face—her braid had unraveled too much to keep it from her eyes.

"Thanks. What about you? Where do you come from, Kella Hylde-born?"

Kella giggled. "I've been traveling with the raiders all my life. My mom said she thought about settling down in a town when she found out she was pregnant, but she decided not to. I'm glad she didn't. The towns we pass through all feel so dull. Out here there's more adventure. I like it most of the time." She tossed a piece of copper back into the pile of scrap. "Sometimes I just wish I had friends. People my age, I mean."

Oleja couldn't help but give the girl a sad smile. "I know the feeling."

The space between them fell silent for a few minutes.

"What about your dad?" asked Oleja.

Kella shrugged. "Never had one. Well, I guess I did, but I never met him. My mom says he was just some guy she met while passing through a town once. She never saw him again. I had another mom, though. She joined the raiders just before I was born. She and my mom raised me together."

A question hung in the air, shrouded in a cloak of sadness that Oleja was worried to pull aside. She didn't want to pry, but curiosity got the better of her.

"What happened to her?"

Kella laid her pliers in the dirt alongside the twisted piece of metal she poked at. "About three years ago, she was scouting ahead for the group. She ran into a pack of earthborn. They killed her."

Oleja reached out a hand to Kella. Kella took it in her own.

"I'm so sorry, Kella. I know your pain. I lost both of my parents when I was still a young girl. They were in the mines and there was a cave-in. They both died, leaving me alone."

"I'm sorry."

Oleja gave Kella's hand a squeeze as a single tear fell from the younger girl's cheek and into the sand. "We are alive and well. And we will do great things in their memories." Kella nodded. Oleja released her hand and began repacking her bag.

"Thank you for teaching me," said Kella. "I didn't make anything useful—just freshly bent metal. But I'd like to keep learning. And to learn your way of shooting. Don't think you can get out of that. Remember, I said I'll hunt you down."

They laughed together until Hylde came over from her seat by the fire and asked what sparked so much excitement. Kella showed off her piece of bent metal, which Oleja insisted she keep despite the other girl reassuring Oleja that it served no purpose whatsoever. They agreed the time had come to retire for the night, and once Oleja gathered the rest of her things, they parted ways and found their tents.

Over the following days, Kella sat with Oleja as she worked on the glider in the evenings. Kella perfected her bent-metal-making technique while Oleja's glider began to take shape. She completed the frame, though it still lacked springs, straps, the fabric, and the release mechanism inside, leaving it still a ways off from being complete.

Two days from when Kella first sat with Oleja to tinker, as they crested a hilltop, Oleja beheld a scene that sucked her breath from her lungs. Below them lay a massive expanse of glittering blue water that stretched at least two miles across before the ground continued on the other side. It wasn't as large as the one she saw during her glider flight, but impressive nonetheless. A lake, if she remembered the term correctly. Even if she didn't, Wulshe made sure to inform her of the name, as he did with every simple object that crossed their path.

But not even his sarcastic remarks could ruin the view before her.

CHAPTER TWELVE

"Hmm. I thought the lake would be dry." Casmia held her map close to her face, eyebrows pinched inwards as she studied it.

Pahlo looked around. "Uh… I think lakes are usually wet…"

Casmia scoffed. "Well, yes, the ones that still exist. But this map is from the Old World. Most bodies of water out here in the desert have dried up—or partially dried up— since the temperature rose when the shift occurred." She folded up her map in frustration. "All right. I will have to plot a new route around. In the meantime, we will go down to the shore to refill our water supply and rinse off all of this sand."

Oleja surveyed the lake below. It was immense—she couldn't even begin to guess at how much water it contained. Only once had she seen any body of water larger, but she still got the sense that this was nothing particularly special to the other raiders. Though she could hardly imagine such a thing, she figured there must have been larger bodies of water aplenty in the world beyond the desert, out where the temperatures allowed such a thing to thrive.

Though her estimate said that the lake was no more than a few miles across at its narrowest point so far visible, its shape included three long arms. Two stretched to their left and right—north and southeast—while the third pointed straight out ahead of them to the west. To either side and looking ahead, the farthest banks lay somewhere out of sight. A detour to find a new path around could add a full day or more to their trek. And time was still a valuable resource if she wanted to stay ahead of Honn.

They descended to the lake where waves lapped at the rocky, sandy shore. Casmia found a place to sit on a boulder just up the slope. She looked up and down the shoreline, consulting her map between each glance outwards. The rest of the group went right up to the edge of the water.

Trayde and Jeth were the first to kick off their shoes and run into the shallows, but Kella was only a pace and a half behind them. The other raiders followed, though none of them plunged into the water with the same enthusiasm as Trayde or Kella, opting merely to remove their boots and wade in up to their shins. Trayde, Kella, and Jeth, on the other hand, were quickly drenched.

"Do you think you're going to go in and join them?" Pahlo asked Oleja. Only the two of them remained on solid ground, save for Casmia back up the hill.

"I might. I want to. But I—"

"Can't swim?" finished Pahlo.

"No," she admitted.

Pahlo shrugged. "Me neither. I'll wade in if you will, just not past my knees."

"Deal."

They tugged off their boots, gathered up the hems of their robes, and waded into the water. A chill raced through Oleja's skin as she touched the waves—colder than she expected given the heat of the sun and desert air. The burden of the heat melted away as she stepped in deeper and deeper. Chills invaded her entire body despite the water only reaching her shins. Sand comprised much of the lake bottom, soft beneath her feet, but rocks of varying sizes dotted the shallows as well. They were slimy beneath her feet, a lesson she learned the hard way when one nearly brought her down to get a closer look at it.

"Raseari!" called Trayde from behind her. Oleja turned just in time to get hit with a torrent of water. Her soaked clothes clung to her skin. A matted curtain of her hair obscured her vision. She brushed the hair and water from her eyes, dropping the hem of her robe into the water in the process—not that she had any reason to try to keep dry anymore.

Trayde had ditched her sodden robe and now stood before Oleja in her underclothes. She held a metal pail in her hands—the very same that she had just emptied on Oleja. A wide grin carved through her face.

"Bad move, Trayde," she said, and then with an equally wide grin she charged the girl.

Trayde ran through the shallows, and Oleja quickly learned how fast the other girl could run. Oleja struggled just to keep from slipping on the rocks underfoot. Her drenched robe weighed her down, and it wasn't long before she shed it as she ran after Trayde.

As Trayde splashed through the shallows, she stooped to fill her pail again. Oleja did not have long to wonder at her reasoning; a moment later, as she passed Onet, she emptied it above his head and kept running. But while Trayde moved fast, Onet moved faster. In just a few bounds he caught her, grabbing her around the waist and pulling her down into the waves as they both disappeared beneath the surface amidst a huge splash. Both resurfaced a second later, coughing and laughing and gasping for breath.

Oleja fetched her robe, now fully soaked through, and then returned to the shore to wring the water from it and to dry herself off. She looked up the hill to where Casmia still sat, plotting their new course around the lake.

Not only would a detour waste time, but it could give Honn an opportunity to catch up if he cut a few corners in anticipation of the lake and their path. Finding an alternative route would not only negate such consequences, but could also buy her a good margin of extra time. Honn, with his sled and eight coyotes, would have no choice but to go around. Granted, at the moment it looked like she didn't either, but she was craftier than him. She could find an alternative. But what other options did they have?

Several miles separated them from the opposite bank. Even if some in the group could swim that distance, not all of them could, and that didn't even take into account the wagon and all of its cargo or the horses. Oleja walked a circle around the vehicle. Perhaps it could float if she removed the sled runners. She bet it could, in fact—the wooden walls rose high and it looked buoyant enough, minus the long slats of metal fastened to the bottom of course. But their crew consisted of nine people and two horses. It would be a great feat just to fit everyone inside— forget the horses—and with nine people plus all of the gear and loot, they'd all quickly become well-acquainted with the bottom of the lake. Getting everyone across by such means required at least two boats of that size—still not accounting for the horses.

She climbed up inside the wagon. In the dim light, she could just make out the shapes of the various objects stored within. She went shelf-by-shelf, looking for nothing in particular—save for a boat, but something told her none of the boxes hid one. She just needed something to give her an idea, light a spark in her mind that would tell her how to get everything across to the other side of the lake.

Plenty of metal weaponry and scrap filled the boxes, enough so that if the goal was to sink, they'd be all set. Plenty of wood lay about as well, but not enough to build even a small boat or raft.

In a small crate tucked away on the bottom shelf near the corner, Oleja found something smooth and cool. By touch alone she could not identify it, so she pulled the crate from its spot and brought it into the light. The rolled-up bundle inside was a bright, vibrant yellow. Dried mud caked the object in patches, but it crumbled away with the brush of a hand. She lifted the material and unfurled a corner. Stretchy and thin like fabric, yet free of the holes that filled even the finest cloth. She took it from the crate and hopped out of the wagon.

Back at the waterline, she dipped the material into the waves. They lapped at it, but it did not absorb the water. Next, she scooped some up in a pocket of the material and held it up. It did not drip through. The material—whatever it was called—was completely waterproof.

She returned to the wagon and sized it up anew. Coating the wagon in the material might make it more buoyant, but if it could already float that seemed like a foolish waste since it didn't solve the more pressing issue of space. But what about the roof of the wagon? Canvas stretched across the curved wooden frame—nowhere near watertight on its own, but if she removed it from the wagon body and covered it with a layer of the yellow stuff it could serve as a second boat. Together, the two structures could carry all nine of them plus their cargo. But what about the horses?

"Raseari, what are you doing?" Casmia's voice sounded strained—annoyed, but with no conviction, no anger. Like she knew what was to come and lacked the energy to deal with it. Oleja turned to face her.

"I figured out how to get across the lake."

"That's excellent," said Casmia in a dismissive tone.

"And I found a way around. The water level is just low enough that there should be a pass to the north. It will only add a day's walk to our trail. We are still ahead of schedule, but I suggest we get going nonetheless so we can lose as little time as possible. Please gather the others—and remind Trayde she is supposed to be using that pail to refill the water tank."

When Casmia mentioned the pass, it was like the final piece of her plan fell into place. She knew exactly what to do. A glance up to the sky revealed the position of the sun: high overhead, midday.

"I can get us all across the lake by the end of the day. Listen; the wagon will float on its own if we take off the runners. I can turn the roof into a second boat by lining it with this," she held up the yellow material. "Five people can ride in there, along with the two runners for the wagon. Two can go in the wagon and paddle that across with all of the supplies. The last two—probably Trayde and whoever else is best at riding—can take the horses around to the pass. Without the wagon, they will be much faster. They'll meet us on the other side, where we can put the runners back on the wagon, hitch up the horses, and continue on our way."

Casmia looked neither impressed nor convinced.

"Is this about the earthborn again?" she asked, her voice low. Oleja's face fell. She didn't want to show any of her fear, especially not to Casmia.

"Yes, but also in the interest of taking the best route.

This won't pull us off course at all. It's overcoming the obstacle instead of going around."

"My answer is no, Raseari."

"Why?" She kept her voice firm, a challenge rising in her tone.

Casmia narrowed her eyes. "Excuse me?"

"Why? My plan is better."

"Need I remind you who is the leader here?" asked Casmia through gritted teeth.

"Supposedly it's you, but I have yet to see evidence as to why."

The anger that fell over Casmia's face radiated none the same fiery rage that Oleja had seen before. This one embodied the cold and sharpness of steel.

"And I suppose that makes you think the leadership role can fall to you? You have been a part of this group less than a week."

Oleja did not want to waste her precious time arguing with Casmia; enough of it had been lost to that fate already. It was time to act and set her plan into motion. She turned her back on Casmia.

"Trayde, Jeth, Hylde!" she called. "I need some help over here." The three hurried over.

"Raseari!" called Casmia in a stern voice. The trio of raiders looked behind Oleja to Casmia in confusion. Oleja ignored her.

"I need you all to lift this side of the wagon, then the other. I'm taking the runners off—we are going to float it across the lake."

"You absolutely are not," hissed Casmia, grabbing Oleja by the shoulder and spinning her around to face her. "This is my wagon. This is my crew. You will do as I say, or you will not be part of it!"

"Actually, this is my wagon," said Trayde. Casmia looked past Oleja to where Trayde stood alongside Hylde and Jeth.

Casmia stared at her open-mouthed for a moment. "Yes, well, I just meant…" She stammered. She grappled for words but found none.

"What is your plan, Oleja?" asked Jeth.

She summarized it for the three of them. Casmia never loosened her grip on Oleja's shoulder. When Oleja finished, they all looked to Casmia. A wild look shone on Trayde's face.

"That's genius and completely reckless," she said. "I'm in. What do I do?"

Jeth held up a hand. "Casmia?"

Casmia explained her route, though Oleja had already told them about the pass to the north as part of her plan, leaving Casmia with little left to share. Bids for her own plan peppered her speech—saying it would take "a day *or less*" despite what she told Oleja, referring to her plan as "the safest route," and wrapping it up with a reminder that she was the leader and they always relied on her for direction, which she never failed to "provide expertly." When she concluded her speech, the other three looked around uncomfortably, and Oleja started to doubt whether or not she'd have their backup. They would side with Casmia purely for the sake of preserving whatever establishment of leadership she clung to, dragging Oleja along on their day-long detour.

"What is wrong with Oleja's plan?" Jeth asked Casmia.

"It's completely and unnecessarily reckless!"

Jeth considered this. "But we would test the buoyancy of the two crafts while still in shallow waters. We aren't throwing them right out into the middle of the lake and hoping they float. If they don't, we will know it pretty quickly. We can pull them back in, put the wagon back together, and go the long way. Your plan doesn't have an abundance of concern for time, so at least testing her idea shouldn't be a problem."

Oleja breathed out a sigh of relief. At least Jeth and Trayde stood by her.

Casmia shifted uncomfortably. "Fine. But if everything sinks, I will be collecting repayment *in full* for the damages."

They jumped into action immediately. Trayde unhitched the horses and then joined Jeth and Hylde in lifting the wagon. It took more muscle than Oleja initially expected, but with the others joining in they managed to get it off the ground just enough. Oleja rolled underneath and made quick work of removing the first runner. She had built them to come on and off relatively easily, knowing that when they reached the edge of the desert they would want to switch back to the wheels—after all, having both on hand allowed for better travel over various types of terrain. Once both runners lay in the dirt off to the side, they set to work on the roof.

Removing the roof proved easy as well. Wrapping the material around it presented them with a challenge. The material turned out to be just barely too small, but with the stretchiness they managed to pull it to fit. Keeping it taut while fastening it to the frame took many hands, however, though fortunately they were in no short supply. Within the hour, both boats sat in position on the shore, ready to sail.

They sifted through the scrap wood available on the wagon and selected the pieces that would serve best as paddles. Oleja also divided up roles to the raiders: Trayde and Pahlo would ride the horses around the lake and across the pass to meet them; she and Onet would ride in the wagon; the others would ride in the roof. As a final preparation, Oleja turned the knob on the spigot attached to the water drum and let the drinking water drain out onto the beach. They could refill it from the lake on the other side, as they intended to do on the beach already before Trayde got distracted and put the pail to more chaotic use, but this way the wagon did not bear the added weight.

When at last the time came to put the boats in the water, Oleja just prayed that both crafts would float. She could afford neither the embarrassment nor the fine from Casmia.

Thankfully, luck joined Oleja's side of the brewing feud.

Both boats held, bobbing gently in the waves. A round of cheers arose from many of the raiders as the excitement of the plan took off. As it turned out, not one of them had ever been in a boat aside from Onet.

The group waved to Pahlo and Trayde back on the shore as they paddled into the water. When they were certain the makeshift boats were in no immediate danger of becoming decorations for the depths and that they would not need to revert to Casmia's detour, the horse riding pair rode off at top speed, racing along the bank as they headed north before finally vanishing in a cloud of dust in the distance. The groups in the boats continued paddling.

The wagon-boat moved slower than the other, both due to its weight and having only two passengers to row. Oleja kept her eyes on the shore ahead as she dug into the water, pushing her weight against the long, wide wooden board she held with each motion of her arms. Her muscles ached but the repetition of the movements helped. She let her mind drift as her body took over the motions.

An hour passed and the western shore neared. The travel went by at a slow, dull crawl, providing no new scenery in the identical waves. Still, the day-long land route would have taken longer. Oleja's arms felt like they had acquired a nasty sunburn, though only the fire in her muscles burned her as they worked overtime to keep the wagon-boat moving towards the shore.

As she paddled, a chill seeped through her boots.

Oleja looked down. Crystal-clear water rose up from the wooden floor of the wagon—no more than an inch or two deep, but she would have much preferred it to be zero inches deep. She didn't need to be overly familiar with boats to know that water did not belong on the inside.

The wagon tipped deeper on Oleja's side just enough

that the water level had not yet risen high to reach Onet. He stood at his side, still unaware of their predicament as he remained equally focused on rowing as Oleja had been moments prior. Oleja looked ahead to the other boat, paddling along just in front of them. She didn't want to alert them if it wasn't dire.

"Onet," she said, keeping her voice calm and low enough that the others wouldn't hear her.

"What?" he asked without shifting his gaze.

"We may have a small issue." At that, he turned.

"Uh oh. That's not good," he said, looking down at the water as panic blossomed on his face. The water was getting deeper, she could feel it.

"We need to make the boat lighter," said Oleja, but no plans for how to do so came to her, save throwing their cargo overboard—a good way to stoke a fierce rage in Casmia.

Onet looked ahead to the other boat. "They are floating fine, let's hand some stuff off to them."

Oleja bit her tongue before she could protest. Now was not the time for pride to take the reins—she couldn't swim. If they sank, more than just cargo would sink to the bottom.

"Jeth!" called Onet. "Can you pull your boat over here beside us? We are taking on some water; we are going to pass a few crates over."

"You're taking on water? How much?" asked Hylde, concern rising in her voice.

"Not much," Oleja called over. "A few inches at most." She looked past the other boat to the shore. They had crossed the halfway mark, but the water level inside rose quickly. They would need to unload more than a few crates.

The other boat got into position and they handed over crates until it bobbed as low in the water as they ruled safe.

"That's all we can take," said Wulshe, scratching a hand through his golden beard. "How's the water situation?" Oleja looked down. Water covered the entire floor now and rose to her ankles in the deepest places. Her heart pounded in her chest. Asking to join the other boat would be cowardly, a defeat. She formed this plan; she would go down with it before letting Casmia prove her wrong. Casmia remained quiet through the whole ordeal, yet the tension she exuded grew more palpable with every glance she stole.

They kept paddling. Adrenaline fueled their movements and gave them fresh steam, but not enough. When the water pooled around her shins, Oleja knew that little time remained to get them to the other side.

"Keep rowing," she said to Onet as she threw down her paddle and seized the nearest box. Metal scraps rattled around inside. She dumped them overboard.

"Raseari, stop!" shouted Casmia, her first words since leaving the shore.

"Would you rather see them drown?" asked Hylde, who stood beside her. "Oleja, Quinje, can you swim?" Onet's answer provided an ounce of reassurance to the situation. Oleja's did not carry so much hope. She dumped another crate overboard. Casmia groaned in frustration and slumped against the side of her boat.

After grabbing a large metal bucket filled with an assortment of spare weapons and sending that to the depths as well, Oleja took her oar back up and continued rowing. Perhaps it was a pure manifestation of optimism, but she almost thought she felt the water level stop rising.

By some stroke of luck, they took on only a small amount of additional water before the bottom of the wagon scraped against the sand of the western bank. The crew from the other boat stood ready when they arrived and pulled the wagon as far onto the beach as they could, though the water inside made the boat heavier. Onet opened the back gate and the water poured out in a surge, taking with it some loose items that Wulshe and Kella quickly scooped up. With the wagon fully ashore, Oleja jumped out of the back and flopped down in the sand, letting her breathing return to normal.

"Rough sailing?" asked Trayde, pulling up on her horse.

"They lost several crates of our loot," said Casmia. "Who *knows* how much was lost to the bottom of the lake. This is why I advised taking the safe route and going around."

"Ah we didn't lose all that much," said Wulshe. "And what an adventure!"

"For you, perhaps. You rode in the dry boat," said Onet, wringing out the drenched hem of his robe onto the other man's shoes. Wulshe shoved him off with a huff of laughter.

Before they reattached the roof or reloaded the cargo from the roof-boat onto the wagon, the party lifted it so that

Oleja could refasten the runners to the bottom. The sun sank beneath the westward-pointing limb of the lake as they got the wagon reassembled and replenished their supply of water. Hylde wound her way around the outside of the wagon, inspecting the sides.

"Here! I found the leak," she said, pointing. The party crowded around to see. "Two holes here on the side." She poked her finger into each one in turn. Casmia stooped to inspect them.

Oleja didn't need to look to know exactly what they were—the holes from her mobile tinkering tray, the modification she and Trayde put together. Her own foolishness swirled around her, drowning her in embarrassment. She nearly sank the entire wagon because she forgot about the tiny holes that she herself carved in the side. With a quick glance, she met Trayde's eyes. Understanding, regret, and just a hint of amusement played out on the girl's face in a great conflicting battle. Foolish, but they all survived in the end—minus the belongings that now decorated the dark depths of the lake. Perhaps one day when it had truly dried up, Casmia could return and reclaim them.

If she could manage it, and if Trayde's face did not betray her involvement, Oleja intended to keep the nature of the holes a secret from Casmia. The raider captain had spat enough fire in her direction. And Oleja, caught in the midst of the feud kindled between them, already sank so far in over her head that she might as well have been alongside the cast out items at the bottom of the lake.

CHAPTER THIRTEEN

The tension in the air followed them, too stubborn to stay behind. It weighed heavy enough upon them that if Oleja had found a means by which to throw it over the side of the wagon back in the middle of the lake, its absence alone would have lifted them up out of their predicament and—quite likely—into the sky.

They followed along the lakeshore heading west. The terrain on their right was rocky and steep, the base of a line of hills. In some places the slopes ran right up to the waterline, forcing them up towards the peaks until they could descend back to the banks.

Night descended in full shortly after. They made camp on a dry spot of land near the water, far enough away that they were in no great danger of finding their campsite splashed; they all agreed they'd had enough unplanned water for the day.

"Gleathon, Trayde, Dirin—pull out the tents and get

them set up here," said Casmia. "That is, if we still have them."

Oleja shot her a look, but Casmia failed to notice, or at least pretended she did. Oleja had made sure not to throw anything important into the lake, only extra loot from the ruins. Tents were important supplies and would have been among the last things to go.

The trio set to work on the tents. Hylde got a fire started while Onet and Kella prepared their supper. Casmia pulled Jeth aside to discuss some features on her map, leaving Oleja alone without a duty. She highly doubted it was by anything but explicit design. After a few minutes jumping between groups and attempting to look busy, she gave up and wandered down to the water's edge. Slick gravel blanketed the beach. Water ran between the rocks, rippling and pooling in tiny channels as waves sloshed against the land. Rocks more significant in size dotted the dark shoreline, and on one around which the waves surged in gentle rhythm, Oleja found a place to sit.

She sat cross-legged at first, keeping her feet from the water that flowed around her, but soon pulled off her boots and lowered her feet to let the cold water run over them.

Ude would have liked it by the lake. He always enjoyed sitting by the village river. In his age, he was no longer expected to work in the mines. He sometimes spent his days making clothes or pottery, and he rather enjoyed hanging around Oleja's workshop, carving new scenes into her workbench or prodding her for a nerve to strike, but no rule required him to do more for the village. Leisure was the gift of living to see an old age, reserved for those lucky enough to bypass the most common cause of death: mining accidents. In Ude's case, few in the village were particularly happy about his luck. They disliked his presence enough when he contributed to their survival—having him around as a freeloader did no favors for their detestation of him. Of all the reasons they wrongfully wanted him dead, it just added another item to the list.

But Ude ignored them and enjoyed his time nonetheless. His days spent at the riverside were his favorites—at least he told Oleja so. He could watch the water course by for hours, wave caps gleaming in the midday sun. Oleja sat with him sometimes. She couldn't stand to do it often—the act of sitting and watching the water seemed too unproductive for her. She needed to do something—to feel like her time meant something. But sometimes, on slow days, she could sit with him for a short while. During those times he told her about the river—something he seemed to be able to do at great length, despite how clearly defined and uninteresting it seemed to her. He liked to watch it, he said, because it was the only thing that came and went from the village. Sure, births and deaths created a cycle of faces— skyborn children marking the most unique of the bunch. The eclipsers lowered down food, and threw junk into The Heap, but once those things arrived, they never left. The river was just passing through. It came in through the grate in the north wall, ran down the length of the canyon, and then left, out through the grate in the south wall and back into the world. Neither the eclipsers nor the canyon walls made any effort to hold it back; they allowed it to move about as it pleased. The river was free.

News of the outside world never came to the village, but Ude said he learned of it from the voice of the river, from the words it spoke as it flowed over the shores and pooled through the channels. Sometimes Oleja thought for sure the man had lost it.

She kicked up a wave of water, sending ripples across the surface. She would see Ude again. She had to go back, and when she did, he'd be there waiting. He couldn't exactly go anywhere. But when she saw him again, she could never admit to how much she missed his company in her time away. He'd never let that one go.

Footsteps crunching in the gravel caught her attention.

"Food's ready," said Hylde.

Oleja turned her head to the side an inch, though not enough to see the woman behind her. "Thank you. I will be over in a moment."

Hylde did not leave immediately. Oleja was about to ask if she needed something else when she spoke again.

"You're thinking about someone you miss," she said, her voice quiet. "Is it your parents?"

"In a sense, yes."

Hylde stepped up to the waterline to stand beside Oleja. The waves swelled around her bare feet.

"I'm sorry if it's not my place. Kella told me about the conversation the two of you had the other night. Forgive her if it was not something you wanted her to share, I did pry from her the source of her tears."

"It's all right, it's no big secret."

Hylde nodded. "We all had a stressful afternoon—you and Quinje most of all. Sometimes we think of those we miss in the wake of fear." Hylde paused as she worked through her next words. "I'm sorry about your parents. Losing those we love is never easy. And I'm sorry about Casmia. She tries her best, and most of the time she does have everyone's best interest in mind, but she doesn't take well to being challenged. Concerning herself more with the cargo than with yours and Quinje's lives, though—I cannot condone that."

Any words Oleja could have strung together into a response refused to come to her. She nodded instead.

"I will leave and give you a few more moments alone," said Hylde. "But just know that should you ever need it, for a moment of advice or for a lifetime, you are welcome to come to me if you need a mother."

If Oleja had been unable to find the right words before, words may as well have not existed at all in the moments that followed. Hylde took her leave as she said she would, but somehow Oleja felt her presence there for many long minutes after.

***

Morning passed in a blur, and as the sun climbed to midday its rays subjected the party to their hottest day yet. As they walked, Oleja noticed how different the terrain had become compared to the canyon. It had been a steady change, making it hard to detect overtime, but as she thought back to the rusty color of the sand and stone of the canyon and surrounding wilderness, she realized that the orange color had faded over the course of her travels. Now, brown rock and beige sand comprised the landscape. Some pockets still retained that orange hue of her village, but in most places that color was muted or gone.

The heat grew harsher as well. Even under her robe—which had served well so far in keeping her cool—sweat dripped down her forehead and spine, soaking into her clothes and adding to the discomfort. Late afternoon marked their parting from the shores of the lake, which did them no favors in dealing with the heat. Without the ability to stray down to the waterline to splash water on their faces, trudging over the hills and through the sand became even more unbearable. But as they crested a tall range of hills, they got their first glimpse of the destination Casmia had promised.

Ruins rose up on the horizon. None of them had doubted for a moment that ruins marked the end of their path; the question revolved more around what made them so noteworthy. What set them apart as awe-inspiring, "something like none of them had ever seen" as Casmia claimed, was the immensity of them. Towers stood taller than any hill, some perhaps even taller than the walls of the canyon Oleja had spent her years looking up at. They cast enormous dark shadows across a flat, sandy landscape below, dotted with smaller crumbling structures, though even the smallest of them looked several times larger than those in the other ruins. Still, few looked to retain the elements of the buildings they once were. Imagining them in their prime painted an image beyond belief. How could anyone have made structures so tall?

They couldn't reach the ruins by nightfall, though the sight of their destination increased the morale that suffered in the heat, which kept them moving until darkness fell. With the darkness came cooler air—a relief beyond words.

They made camp and talked excitedly about the ruins over their meal, theorizing about life in the Old World. No one, not even Casmia, could guess at why anyone needed buildings so large. Oleja doubted there were enough people alive in the entire world to fill even one.

After eating, Oleja sat to the side with Kella to work on her glider. Kella worked diligently on a contraption of unknown function, though it included a bit that spun which made it neat enough all on its own as Oleja told her. Her glider was coming together nicely as well—she finished the frame, fastened all of the hinges into place, which held the arms in their proper spots, and built the release mechanism, though it shifted about loosely without a spring. She still worked to whittle away extra wood on the sides of the frame to keep the arms from scraping on them as they swung out. After that, she needed to add the springs— which she had collected most of, though not all—the straps, and then stretch the fabric across the arms and fasten it into place.

"How does this look?" asked Kella. She pushed her

work over for Oleja to see. The purpose still remained a mystery despite the evening's additions.

"Looks great," said Oleja, hoping her smile said more than her lack of words. Kella pulled it back close and set to work tightening some loose bits.

She flipped it around, letting the spinning element whirl about. "When is my first lesson with my bow?" she asked, though she kept her focus on her work.

"You're persistent," said Oleja. "Dedication is the sign of a good student. How about tomorrow night in the ruins after our day's work?"

Kella threw her hands in the air. "Yes! Finally. And I'll hold you to it."

"I expect nothing less, Sky-eyes."

Thunder rolled across the land. Oleja looked at the night sky. Clouds were few and far between, and no streaks of lightning cut through the blackness. A crashing in the brush off in the shadows snapped her attention back to the earth. Not thunder, a growl. Oleja got to her feet in an instant, maneuvering between Kella and the noise.

Black and yellow streaks emerged from the brush. Clawed feet dug into the sand. Beady black eyes found Oleja's. She nocked an arrow.

"On your right!" shouted Onet as a blur cut through the shadows in her peripherals. A second mutant lunged for her, but just before it struck her a spear sailed through the air, finding its mark deep in the exposed underbelly of the creature. It roared as it staggered back into the long dry grass, but two more took its place, flanking it as they stepped forth.

The raiders raced forwards with weapons drawn—Onet with a second spear at his side, Wulshe and Trayde each with a sword, and Jeth with two. Hylde grabbed two small axes that she typically used to cut up branches for their fires. Even Pahlo, though he moved forward in timid hesitation, wielded a sword given to him by Casmia and which Jeth and Wulshe trained him in the use of. Oleja drew back her arrow and aimed for the eye of the leading beast.

"Raseari!" shouted Casmia, the tone of frustration she so commonly wore already plain in her voice. "Where is my sword?"

Oleja loosed her arrow. It caught the mutant in the shoulder and its advance slowed. "How should I know?" she shouted back without shifting her gaze.

"It was in the wagon you so *kindly* unloaded!"

Oleja fired another arrow into the mutant's ribs. It screeched and clawed at the wound.

"I only threw spares overboard!"

"My sword is *not* a *spare*!"

"Well good, then I didn't throw it overboard!"

The mutant was on her now, lashing out with razor-like claws. With her free hand, Oleja drew her curved knife and caught the advancing strike, slicing into the soft scales of the beast's palm. Trayde finished the job—with two swift strikes, the mutant's head found itself no longer attached to the rest of it, a sure sign that they no longer needed to worry about it attacking.

Oleja risked a glance back to where Casmia's voice came from. The woman tore through the contents of the wagon, but it seemed her luck was nowhere to be found.

Dropping her knife into the sand, Oleja went for another arrow and unloaded it into the hide of the first mutant, which Wulshe staved off with his sword as it charged him. The arrow stuck in its neck and the beast recoiled, giving Wulshe an opening to slice a cut across its right eye and jaw. An axe flew through the air and sunk deep into the thing's face. It twitched as it fell to the ground, dark blood dripping down its snout and staining the sand below it.

Another beast snapped at Oleja. She sidestepped the blow. Jeth cleaved at it with his swords, but it skirted underneath and swiped at his legs. Sharp claws raked across his right thigh, eliciting a grunt as blood bloomed across the front of his white robe, staining the tattered fabric with red streaks. He plunged a blade into its shoulder. It hissed and stepped back.

Oleja kicked the beast hard in the snout, causing it to whirl and face her. She unloaded an arrow into its foreleg, and as it reared up, she sent another straight through its throat. It fell into the sand, dead.

The one with Onet's spear in its belly emitted a low, rumbling growl as Pahlo brandished his sword at it. The beast tried to slam him with its tail, but he scampered back. Then, as if remembering the blade in his hands, he swung, cutting a deep gash in its tail and side. As Oleja reached for another arrow, movement on her right caught her attention.

Kella rushed forward, Oleja's knife in her hands. The mutant turned to see her as she ran up and thrust the blade forward. It sank to the hilt into the scaly neck, and at last all four of the beasts lay still.

Oleja's breaths came heavy. The other raiders around her echoed her gasping. Wulshe and Hylde went to assist Jeth in bandaging and cleaning his wound.

"Sorry," said Kella, approaching Oleja with the knife held out and her head tilted down, though it didn't hide the smile playing at the edges of her lips. "I saw it on the ground and grabbed it. I wanted to help."

"Don't apologize, that was fantastic!" Oleja took the knife back and sheathed it. "We will make you a master archer soon, and then you won't have to go around picking up other people's weapons from the ground." Kella beamed, but the exchange was cut short when Casmia approached them.

"Raseari, would you like to tell me where my sword is?" she asked.

"Probably exactly where you left it. I didn't throw it into the lake."

"Hmm. Well, the funny thing is that I *checked* where I left it, and it doesn't seem to be there. But I distinctly remember watching you throw plenty of things to the bottom of the lake. Why don't you go check down there for me?" Malice dripped from her words.

"Was it in the big metal bucket in the corner? About…" Oleja made the shape with her arms, "this big?"

"No, those were all spares. Mine was on the shelf by the gate."

"Then that's where it should still be, because the only swords I threw overboard were those in the bucket."

Casmia narrowed her eyes as she studied Oleja, her gaze cold and unwavering. "That's a lie and you know it."

Heat rose in Oleja's face. "I am not a liar."

"I have had it, Raseari." Her voice rose with every word. Everyone's eyes went to the two of them. Kella inched backwards, trying her best to remove herself from the confrontation.

"Maybe the sword just got jostled around when we lifted the wagon?" suggested Pahlo, doing his best to diffuse the situation. "It could have fallen behind the shelves. I'll help you look."

"That's *enough*, Dirin!" she barked, and Pahlo jumped in surprise. "I know *exactly* where it is! She threw it into the lake to save her own ass." She turned her attention back to Oleja, eyes wide and lips drawn tight. "And now you are going to go back there and retrieve it. Maybe if we're all lucky you'll suck in some water while you're down there!"

"Casmia, enough!" shouted Hylde. "If she threw the sword into the water, it was an accident and nothing more. Do not speak to her as if her death would be a blessing to you."

Casmia stood in silence for a moment, surveying the rest of them each in turn. Her eyes fell on Oleja last.

184

SKYBORN

"I am going to ride out and scout ahead," she said, her voice quieter now but just as sharp. "I need the air." She climbed atop a horse and rode off without another word, but just before her departure she gave Oleja one final look. Something shone in her eyes that Oleja didn't like. Something had changed.

It struck fear in her.

CHAPTER FOURTEEN

Quite to Oleja's dismay, she was the one on watch when Casmia returned.

The hour grew late; her watch came second after Jeth's. The sound of hooves on the sand drew steadily nearer, but she did not look. She knew who approached.

Thankfully, Casmia seemed to have exactly as much desire to talk to Oleja as Oleja had to talk to her. She disappeared into her tent without a word.

After Oleja's watch wound to a close, she woke Hylde and retired to her tent. Lying down at last atop the blanket that separated her from the ground provided a great relief, and sleep did not dawdle in its arrival.

She was up again at first light. Casmia seemed perfectly happy to ignore the previous night's quarrels as she chatted with the rest of the group over breakfast, though none could deny her curtness with Oleja. Oleja expected nothing less—quite honestly, she was surprised Casmia regarded her in any way at all.

They set off soon after, watching the towers grow steadily closer on the horizon. They cast great shadowed streaks upon the land in the light of the low morning sun. The size of the structures grew more and more impressive the closer they got, and soon they blotted out the clear blue sky as the group traded shrubs and clumps of dried grass for the crumbled remains of buildings. The ruins started out low and squat like those they had seen before, but the deeper into the town they got, the taller they became.

Buildings in this town were only in slightly less disrepair than those in the others they'd passed through. The smaller structures lay in the same familiar state of rubble. Scanning through the remains, Oleja concluded that in their prime, stone and wood and other such materials made up the buildings, but there seemed to be a heavier emphasis on metal as a building material compared to the other ruins. The towers stood even further apart from the norm, displaying a different style of construction. Even as they remained at a distance, Oleja could tell that they were built sturdier—they had to be in order to hold up what must have amounted to a village's worth of weight above their foundations. Huge metal beams larger around than Oleja's own body rose up, rusted and corroding but still holding firm. Stone adorned the sides in some places, but it grew sparser on the higher floors. Much of the sides were reduced to open ledges at each floor—windows, once, if Oleja guessed correctly. In a few openings, a faint glittering rimmed the edges, possibly indicating the remains of glass panes.

Glass was not a common material back in her village. In most cases, residents omitted it as an addition to their windows in favor of wide openings through which as much air could enter as possible. Spending their days in the mines, the people of the village liked to get fresh air when they could. Glass panes found a home in the windows of the food storage rooms, where keeping bugs out was a must, as well as certain areas for the sick where they blocked the dusty sand kicked up by an army of miners passing through the street, protecting the fragile lungs of the sick within. Oleja had also come across her fair share of encounters with glass while sifting through The Heap. It provided an ever-present threat to her exposed skin, always seeming to find the perfect place to bite when she let her guard down and reached blindly into a crevice in the mound of scrap. Seeing indication that the material found regular use here struck her as odd. After creating such an immense and impressive tower, why block the windows off and keep the air out?

Many of the larger towers were in decent shape, though luck didn't favor others so fondly. Scattered throughout the ruins lay evidence that such a structure had met its demise somewhere in the past. Long ridges of metal columns and boulder-sized chunks of rubble rose up in snaking heaps impossible to cross with the wagon and horses in tow. Such walls were not excessive in number, though the few that cut through the ruins turned the terrain maze-like.

The area over which the ruins stretched was even more immense than the towers were tall. While one could pass through the other ruined towns from one end to the other in around an hour, the party walked through the maze of rubble for the same amount of time and Oleja guessed they had yet to reach the center.

Casmia called a halt amidst a clearing in the rubble. Stone bricks comprised the ground underfoot, dusted with a layer of small wispy sand dunes that shifted beneath their feet. Columns rose up in a semicircle. Oleja slowed and pretended to admire one as the rest of the group congregated in the middle.

"We will leave the wagon here. This is our meeting place for sundown," said Casmia, giving the same speech she seemed to give at every new location. "Jeth, you're with Gleathon. Onet, with Dirin. Hylde…"

Oleja didn't stick around to hear any more. She had her own work to do, for which she needed to go off alone. The party had an odd number of members anyway—everyone could still work with a partner even if she went out by herself. It didn't matter that much. And besides, she had no chance of redeeming herself in Casmia's eyes anymore. She slipped around behind the column and then off down a narrow passage between two walls. On the other side, she broke into a jog and made for the center of the ruins where the towers clustered in the greatest number.

Now that she could see them up close and get a better

sense for their height, she knew without question that the tallest among them would rise up out of the canyon and then several hundred feet beyond. One of the towers in particular caught her attention, and not only because it stood the tallest. Three pillars of stone braced the sides in a triangle, though constructed so they curved inwards as they reached for the halfway point, then back out as they stretched along the upper half. The pillars retained a decent condition, though some portions looked to be of questionable integrity. Between them, at the heart of the tower, was the main body of the structure. Stone walls chipped away, leaving gaping holes through which she spied a staircase of stone and metal alongside other twisted beams and debris. At the top, a circular metal hull rested atop the pillars. The whole tower rose up out of a mound of stone and what looked to be the remains of a sagging building, still impossibly tall yet looking hunched beside the structure amidst its remains.

She couldn't help but sway her feet towards it. Not in her entire lifetime could she imagine building something so massive. It was incredible.

As she gravitated towards the tower, she passed something else that caught her eye. The remains of a building, now reduced to rubble just the same as those around it, sat squashed between two larger crumbling structures to either side. The rough shape of three walls stood intact, though the fourth and the ceiling they held aloft looked less like a wall and a ceiling and more like overburden from the mines. Buried beneath them, with only a corner visible, poked one of the metal machines that perplexed her. Though they littered the world with no great rarity—in fact, they seemed to be just about everywhere—this one, buried under the remains of the ceiling, looked to be in fair condition. After a bit of digging and shoving aside larger chunks of debris, she found her assumptions to be correct—but also that the thing was in far better condition than expected.

Her excavation efforts revealed a crevice just big enough for her to squeeze through. Deeper inside the ruined building, the roof still clung to the standing walls, leaving an open space that remained untouched by the collapsing ceiling. She crawled inside to the long-lost room beyond. Craters pocked the machine's front half, scars left over from the collapse of the roof above it, and rust leeched out in rings from those blemishes, but beyond that it seemed to have minimal corrosion, and the back portion remained free of dents. Faded blue paint covered parts of the surface, though it took blowing off a thick layer of dust and sand to see it. Some of the machines she had come across retained shards of glass around the openings, never anything more, but a full pane filled the largest open section of this one with only minimal cracking as damage. Inside ran rows of what looked like chairs.

She brushed her hand along the surface of the metal. A handle adorned the side, and she tugged on it—gently at first, but when that offered no reward, she pulled harder. A large panel on the side groaned as it swung outwards a few inches, then with a loud *crack* it came off in her hand. The unexpected weight pulled her down, but she righted herself and looked inside. Deep earthy smells found her nose. She leaned through the opening.

A rough, cracked padding covered the chairs—leather, she realized after a moment. She pulled out her knife and began carving strips from the seatback. Leather would make much finer straps for her glider than the coarse rope of her previous version.

Back outside the machine, she scanned the rest of the room. Tools leaned against the wall in the corner. Rows of warped shelves filled the back wall, many broken, spilling their contents down onto the shelf below and the floor. Odds and ends covered what remained of the shelves, and though she couldn't name most of the contents, Oleja approached the assortment and surveyed the mess. To many of the items she gave little more than a glance. Some she picked up, examined, but ultimately tossed into the corner after seeing their uselessness on full display. She hefted a rusted metal box-like contraption into her hands and flipped it over. Rattling parts clattered together inside, creaking as they shifted, stretching in their first chance to move for generations. Knowing not what to do with such an item, Oleja cast it aside into the growing heap of discarded things.

When it struck the floor, the box burst apart, launching bits of shrapnel out in every direction, though none carried the force to wound her. Oleja looked down at the weak box, destroyed by so little force. But just as quickly as she lost interest in the thing, that interest returned, rolling across the floor in the form of a single small spring.

Oleja picked it up and tested the resistance. It was nowhere near strong enough to serve as one of the springs in her glider limbs, but she could use it for the release mechanism, for which it would serve perfectly. She knelt and inspected the carcass of the shattered box to find a second spring, which she also took. After another quick perusal of the room, she grabbed her things and headed out.

Back outside, she returned to her path for the tower. She unhooked the body of her glider from where she'd bound it to the side of her tinkering bag and hefted it up under one arm. She had all of the pieces she needed; now it was only a matter of getting it all put together.

At the base of the tower, she looked up. Vertigo swayed her on her feet. The mound of rubble surrounding the tower was nothing compared to The Heap, and she prepared to climb it in order to reach the tower's base before realizing that the other side of the structure stood exposed. The stone wall along the ground was intact and impenetrable, but up a few feet the stone split along a crack and an opening led inside to a landing on the staircase. If she jumped, she could just catch the lip of the ledge with her fingers. Doing so, she managed to haul herself up and enter the tower.

The staircase inside had seen better days—but then again, so had everything they encountered in the ruins. Metal made up the frame and railing, while the stairs themselves were stone. Cracks and missing chunks left only the lattice frame in some spots, making it a trickier climb—one where she watched her step with careful attention to avoid losing a foot or the rest of the life attached to it. Echoes wafted up and down the stairwell in some spots, though most of the time the open and crumbling walls swallowed up the sound.

At around the fifth or sixth story, she came upon a landing where the surrounding walls had fallen away entirely. She sat cross-legged on the floor there and set her glider out in front of her. A gentle breeze swept in through the open hole in the wall. She smiled to herself.

The frame was finished; the arms and hinges swung out freely, no longer scraping on the body of the device. Except for the addition of the springs, the release mechanism sat nicely in place and functioned properly. All the glider needed now were the springs, straps, and the fabric wings to finish it off.

First came the springs. Each fit into place smoothly as she attached them in turn. The work came with its share of struggles—each slip of her fingers resulted in the spring leaping from its spot. A few times, one of them nearly sailed straight over the ledge and into the pile of rubble below, but fortunately she kept the runaways corralled every time. With all of the springs in place, she pulled the cord. Both arms sprung outwards with great force and snapped into place. Perfect.

Next came the straps. The leather made a much finer addition, better than the itchy rope that burned her shoulders. She lined up one of the shoulder straps and fastened it down, then lifted it to test it out. It fit snugly, if a bit too much so. No great issue—she could loosen it.

A whistle cut through the air as something struck the metal railing next to her. The sound reverberated through the stairwell. A crossbow bolt clattered to the floor.

Oleja's heartbeat paused as she saw the dart lying there on the floor, then raced to make up for lost time. She ducked low and looked out through the hole in the wall. A moment of scanning the ground showed nothing, but then she saw him.

Honn.

He crouched amidst the rubble, taking cover behind a huge arced piece of metal. His armor glinted in the sunlight, and with his helmet visor raised, she saw his face clearly. A look of amusement played on his features. The two of them locked eyes.

When she saw him, he leapt up and raced across the uneven ground. At the base of the tower, he jumped and vanished from view. Oleja could no longer see him, but she could hear him. His thick-soled boots struck the metal and stone stairs below her, sending echoes up the chamber. And then he began to climb.

Oleja had all of her belongings in her arms within seconds. With her bag and bow over her shoulder, quiver on her back, and her glider in her arms, she bolted up the stairs.

There was only one way down. One staircase, and she shared it with Honn. It was fight or die.

No—it was fight, die, or *jump*. She had her glider, she just needed to finish it. But on what surface? Sprinting full-speed up a broken staircase while pursued by a bloodthirsty eclipser hunter did not create the calm environment she needed in order to concentrate and build a device to gamble her life on the functionality of. Besides, it still needed three more straps and the entire fabric sail.

Well, it was that or die. Die and never free her people from the canyon, never be the hero, never return to prove to Ude that she lived past her escape.

She held the body of the glider out in front of her with one arm and pulled a leather strap from her bag with the other hand. Loud footsteps pounded on the stairs below. With one finger, she held the strap in place, and then drew a nail and her hammer from her bag. Shifting her fingers, she got the nail in place, and took up the hammer with her full grip. Two swift strikes sunk the nail into the wood, though her fingers were not spared from the blow. She shook off the pain; more pressing matters loomed behind her. If Honn caught up to her, he'd do more than tap her fingers with a hammer.

She put another nail through the top of the strap and then did the same to the bottom. Shoddy work, but it would probably hold her in flight. It had to.

"Canyon girl!" Honn bellowed from below. "Where do you expect to run to? You have nowhere to go!" He sounded closer than she'd anticipated—a flight or two down and no more.

She reached a landing and found a large chunk of

rubble blocking part of the next leg of stairs. The gap provided just enough room for her to squeeze through, but she paused for half a second as an idea formed in her brain.

Bracing herself on the wall, she used her leg to shake the stone. It wobbled back and forth, and then leaned. With one huge shove she sent it toppling from the ledge and down the staircase. It bounced off the first set of stairs and slammed into the one below it, taking a bite out of the stone and metal framework, which collapsed into the level below. Honn howled. It sounded like he had been struck. Oleja didn't stick around to find out.

Honn's thunderous footfalls returned a moment later, though his gait had changed. Injured now, and slower, though he kept coming with a fierce speed. But any scrap of time she could amass was well worth it.

Oleja let one arm of the glider extend out in front of her. She pulled the fabric from her bag. Right now, that was the most important element of the device. She'd finish the leg straps if time stayed on her side.

Using the same awkward maneuvers as before, she slowly began fixing the fabric to the arm. Every slip of her fingers—every mistake—only frustrated her more. It was not working. She needed a surface to work on.

Her legs ached as she pushed herself faster. She took the steps two at a time, careful to avoid the pitfalls of the ancient stairs. One wrong step and she could lose her lead on the eclipser, falling right into his grasp and, likely, the wrong end of his blade. She ignored the protests from her legs and kept going, adrenaline fueling her bounds up to the tower's pinnacle.

When she burst through a door at the top of the stairs, she found herself on a wide circular floor. A lattice of metal beams crisscrossed the circumference—windows of a sort, though open to the air. A strong gust whipped loose strands of her dark hair about her face and tugged on the fabric that hung haphazardly affixed to her glider. She moved towards the edge. The heights slung a dizziness about her head. Should her glider fail and send her on the quick route to the ground, her chances of survival totaled a clean zero.

Oleja threw her things to the floor and resumed her furious work. The wind masked the sounds of Honn's approach. Exactly when he'd reach the floor would be a surprise. Until then, she had work to do.

Her hands flew over the frame, pulling the fabric into place. Sweat beaded on her brow. The wind swept it away. Footsteps hit the floor, sending tremors through the structure. Oleja hurriedly wrapped up the last of the fabric and collapsed the glider wings. Two straps would have to do.

Honn kicked open the door.

Oleja strapped on her glider.

With a cruel scraping sound, Honn slid two swords from sheaths at either hip. He grinned. Oleja pulled her bow off her shoulder and drew an arrow, clasping the cover over her quiver once she retrieved one. It was going to be a bumpy ride.

"Did you think you left me behind?" asked Honn with a

sneer, speaking loudly to make his voice heard over the wind.

"Hoped, but never thought," said Oleja, backing up slowly. She couldn't make her plans clear or he'd charge her or go for the crossbow at his hip. As she sized him up, she noticed something. The armor along his left hip and leg bent sharply, and blood trickled out from the gaps. The metal parted just enough around the thigh to expose some of his grey skin and torn brown pants—the results of her rubble cave-in.

A loud bang sounded as the door flew open again. Oleja looked past Honn. Pahlo stood in the doorway. Honn didn't even bother to look back over his shoulder. But Pahlo was a far cry from the force needed to bring down the trained eclipser soldier.

Casmia filed in behind him, and then the rest of the raiders, all breathing heavily and clutching their weapons. Even Kella stood amongst them, her eyes wide yet determined. Oleja grinned. They had him well outnumbered, and hopefully out-skilled. Honn didn't flinch.

"Attack to kill!" shouted Oleja. Several of the raiders lurched forward. They paused as Casmia raised a hand.

"They don't act on your command, Raseari," she said. Honn kept coming. Oleja kept retreating.

Was she serious? Was it not clear what they should be doing? They hated the earthborn whether this one in particular was an enemy of Oleja or not. Honn still didn't look back to size up the new opponents or guard against their attacks. What was going on?

"You don't see what is happening here, do you?" asked Honn with a smirk.

"What is there to see? You're about to die." Her voice wavered. She couldn't imbue her words with sureness if she didn't possess it.

"This is what happens to lowly digging worms who try to play the hero. You make *enemies*. Even where you don't expect them."

Realization hit Oleja like a ceiling of stone crashing down on her. She looked to Casmia.

"What did you do?" she asked the woman, fear and anger rising in her voice.

"What was best for my crew. You fetch a high price, Raseari. Weapons, ores—materials to replace the ones you lost—and safe passage through the earthborn lands to the east. We have lost faithful members of our crew in similar territory." She looked to Hylde and Kella. "Now we won't have to face that tragedy again."

Oleja's foot found the edge of the platform. Behind her was only the sky. She set her jaw and drew her focus away from the raiders. She didn't need them. She didn't need anyone. Her escape plan would have worked out fine whether they came after her or not, and her plan to save her people would be no different. This was why she worked alone. The sky behind her was all she needed.

Honn kept coming. The raiders all looked between Oleja

and Casmia. Oleja drew back her bow and aimed at Honn's face. He dropped his visor.

At the last second, she shifted her aim to the gap in his dented armor and fired. The arrow sank deep into his flesh, spilling dark blood anew that ran down the polished armor that clad his leg. He roared in pain and fell forward. And she saw nothing more.

She jumped.

The ground raced to meet her. With her free hand, she reached behind her and pulled the cord on the glider. The wings deployed in an instant, the frame rattling as the wings caught the air. Her legs, floating freely without straps, fell down beneath her—surely not a dignified position, but it didn't matter as the wind caught her and propelled her forward, carrying her along with it as it blew northwest.

At her altitude, she could cover a great distance before she reached the ground, and unlike last time, she wanted the glider to take her as far as it could. The wind blew strong and kept her descent slow.

It would be a while before her feet found the ground again.

CHAPTER FIFTEEN

No doubt about it—controlled landings were far better than crash landings.

The new glider shook and rattled, rickety in its hastily-finished state, but by some miracle it held together. Perhaps she had her "skyborn talent" to thank if what that one kid said was true. She almost laughed thinking about it, but the feeling evaporated almost immediately. She was in no laughing situation. Only anger coursed through her now.

They betrayed her. All of them. Sure, she expected it from Casmia, but Pahlo? Kella? Hylde? They conspired behind her back to sell her to Honn, thinking only of their own selfish wants. Casmia could have dozens of weapons to replace her lost sword—which *she* misplaced, not Oleja. Hylde could make sure she never lost another person she loved to the eclipsers, and Kella would sleep well knowing her birth mother was spared from the same fate as the mother she already lost. And of course, Pahlo just wanted to save his own skin—Honn pursued Oleja, not him, and if he acted in a way that pleased the hunter, he could ensure that neither Honn nor any other eclipser changed their mind and went after him once they apprehended their primary target. Oleja just hoped her escape meant the deal collapsed and that no one could get what they were all too willing to sacrifice her for. She couldn't bear the idea of Casmia receiving her reward in metals that Oleja herself hauled out of the earth with her own shackled hands.

Honn would die, if he hadn't already. He had no hope of surviving his predicament. He bled heavily with an arrow in his leg at least a thousand feet in the air. Stairs would be his end, and plenty of them stood between him and his sled. The raiders wouldn't help him—clearly they operated on a skewed sense of alliance, but they weren't *that* stupid. After Oleja slipped through his fingers, nothing held him to his deal. He could turn on them, and even injured he'd be able to take out at least one of them, perhaps more, before they could finish Oleja's job. They could leave him there to die and shed no more worry in his direction. They could even loot his sled back down on the ground. All thanks to Oleja.

She was outside the ruins now. The wind carried her longer than she'd hoped, oftentimes keeping her from losing any elevation at all. The towering husks of the old towers now rose up as vague shapes behind her. Sand surrounded her—not that she was used to anything different—though no scraggly shrubs or patches of dry grass broke up the terrain, only sand, strewn in wavy lines by the wind.

For once, she had options in where to turn her path. Honn was out of the way. She could return to her village, alone, just as she wanted to. Or she could turn elsewhere—seek out a spot of refuge from the desert heat and plot her next move.

Her first concern should be water. She replenished her clay canteen and waterskin shortly before slipping away from the raiders and had hardly touched either since. She didn't have a lot, but the water could last her a day comfortably, more if she rationed it. The closest water source she knew the location of was the lake. Getting back to the ruins would take the remainder of the day, and reaching the lake meant another several hours' walk from there. Doable, certainly, but it came with one major deterrent: passing back southeast meant going past the raiders and risk running into them. Such a confrontation sounded awkward at the very least.

Going back through the ruins to the lake also made up the first leg of the trip back to her village. If that was her path, nothing stood between her and whatever awaited her upon return. Against the eclipsers and their defenses, she'd have only herself, her wits, and the things she carried.

Normally she'd have confidence in such an arsenal, but the lightness of her quiver posited a counterargument. Aside from her bow, she had her knife for a weapon and nothing more. And her armor still collected dust in a hole back in the canyon. If she planned to fight her way singlehandedly through whatever protections the eclipsers put in place to keep her from the gate, it would be tricky.

She could piece together new arrows in the desert, but for that she required time and many resources she didn't presently have. Following in the raiders' footsteps and looting for parts could be an option, but during that time she'd need to survive in the wilderness alone. As long as she set up camp by a water source, she'd take care of that need, but ensuring a reliable stash of food was more difficult. She carried enough rations for a few days at best. Hunting would be a necessity.

All of that made up one of her options, but she had another. She could go to the civilization of people in the mountains that Casmia mentioned—northwest, according to her direction, though Oleja knew not how far. The journey pointed through land unexplored to her, and without a map for guidance, she'd have to find her way on her own. But according to the raiders, food and water were more plentiful outside of the desert, making survival easier. At least, assuming they didn't lie to her about that as well.

If she managed to reach the town in the mountains, she could trade with the people and plan her next move from there, conserving her energy without having to divert so much of it to staying alive. And as a bonus, if she took that path, she wouldn't have to wander back past the raiders.

Setting her course for the mountains seemed like the best option. If nothing else, it would get her out of the desert heat while she readied to take on the eclipsers. She just hated that it meant moving farther away from her village, further from her time to be the gallant hero leading them to safety. Though her heart felt as if her village tugged in the other direction, she turned northwest and continued on the route that the wind had already brought her down. First things first, she needed to get out of the desert. Once she accomplished that, then she would worry about her people.

She tried her best to brush off the uncertainty she felt. Confidence was the key to bringing down the eclipsers and freeing her people. She needed to plan, and couldn't do it if she struggled just to keep herself alive. Making for the mountains was the right choice.

The sun indicated that the hour ticked passed midday now. Thinking back to that morning, before they even reached the ruins—it felt like ages ago. She was better off now—back in control of where she went and what she did. She should never have started traveling with the raiders to begin with. Nothing but insects, they lived like mites, crawling through the trash looking for something they could use for their own benefit. Oleja was not a scrap pulled from the trash, and she wouldn't fetch a deal for anyone. Never again would she be a pawn in someone else's game, not ordered to mine or thrown about in a barter. She was the one playing the game now, and it didn't matter what it took to win; she would do it.

Time wore on as she walked. All of her gear weighed her down. Glider, quiver, bag—she forgot how it felt to bear so much. Looser sand composed the ground underfoot now, and it made her slide with each step. Though she still wore the raider's outfit—and planned to wear it while it still served her, because suffering the heat for the sake of pettiness clearly indicated a fool—the sun beat down hard upon her and only made the walk more miserable. Sweat soaked into the fabric. She could almost feel the weight it added. The heat only seemed to grow in intensity the farther west she went, and if that was truly the pattern to expect for the trail ahead, she had half a mind to turn and reverse course, going instead back east to where the sun treated her more kindly. Supposedly cooler air settled in the mountains—if she still trusted the words of the raiders— which meant that sooner or later the temperature had to start decreasing as she moved westward. With any luck, that leaned to the sooner side of things rather than the later. Water was not a resource she had in abundance, so she preferred not to sweat all of it out the second it passed through her lips.

Sunset marked the impending arrival of cooler temperatures, but it also meant that while the sun sat lower in the sky, it shone in her eyes as she continued on her course. Squinting made the muscles in her face ache, and before long she gave in and resorted to keeping them shut as she walked through the barren landscape. There was no threat of crashing into anything given that doing so required something to crash into, but she opened her eyes and blinked into the light every so often just to check and make sure. Each time, nothing but the sight of more sand greeted her. If she never looked upon another patch of sand again, she would offer no complaints. Even the hills off to her left and right promised more interesting sights, but the frequent ascent and descent over each rolling peak would only double the distance she had to cross, and that was not a tradeoff she had yet resigned herself to making. Although she'd be lying if she said she wasn't getting there.

A rattling sound seized her heart and she snapped her eyes open. The bright red-orange light of the low sun left her blind. She blinked as the sandy landscape came into focus, but no snake lay before her. Turning her head, she scanned her surroundings, but saw nothing but sand.

Then the ground before her started to ripple like waves as the sand shifted and a long body emerged. Scales appeared, hardly a shade removed from the color of the sand. Thicker around than her arm and nearly twice as long as she stood tall, it surfaced, bearing fangs and a jaw that looked powerful enough to sever a hand in one clean stroke. This beast was no rattlesnake, at least not anything like those she'd seen before. The size, of course, gave the first indicator, but it also had a rigid back and wider head. Fear pulled her backwards, though slowly. She knew how fast snakes could strike, and no more than a foot lay between her and the thing's mouth. Rattlesnake venom was deadly in many of the cases she saw back in the village, and the few who lived owed thanks to immediate help from others. Oleja was alone.

This must have been a mutant, like the Gila monsters and the eclipsers. The raiders mentioned mutant rattlesnakes, and one of them said something about the venom taking on different properties. The details were lost to her as her mind prioritized yelling at her to get out of its striking range.

A forked tongue flicked between its teeth and it rattled again. The rattle sang a shrill note, a different sound than its non-mutated counterparts. Slowly, carefully, she drew an arrow and nocked it. She kept her movements as unthreatening as she could manage while preparing to kill. She raised her bow and aimed for the head.

The snake lunged. The suddenness made her jump and she fired. A fountain of sand sprayed up as the arrow sunk into the ground. The snake had better aim.

Pain flared through her left leg. Oleja screamed and dropped to the ground. The snake writhed, twisting its body around as she pulled it through the sand, but its grip on her leg clamped too tight, and its long, sharp fangs were buried deep in her flesh. Dropping her bow, she went instead for her knife. Blade in hand, she swung blindly, the pain clouding her vision. The snake fell still.

Oleja looked down. The head hung limp and only half-attached to the body, the other half cut through by the blade of her knife. As it died, the snake's hold on her loosened, but the fangs held it pinned to her leg. She pried it out quickly with the tip of her knife, sending another bout of pain rearing through her. Blood dripped from two fine holes.

What had the raiders said about mutant rattlesnake venom? Her head spun. She couldn't remember. The group's faces blurred together, and their names disappeared in the sand.

Her breaths came quick and ragged. She needed a bandage on her wound. She could walk if she just bandaged herself. The venom wouldn't kill her. She was going to be fine. If anyone could tough their way through it, she could. Death was not an option. Never had been, never would be.

Bandage.

She found a scrap of some old fabric in her bag, perhaps once attached to a tattered bit of clothing. Pants, maybe? It didn't matter. She wrapped it tight around her wound. Blood stained it through in moments. It didn't matter. She got to her feet.

Her vision went fuzzy. No, it was only the sand, everywhere she looked. Or maybe it was the sand *and* her vision was fuzzy. She couldn't tell.

How long ago did she last drink water? Her mouth felt so dry. She tried to pull the cotton out, but it moved deeper, deeper into her throat until it stuck there and she couldn't breathe. She coughed, and the action made her lurch forward.

She stumbled two steps forward, and then two more. Her left foot only stepped on spikes; hot sand and nails coated the bottom of that foot. She looked back up. She had to go towards the sun—she had to keep moving.

More pain. Her left leg threatened to give out. She clenched her teeth and pushed through the pain and the shaking of her mind. This wouldn't be her end, she had so much more to do. Her people were out there. She was going to rescue them, be the hero. She needed to be the hero. Like

Tor. Ude still waited for her. He believed in her, he had to know she'd get back there. No matter what it took. A little pain in her leg was nothing.

The ground swung up and slammed her hard in the face and chest.

Dark holes in the ground swallowed her eyes.

CHAPTER SIXTEEN

Oleja awoke deep in the mines. There were no torches around, and she couldn't find any on her person. Cotton still stuck in her throat. She coughed and gagged, trying to free it before it wedged itself deeper. It was too stubborn. Why was she covered in so much sand?

She shook herself off and looked around. She had to follow the sun. How was she supposed to do that if she couldn't see it? Panic thrashed inside of her, slamming against her chest from the inside, threatening to burst out. She pressed her palms to her ribcage, reinforcing it, trying to keep herself in one piece.

The sun. She had to find the sun. In haste, she got to her feet. Silver light exploded in her vision and she fell back to the ground. She needed to breathe and clear her mind. Something stuck to her face, wrapped around her head, keeping her from thinking clearly. For a moment, she sat still. Air couldn't reach her lungs; cotton still blocked the way. She coughed. Gritty sand filled her mouth. From her canteen, she took a swig, and the cotton dissolved. She gasped for air.

No stone surrounded her, only darkness. Was it night? She thought she remembered falling asleep, but where, and when? Lights hung in the sky—yes, stars, but too dim. Pink light tinted the sky.

The sun. That was where she had to go. Was it the east or the west where the sun rose? She couldn't recall. But she had to go to the sun.

She tried to stand again, slower now, wobbly on her feet. Rumors back in her village talked about the whole ground shaking underfoot as the earth moved, "quakes" or something like that. Was this one? Were they real? Her leg throbbed. She clenched her teeth. They cracked, shattering, falling from her mouth in shards. She ran her tongue over the sharp remains, slicing it raw. Metallic blood filled her mouth. She spat red-tinged saliva into the sand.

Footsteps sounded in the sand behind her. Oleja turned, only to come face-to-face with an eclipser.

He leveled a spear as he charged her. Oleja raised a sword in her right hand, bracing a shield against her body with her left. A jagged line cut across the face of the shield, glowing white-hot. It cast the eclipser in bright light. He blinked and held up an arm to cover his face. Oleja lunged.

The eclipser fell, a victim of her swift strikes. She bashed him in the head with her shield as he fell, knocking him out cold. She turned back to the sun and ran.

Two more eclipsers rose up out of the sand. Fangs stuck

out as they sneered at her, showing off forked tongues. One swung her spear, but it glanced off Oleja's helmet. Oleja ducked low and brought her sword up into the eclipser's stomach. The second jabbed at her. The spearhead pierced her left side. Oleja brought the edge of her shield down hard on the shaft, snapping the wood in two. She kicked the eclipser's kneecap and he fell to one knee. One quick blow and it was over.

The skin around her spear wound knitted itself back together until only a thick scar remained.

She kept moving. The sand around her rippled like the surface of the lake, with peaks of sand rising and falling, making her path hard. She staggered left and right, swaying over the uneven ground. Waves grabbed at her feet, attempting to pull her under, but she kicked them off. Sand sprayed out as she crushed the current under the soles of her boots.

Someone whispered her name, their voice cracking and hoarse. She looked up. A hoard of eclipsers stood before her. Ude lay at their feet. The ground would not be still—it surged up in pulsing, pounding spikes that grew and contracted with her heartbeat. The eclipsers charged. Oleja stood fast.

She felled the monsters left and right, taking hits but shedding more of her enemies' blood than they drew from her. Their blades crashed against her armor. With each one she killed, two more rushed in to take its place. But that was just two more she got to kill.

When the last one fell, she stood in the center of a field

of bodies. Ragged breathing tore at her lungs. Her people stood in a wide ring around her, encircling the carnage.

"Hero," voices echoed. "Oleja, skyborn, hero. *Hero*."

Pride swelled in her chest. They were free. She was the hero.

A shadow swallowed her. Something loomed above. She turned. The largest eclipser she had ever seen stood there, at least twenty feet tall and wielding a sword longer than she was tall. He grinned. Oleja lifted her own blade.

The giant swung his sword down at her. She blocked it with hers. The force knocked her to the ground.

Oleja's sword fell in two halves at her sides, cut clean through by the dominant blade of the giant eclipser. Oleja raised her shield, ready to deflect the next blow, but he didn't swing at her again, only laughed. He turned to the people in the ring around her.

With low sweeps back and forth he cut them down, dozens falling with each pendulous arc of his cruel steel blade. Oleja screamed for him to stop, clawing herself up to her feet. The pain still burned in her leg. She didn't care. She hadn't come so far for this to be the ending.

She swung punch after punch at the giant's legs, but they were as thick around as she was, and he didn't so much as flinch. Using the edge of her shield, she struck his calves, first with one hand but then using the other to deliver more force. Nothing worked. The giant kept on killing.

The people didn't even move out of the way, just stood and let themselves die at the hands of this tyrant. Oleja shouted to them, first to fight at her side, but when they made no move to do so her pleas morphed into calls to flee. None of them budged an inch, at least not until the sword cleaved through their bodies and left them in a crumpled, shredded heap on the ground.

With a fierce battle cry, Trayde vaulted over Oleja's head and thrust her sword deep into the giant's ribcage. He grunted and turned his attention at last away from the people of the village.

Onet and Wulshe surged forward and struck the leg opposite Oleja. Hylde's axes arched through the air and imbedded in the giant's flesh, one in either shoulder. Arrows came in volleys, shot by Kella standing tall atop a pillar of pure white stone. Jeth rode in atop a horse and wound around the giant's legs, slicing long gashes into his grey skin. The giant roared in agony.

A shadow swooped overhead. Oleja looked up. Casmia soared past, Oleja's glider strapped to her back, sword out in front of her. Shouting in fury, she collided with the giant's face, her sword piercing the soft flesh of his cheek.

The giant fell to one knee. His palm struck the sand, steadying himself. A glint flashed in his eyes and he dug his fingers deep into the sand and pulled forth a boulder. Without looking, he flung it out to his left. A cry of pain echoed from somewhere out of sight, and then Oleja ran towards it, though she did not know why.

Pahlo lay at the end of her path, crushed beneath the boulder. Tears soaked his eyes. He looked up to Oleja.

"We came to help."

"I don't need help." It sounded like her voice, but she didn't remember saying the words, or even thinking them for that matter.

"Raseari!" shouted Casmia's voice. Oleja turned.

The giant hunched over, down on both knees. The raiders still hacked at his body, spewing dark blood across the sand, staining it as black as the night. The giant's eyes focused on her, unblinking, unwavering.

"Raseari," said Casmia again, but it was the giant's lips that moved. "You haven't won. You never will. Your path leads to me, and you can never bring me down."

And then the sand turned to water again. It rippled and shook. A column rose up as if the grains were caught in a vortex of wind, dancing and shaking as it rose higher and higher, and then it doubled back down. Fangs sprouted; eyes gleamed—a rattlesnake. In one massive bite it crashed against the giant and swallowed him down. When the sand settled, nothing remained. Even Pahlo and the boulder were gone.

A rumble swept in from the horizon. Oleja looked. A blast rose up there, sand billowing into the sky. Light flared, growing brighter and brighter and brighter until it forced her to close her eyes. Even with her eyelids pressed shut it was as bright as day. Then the sand hit her, a massive wave of wind-whipped sand pounding against her, cutting up her skin, forcing her down as her legs failed and she collapsed. The light did not let up. The wind howled in her ears. And then it was over just as quickly as it started. Oleja opened her eyes slowly. The world was still. She got to her feet.

Dawn broke the sky into fragments. Golden light bathed the land. Oleja still had no teeth left in her mouth. She shambled towards the sun.

Many times, she found herself at the edge of a deep crevice that demanded she scale down one side and back up the other in order to cross. She found Pahlo's body at the bottom every time. The crevices were so many in number that it became infuriating. At the lip of her ninth or tenth, she became so fed up that she jumped. The pain in her leg got more intense, but otherwise she found that the hundred or so foot drops took little toll on her. What was more, they were just as easy to jump back out of with a single bound. This discovery made her passage much faster.

By midday she gained the good sense to realize that she could not follow the sun straight up. It didn't matter for long, because just as soon as the sun reached the top of its arc, it slowed, stopped, and then reversed course back down through the sky. She kept on her path.

When the sun dipped low to the ground again late in the day, it turned the sky orange, not the pink or gold from before. Hills marked the horizon, and for a while the sun sat atop them until Oleja went up to join it and it ran off to the next ridge. Amongst the rocky peaks she found a pool of water—nothing near as massive as the lake, but it looked to be liquid no matter how long she stared, so she went to the bank and tested it hesitantly with the tips of her fingers.

It was cool. The single touch drew all the heat from

Oleja's body and sucked it into the water where it sank to the depths. Oleja knelt and cupped some in her hands to splash across her face.

The chill raced through her body, and when she looked back up, the world came into focus. She groaned. *Hallucinations.* Hylde had told her about the mutant rattlesnake venom. Instead of outright death, it brought on intense hallucinations—certainly the better option in Oleja's opinion. She leaned back and looked at the sky. The sun started to taunt her again.

She looked down at her wound. Two red puncture marks marred her calf. Beneath the heavy coat of sand, the skin around them was swollen and raised, flushed red and splotchy, with a sticky oily fluid now leaking from the holes in place of blood. Hadn't she covered it? When did the bandage fall off? She could recall only a blur when trying to remember the events of the day's walk.

For the first time so far that day she realized how exhausted she was. Her eyelids insisted on sleep. It didn't help that her head still spun.

After a few gulps of water from the pool, she immersed her leg in the shallows. Grains of sand floated off and swirled around in the gentle waves. She wiped away the rest of the sand, brushing her hands slowly over her infected wound. Her body shook as the pain bit through her leg anew, causing her to grimace. She could do nothing else to treat the infection, so after a short while in the refreshing water she pulled it out and dried off gingerly. The water that dripped off into the sand caused bright green sprouts to grow. She waved her hand through them angrily and they dissipated just as quickly as they appeared.

From her touch, blood beaded fresh on her scabbed puncture wounds and raced in two lines down her shin. A quick check through her bag confirmed what she already feared—she had no suitable fabric for a bandage. She did find a family of rodents living inside the pocket, however. She ignored them.

A bit of wood lay nearby, an old dead shrub that she could be fairly certain was real. From it, she took several sturdy branches and broke them into shorter segments, which she arranged on a flat spot of ground near the shore of the pool. A bit of smaller kindling from her bag and then a few strikes on a piece of flint got a fire going. Oleja took out her pliers and a small sheet of metal. She held it in the fire for a while and watched it glow hotter and hotter. When she deemed it sufficient, she withdrew it, and after a brief second of preparation, she pressed it to her bleeding wounds.

The metal kissed her skin with a sizzle. A muted grunt passed her lips but nothing more. The fire giggled at her. She had half a mind to douse it then and there.

With a flick of her wrist, she sent the bit of metal into the pool. It struck the surface with a hiss and a wisp of steam and then vanished below the surface, sinking to the depths. She put her pliers back in her bag and settled in beside the fire.

In her bag she carried enough food for another two days

if rationed meagerly, more if she pushed her daily allotment to precarious levels. She hadn't seen an animal that she knew was real since the rattlesnake. In her panic and delirium, the thought to take the meat from it to eat never occurred to her. Would eating the mutant snake meat even be a good idea? Rattlesnake meat was safe despite the deadly venom, but what of mutant rattlesnake meat? She had no idea. Questions of that sort were the type that the raiders or Pahlo always knew the answer to. Too bad they were mutinous insufferable cowards.

She lay back and looked up to the sky again. Darkness had settled over the world, bringing along a few stars. They danced together in the sky, spinning and twinkling and merging and splitting. Oleja let them have their fun; she was too tired to make them stop.

CHAPTER SEVENTEEN

Morning brought little in the way of good news. She had water, yes, but her food supply only got lower and her wound only more infected. There was a special sort of frustration reserved for waking up starving to find a great pile of fruit beside your head, only to take a bite and discover the perfect, juicy, vibrant-colored snack had the taste and texture of a rock—which, as it turned out, was exactly what they were. With that event came the understanding that the venom maintained some degree of hold over her, which fell into the category of "not good news."

She ate a bit of salted meat for her breakfast, along with a small handful of nuts—hardly enough to keep up her strength, and far less than she ate even as a slave under the eclipsers' rule, but she didn't dare allow herself more without knowing when she'd have her next opportunity to replenish her supply of food. All she carried with her now was a small bundle of rations from the raiders. They ate communal meals, but each of them held onto a pouch containing a few days' rations to snack on or in case they got separated from the group—or, it seemed, in case they were betrayed and sent on their way without so much as a farewell aside from the less-than-friendly eclipser hunter invited along who seemed all too eager to say goodbye to her quite permanently. Turning the tables on him was the least she could do to show her gratitude.

After breakfast she went to the edge of the pool and dipped her leg in the shallows again. A heavy layer of heat lay just beneath the skin, but the cool water quenched it and soothed the pain. With the wound cauterized, she no longer feared anything getting inside—nor bleeding though a bandage—but it looked no less infected. Even if she didn't need it, a bandage added a layer of protection. She looked through her bag again.

The only fabric inside that wasn't coarse and porous burlap was her old shirt and pants. Tears and holes riddled the shirt, and even the swaths still holding together bore a multitude of stains—mud, clay, blood. Condition aside, only a slightly finer variety of itchy burlap composed the garment. The pants hardly provided a better option—a stronger material, but rigid in its own right and just as stained and dirtied as the shirt.

The robe she wore was newer and therefore cleaner by a hair. The fabric was certainly softer as well, less likely to chafe her raw wound. Though she still relied on it to keep her cool and protected from the sun, using some of the material for a bandage seemed like the best option in her collection of bad ones. With a sigh, she took her knife and began cutting strips from the hem around her calves. In order to get enough to cover the full length of the wound and infected area, she had to cut a few inches off, bringing the hem up to her knees. That still only gave her enough fabric for one bandage after she wrapped it around enough times to keep the sand and other debris from getting in. Knowing she would regret it, but resolving to do what she had to, she cut another two bandages from the fraying edge hanging about her knees, giving her spares to replace the worn one with when they got too caked in sweat, grime, and blood.

Perhaps she could have opted to leave the robe mostly intact and cut what she needed when she needed it, but the fabric was in desperate need of a wash, especially if she wanted to use it to cover her wound and not worsen the infection. She could wash it now in the pool, but even an hour of walking through the desert promised to have it right back to looking like she rolled through the mud in it, and she couldn't carry water designated for use in washing her clothes. As much water as possible had to go with her in some way, and every drop of it was for drinking. Cutting the bandages now and washing them while she could, then storing them safely in her bag sounded best. She would just have to suffer the heat later.

From what little she recalled of the previous day's journey, she remembered it being hot. Not that that was a hard conclusion to make; she could have guessed as much and considered it correct with a realistic degree of certainty. Mind-melting heat had hounded her steps every day since her flight from the canyon. The farther west she went, the worse it got. She just hoped to leave it behind soon.

She scrubbed the muck from the freshly cut bandages. Brown and orange dirt seeped into the clear water, turning it murky and opaque. She kept scrubbing until the water around the bandages ran clear, then held them aloft one by one and wrung the water out. Still damp, she tied one around her wound—tight enough to keep it from slipping, but not so tight that it irritated her raw skin. She folded the other two and stowed them in her bag. After drinking her fill and replenishing the water supply in both her canteen and waterskin, she began the next leg of her journey.

She made slow progress, especially down the slope of the hills. Every step made her wince. Pain throbbed in her leg and leaked up into her hip and side. She did her best to ignore it, reminding herself who she was and what she had set out to do, clenching her muscles and filling herself anew with determination—the only thing she had left to get herself through the desert. *Oleja Raseari, skyborn, slayer of Honn, hero of the people of the canyon.* She pushed on.

In the haze of the day before, she'd deviated from her intended path. She could recall a burning need to follow the sun, though in her state of delirium she missed the fact that that was the aim of the previous evening, when the sun lay in the west, and should not have carried over into the morning, when it rose in the east. Even still, she wanted to go northwest, not due west, and pre-bite Oleja knew that without strain, yet post-bite Oleja did not. Somehow, by some great stroke of luck, her hallucinations afforded her one single favor: for the entire first half of the day, she seemed to have thought she saw the sun rising in the west. No doubt it truly rose in the east as usual, but until it arrived in the western half of the sky at midday, her hallucinations gave her a false sun to chase, keeping her relatively on course. Although, of that she could not be entirely certain, but given what she remembered, and by all manners of calculation, it seemed she traveled a good deal farther west than she would have if her path took her in a circle or otherwise unproductive shape. However, while her hallucinations and muddy-minded obsessions kept her on a course west, it appeared she made little progress north, leaving her south of where she meant to be—no great loss, so long as it did not spell her demise. All she could do now was point her path northwest with heavy emphasis on "north" and continue on at a slow, limping pace.

The sun rose higher and the air grew hotter. Her robe, which now fell only just past her mid-thigh, still managed to keep some of the heat off her upper body, but her legs remained quite exposed. She knew she looked foolish in her altered outfit, but with no one around to see it, what did it matter?

Occasionally a moment of dizziness hit her, and she stumbled more than usual. All at once the sky upended itself, dragging the earth by the horizon and flipping it over her head as if trying to pull a blanket down on her and trap her. After a few seconds, the spinning faded and she was able to continue on, cursing herself for getting bitten in the first place. She didn't know how long the aftereffects of the venom lasted, but they couldn't go away fast enough.

Hours passed. Her waterskin drained more rapidly than she wanted it to, but no amount of cursing at it replenished the contents. She had yet to start on her canteen, but the location of her next water source would remain a mystery until she got nearly close enough to drink from it, be that hours away or days. Being stranded alone without any water at all could be her end, and she would not let that happen. She cut her water intake down, going longer and longer between drinks, and paring down those drinks from two gulps, to one and a sip, then to just one, then to only a few sips. Sweat poured from her skin as the heat rose in intensity. Part of her considered drinking it. She licked a runaway drop as it curved past her lips. The salt entertained her taste buds, tangy on her tongue, but it leeched what little moisture coated her mouth and only left her with a redoubled need to pull out her waterskin and down it all in a few swift gulps. She could not risk that. She had to ration it.

An ache began in her head, mild at first but slowly rising, clawing its way through her skull as it pounded against her scalp, demanding she drink more water. Looking at the sunlight reflected on the bright golden sand empowered the aching, but she didn't dare close her eyes; she had learned that lesson through the most ruthless manner.

Soon, the sun's touch passed beyond anything she had

ever felt—beyond the heat of the forge back in the village, beyond the days spent walking beneath the sun's intense glare alongside the raiders; like the heat of holding metal in a fire while waiting for it to become malleable, but she was without tools and used her hands instead. Even that might have been preferable to the murderous eyes of the sun trained down on her. Smoke rose from her robe, thin curls at first but soon billowing into her face. Sparks ignited, flames roared, the fabric went up in a blaze.

Oleja yelped and patted at the fire but it spread too fast. Dropping her bow and throwing down her bag, quiver, and glider, she unclasped her belt and threw off the robe in one quick pull. The light fabric fluttered down into the sand, trailed by orange tendrils of flame and dark grey clouds of smoke. She stomped on the fabric and kicked sand onto it. All her weight fell onto her injured leg and she recoiled, hissing in pain as she fell back into the sand. The world spun. Her head lolled. She closed her eyes and let it run its course. When she opened her eyes, the world had re-rooted itself. Her robe lay in the sand, torn somewhat and covered in sand. Not a speck of soot tinged the fabric. It was not scorched—not even so much as singed.

Anger was all that burned her.

Sand clung to her exposed skin, dampened by the coat of sweat that covered her from head to toe. Her head pounded. Her leg burned. She took a meager sip of water.

It felt like the sand had gotten in her mouth and coated the inside all the way down her throat. Her breathing came strained through dry pipes. How she longed to curl up there on the ground and rest. She forced the feeling down, burying it deep in the sand. She could not sleep yet, it would be her end, she knew it. No giving up. She had to keep moving.

A long tear split the front of her robe, and her violent and rapid undressing worsened the fraying at the hem. Though she shook as much sand from it as she could, the grains hid between the fibers, grating on her skin when she put it back on. No amount of shaking it out remedied the problem, and when she picked up her things and tried to keep walking, the sand-filled robe rasped at her skin. Frustrated, she flung it off again and dug out her old clothes. The tank top left much of her skin exposed to the sun. The pants covered her entire legs aside from the holes torn in them, but the heavy fabric quickly proved too hot to wear. Drawing her knife, she made quick, sloppy work of turning them into shorts, stowing the severed portions in her bag. She picked up her belongings again and kept walking.

The sun showed no kindness to her skin, and without her robe blocking the sun and keeping her cool, the heat only became more unbearable. It didn't take long for her skin to redden, cooking under the hot noontime sun, flushing her dark skin with a pink hue. The sunburn hurt with every touch, and all of the equipment strapped to her body felt like knives stabbing her each time it poked her in just the wrong way.

Regardless of how badly she wanted to be out of whatever hell-hole she stumbled through, she could not

CAMERON BOLLING

push herself to go faster no matter how hard she tried. Her leg hurt more and more with each step, and when she pushed herself to move faster, she could feel it grow weaker, threatening to give out beneath her and leave her stranded there to die. Nothing in her bag was big enough to make a crutch, and her bow wasn't sturdy enough to use in such a way, or even as a walking stick. She turned her eyes skyward frequently, hoping to see the sun lowering towards the horizon so that cool air and hope could settle across the world once more. But each time only proved more disappointing than the last. The hour reached midday, and not a minute past it. All of the time she'd spent walking so far that morning felt like weeks. She needed a break, a reprieve from the oppressive heat bearing down on her, adding to the load she already struggled to carry. But nothing broke up the sandy landscape as far as she could see, save for the low hills far in the distance and a small boulder up ahead—the only landmark amidst the field of dry, loose earth.

The boulder rose to chest height, grey and brown and covered in sand. It jutted up from beneath the ground, coming to a point and leaning slightly east so that beneath it, like a small pool of water in the center of an oasis, clung the tiniest sliver of shade. Dropping her tinkering bag and bow, Oleja crouched down and crammed herself face-first against the rough surface, putting as much of her body into the shade as she could—which meant only half of the top of her head and most of her shoulders. She didn't care—it was her first moment of relief since leaving the pool of water at her campsite, save for the few fleeting sips of water she took now and again. The jagged stone pressed against the skin of her chest, shoulders, and forehead. With her sunburn, it felt like the rock carved her skin into slivers. She ignored it and pressed her cheek harder against the surface, thirsty for every inch of shade she could get.

From her bag she withdrew her waterskin and leaned away from the boulder just enough to take another half-sip. She held the water in her mouth for a while and closed her eyes, relishing the feeling, imagining she took gulp after gulp. When she swallowed, the last bit of her hope went with it, down into her empty stomach that groaned for the food she couldn't afford to give it. She lay down in the shade, tucking her knees up to her chest, letting her glider protect her back from the sun. The sand was soft despite the heat packed inside it. She closed her eyes. The feeling of spinning took her and carried her around and around the boulder.

"I'm sorry I've failed," she muttered. To whom, she didn't know—Ude? The people of the village? Her parents? Herself? Perhaps all of them. She didn't open her eyes or look up from the ground. The venom still ran through her system, and she couldn't bear to see any of them; that would be a cruel final trick from her venom-addled eyes. If it was the last thing she did, she would not give up that one last victory.

Then her mind went black.

CHAPTER EIGHTEEN

S omeone was stabbing her. Hadn't she been through enough?

With enough force to open her village gate, Oleja raised her eyelids just a crack. Sand, stone, a deep pink and dark blue sky. No one stood in her line of vision. She let her eyes drift closed again. There wasn't enough left in her to move a finger, let alone her whole body.

Another jab like a cruel-pointed knife pricked at the back of her neck. A spike of searing pain jolted through her. She let out a hoarse groan from deep in her sternum.

This time the stabbing pain erupted in her leg—her right one, the one that still carried its weight and then some. She tried to kick away her assailant—a twitch of her muscles, and nothing more. The prodding came again, more forcefully this time, sending a spark through her. She used it to pull her knees in closer to her chest.

Something grabbed her hair now—not with great force,

merely a tug. It pulled and shook as she felt her braid come further undone. A few strands ripped free from her scalp. From behind her, a sharp screeching hiss sounded in her ear, followed by another stab against her sun-raw neck.

Oleja lifted a hand, so heavy it felt like she wore a glove of iron and stone. She swatted at whatever stood behind her. Soft footfalls danced away in the sand, then hopped right back and poked at her again. With a grunt of pain, Oleja pried herself away from the boulder and forced her head up into the air. She could barely raise it an inch, but it was enough. She turned to look behind her.

A bird looked back. Black and dark brown feathers covered its body, and its head—which looked too small for the rest of it—was stark red like the western sky. It watched her with beady eyes and clicked its white beak, hissing again. She knew the bird: a vulture. They ventured down into the canyon every now and again to pick at the village's endless supply of dead. But she had never seen one so close before. They were ugly.

Two more stalked her from down near her exposed legs. The sound of wings beating in the hot air told her one now sat atop the boulder as well. She dropped her head back into the sand.

It took as much energy as she could scrape together to flip onto her stomach and kick at the birds by her feet. They dodged easily; she was not exactly in peak fighting form. With a deep breath and a grunt of pain, she clawed herself through the sand away from the boulder. Her legs forbade her from standing.

The vultures followed her, four of them in total, all waiting impatiently for their evening meal. Well, they'd have to find it somewhere else, because it wouldn't be her.

She moved only three feet from the boulder before her arms shook so intensely that she couldn't drag herself another inch. Again, she swatted at the vulture hovering around her head, and again it cared little for her movements. Until she stopped moving altogether, it would find no satisfaction in her existence. Breathing hard, she let her head fall into the sand once more. Her bow lay back over by the boulder, deposited on the ground alongside her bag during her haste to get into the shade. Even if she retrieved it, she didn't have the strength to shoot. Strapped to her belt, she still had her knife, but even that she doubted her ability to wield. Her movements came slow, sluggish— the vultures found no difficulty avoiding her swings with her arms or legs, what difference would the knife make?

Killing the birds would fetch her a meal but mustering the strength to kill one called for more energy than she possessed. For now, she just needed to keep them all from eating her. After that, if any of them had a death wish, she'd be happy to oblige, but otherwise shooing them had to suffice. And besides: so far, dehydration had a winning lead over starvation in the race to see what killed her first.

She pressed her forehead to the sand, eyes squeezed shut, breaths still ragged and hoarse as they funneled through a mouth drier than the desert around her. Sweat no longer dampened her forehead—undoubtedly a bad sign. Perhaps it would be best to let herself find her end there in the sand and at least provide one last favor to these hideous birds.

"Not a chance," she muttered aloud. Death was not an option. She reached her hand around to the small of her back, stretching out her aching fingers until they grasped the small cord. She yanked it downwards.

With the force of a strong and distinctly not-dying creature, the wings of her glider unfolded and sprung out to their full span. One of them collided with a vulture, which bleated out a startled hiss before taking to the sky, followed swiftly by the remaining three, all frightened by the sudden movements from what they thought to be their mostly-dead dinner.

The sky faded slowly to deep blue, and at last the heat began to dissipate. Oleja lay motionless until the first chill of night kissed her skin and sent a shiver through her limbs. An ounce of energy filled her. She opened her eyes and set her jaw.

First, she got to her hands and knees. After conquering that, she rose up onto her knees alone. The sand dug into her soft, scorched flesh, pinching at her kneecaps like dozens of tiny needles. She drew what energy she could from the pain and then slowly, one leg at a time, rose up onto shaky legs until she stood tall in the dusk of the desert. Standing, of course, seemed to be the easy part considering the next step demanded she walk tens of miles into the desert. The daunting task almost made her want to lie back down in the sand, but she dropped those thoughts and left them. She could only carry so much; she didn't have the strength to carry doubts as well.

After retrieving her bag and bow and pausing for a modest meal and a quick gulp of water—the most she had afforded herself since shortly after leaving the pool—she set off northwest once more at what felt like a pace of a million miles in each step. At least the temperature had dropped, handing her one single luxury. With each step of her left leg, fresh pain rose up from her wound, reminding her—quite curtly—that she was injured. In her dizzy, dehydrated, sunburnt-state it had nearly slipped her mind.

Another break so soon after setting out was not the best way to cover ground, but she couldn't deny that her body offered no protest. She knelt, untying the sand-coated and sweat-saturated bandage to reveal the infected wound. It certainly looked no better, but at least it remained free of sand—the only spot on her body that such could be said for. Wasting water to wash it again was out of the question, but she removed one of the clean bandages from her bag, wrapped it tightly around the injury, and cast the soiled one aside. The vultures could pick at it if they so wished; she'd give them nothing more.

Darkness descended in full and the stars poked out from behind the curtain of black. The desert almost looked beautiful at night—the distant sand taking on a bluish tint, dark like an expansive lake before her. Thoughts of water only reminded her of the dryness in her throat and dehydration that wracked her body. She vowed not to make that mistake again but took a sip from her waterskin nonetheless to sate her and try to restore some sliver of energy. If she intended to get out of the desert alive, she needed every bit of it she could get, but it was also imperative that she save some for later. Her canteen remained untouched, but her waterskin bordered on emptiness. Within a day from the last water source she drained half of her supply. What if the next chance to refill didn't come for another two or three days? Did she dare cut her consumption down further?

She couldn't have that debate. What little food and water she consumed kept her going, but only barely. Cutting it to even smaller portions could be just as deadly as the heat or her infected wound or running out of food and water entirely. For now, she had to maintain her portions, but if the environment continued to act as hostile as it seemed determined to be, she'd reevaluate her choices then.

The night wore on beneath her feet, albeit slowly. Every hour that passed felt like ten, and by the time morning neared she doubted whether the majority of the venom had truly worn off—she felt sure that day had arrived already, and she only saw night as a hallucination. But when the stars began to fade, she knew day approached at last.

Rocky hills closed in more and more as she walked, nearing on the left and right as if attempting to clamp in, flanking her as they went in for the kill. She had avoided them so far, opting to walk through the sandy valley on even terrain to ease the strain on her leg. Granted, no path made for an "easy" walk with her leg, but the slopes meant harsh ascents and descents, so she chose the gentler route. Fortunately, the valley so far followed a rough course northwest, creating a perfect road for her to travel. Now it looked like she had no choice but to head up into the hills— at least for the time being, until she came down the other side.

The sky turned a deep shade of blue as the sun began to stir. She reached the slopes soon after and began to climb. Great weights seemed to drag behind her in the dirt, pulling her back down the other way with every step. If her body protested before, it was a full-blown riot now.

Up in the hills, some scraggly shrubs clung to patches of softer dirt or emerged triumphantly from cracks in the hard stone ground—the first of their kind she'd encountered since just after leaving the last of the ruins and the raiders behind. Some hope bubbled up within her. Where there were plants, there must also be water in some quantity. At the very least, if they could survive there, so could she.

No water presented itself, but as she neared the hill's peak, a sound caught her ear: crunching, like teeth biting through a tough meal. Oleja nocked an arrow and tested her strength to be sure she could draw back the bow. The action drew heavy breaths from her lungs as she strained, but she managed it, calling upon the splintered bits of energy that returned in the cooler night air and after eating and drinking perhaps more than she should have from her rations. She just prayed whatever made the sound was edible. Even if it wasn't, desperation might have another assessment.

Two ears shot up from behind a low-lying shrub, brown and coated in a thin layer of fuzz. The attached animal sat unmoving out of view. For several long minutes, neither of them moved, not even so much as a twitch. Oleja gave in first, but not in mistake. With the toe of her boot, she scuffed ever so lightly at the ground.

The jackrabbit bounded up the hill a split second later. Oleja took her shot. The rabbit fell forward into the dirt, dead.

She staggered to her kill in haste. Some dark part of her mind compelled her to scoop it up and bite into it as it was, bloody and raw, but she retained just enough sense to silence the commands. Grabbing the hind legs in her fist, she carried the animal higher up the hill to a spot of level ground. There, she gathered up scattered bits of wood and lit a fire, then set to work preparing her supper.

A few times she had watched Pahlo skin and carve animals—including the jackrabbits she felled on their second evening out—but she had never done it on her own. She drew her knife and worked at the pelt, making her moves carefully though unable to quell the haste driven by her empty stomach. In the end, she had a collection of roughly cut pieces of meat, which she skewered and set to cook on a stake over the fire. The remainder of the carcass found a new home down the slope of the hill as far as she could chuck it, which, admittedly, proved to be an embarrassingly short distance given her exhaustion.

Smoke filled the air, richly scented, making Oleja's hunger churn more angrily in her stomach. If any moisture remained in her body, she would have surely been salivating. Instead she got a sour clamminess that emphasized all of the sand residing in every corner of her mouth.

Her thoughts drifted from an assessment of her job skinning the jackrabbit to Pahlo. The boy who had been so eager to help her that he'd been unshakeable when she most wanted to be rid of his aid, the boy who abandoned her and betrayed her, siding with Casmia instead. She wanted to be grateful that she traveled alone at last, free to move about as she pleased, taking care of her needs and then returning to her village to immortalize herself in their stories as a savior and a hero. No one had to be convinced of her actions but her. It was what she'd wanted all along. But he had been so determined to help her, telling her about how he needed to help or save someone in his lifetime. He wanted to free all of the slaves kept down by the eclipsers, but clearly he wanted Casmia's trust and companionship more. He preferred to have weapons and ores. Would he be afforded the same safety passing through the eclipser land that Honn promised the rest of them? Likely, if he gained respect in the eyes of the eclipsers for his assistance in trying to capture the most sought-after runaway slave in the history of their kind. He earned his freedom by selling her out. Now he could do what he pleased, and perhaps one day he'd get his opportunity to save someone while travelling alongside the raiders and looting the Old World's junk to trade. Fulfillment and prosperity found him at her expense.

Unless, of course, the deal fell apart after she escaped. What a sad twist of fate for them all, especially Pahlo. Oleja could not say she pitied him—she certainly did not. Whatever fate fell upon Pahlo and the raiders now, crushing them all under the weight of their guilt, was for good measure. Traitors, all of them—they deserved whatever they got.

Her mind snapped back to the present as a dark shape slunk through the brush beyond the light of her fire. It slunk through her peripherals as she turned, squinting into the darkness, drawing an arrow cautiously from her quiver so as not to make a sound. She watched, though the shadows didn't move.

Then something darted towards her. A blur of brown and grey, hunkering low to the ground, leapt into the light. A coyote—smaller than any of Honn's, which bore bulky muscle, while this one was all tendons and bones. It flicked its brown eyes up to look at her for a split second before zeroing back in on its true aim: the meat cooking over the fire. Oleja raised her bow, an awkward angle while she sat on the ground, but she knew with certainty that she had nowhere near the time she needed for the sluggish process of standing up in her current state.

Two more coyotes emerged—another the same size as the first, and a smaller one. The first crouched low to the ground as Oleja drew back her arrow. The adolescent yipped and the second of the two adults surged forwards just as Oleja released. The arrow caught the first coyote in the neck. The animal staggered and slumped to the ground, its tongue lolling free as its head struck the hard ground. Oleja pulled another arrow from her quiver, but the second of the adults grabbed the stake in its mouth and raced away, the younger one quick on its heels. They vanished before Oleja even loaded her bow.

She shouted out in rage and threw her bow to the ground. The roar of fury had not even quieted before it turned into a sob in her throat. Tears kept at bay—if any even resided within her. She hung her head in her hands. The first food she had come across in days and it was gone, ripped away from her in the jaws of a beast. Could they not just take the discarded carcass? Sliver-sized morsels of meat still clung to the bones, and though scant, the animals would not have the same aversion to eating the flesh raw. No, they had to take her portion, the first real food to cross her path in days. Damned creatures.

With defeat in her eyes, she looked to the felled coyote. It was her only option now.

She skinned it and skewered the meat just the same as she had done with the jackrabbit, though even less meat clung to this creature's bones despite its larger size. Muscle and bone made up the entirety, and the bits of meat she managed to cut away added up to hardly more than scraps. In the end, she amassed enough for a meal or two and set it all to cook. This time, she kept her bow loaded as she sat by the fire, guarding her supper with her life.

The meat was chewy and tough, but given how little sat in her stomach—all of it from the diet of hard bread, salted meat, nuts, and vegetables that comprised her rations—

even the poor-quality, meager scraps of meat satisfied her. She ate half and set aside the remainder for her breakfast— or her lunch, or whatever meal it ended up being.

The sky continued to grow lighter as dawn prepared to give way to the new day. Thoughts of sleep crept into Oleja's mind. She had spent the night walking and needed to rest eventually. Sleeping during the heat of the day and traveling at night sounded like a suitable plan, so long as she could find a place to rest where the sun would not cook her alive while she slept. Even a spot of ample shade would suffice.

A noise down the slope of the hill caught her attention. She looked to the remainder of the coyote meat and picked up her bow from where it leaned against a rock. Nocking an arrow, she waited, watching the slope.

A figure appeared past the lip, dark and shrouded. She squinted into the darkness, bow raised, though she withheld her draw.

"Oleja?"

Her heart skittered to a stop when she heard her name. She knew the voice.

Pahlo stepped into the light.

CHAPTER NINETEEN

The venom was playing tricks on her. It had to be. The real Pahlo couldn't be standing in front of her now—he traveled with the raiders through whatever ruins they picked through that morning.

Oleja closed her eyes and shook her head, but when she looked back up, Pahlo still approached.

"Oleja, are you all right?" he asked, stooping and placing a hand on her shoulder. Even the gentle grip stung her sunburned skin. With his touch, the reality of his presence snapped into clarity in her mind. She shoved his hand away.

"What are you doing here?" She couldn't have hidden the anger in her voice if she'd wanted to. And she didn't.

"I... well I came to find you."

"Exactly. Why?" The words didn't even feel like they came from her mouth. Her tongue and lips were so dry and cracked that a numbness settled over them, cloaking them from all feeling. Words came hoarse from her lips; she certainly didn't sound the part of a person who should be challenging another.

Pahlo contorted his face in confusion. "To help?"

Oleja struggled to get to her feet, but in her anger-blind haste and weakened state she fell back onto the rock she sat on. She didn't make a second attempt. "I don't need your help. I never did. I can handle this on my own—I'm doing fine! So just go back to the raiders, wherever they are, and don't bother me. I don't need you, or them, or anyone else either. I only need me."

Pahlo stared at her for several long moments without speaking. It only infuriated Oleja further.

"How much of the venom is still in your system?" he asked softly.

"None! I'm fine!" she shouted, but then her voice broke as a layer of confusion enveloped her words. "How do you know about the venom?"

Pahlo shrugged. "I found the dead snake, and then after it your path got... weird. I guessed."

Oleja hung her head. "I'm fine. I don't need your help. Go back to Casmia."

Slowly, Pahlo sank to the ground in front of her and settled in, sitting cross-legged. It didn't look like he planned to go anywhere.

"I suppose it looks like a betrayal. That makes sense. But you might want to hear about what happened after you left. Can I tell you?"

Oleja didn't have the strength to protest. "Fine."

Pahlo nodded. "Thank you. Oh, and here you go." He rummaged in his pack—one of the large canvas bags the raiders used to collect loot from the ruins—and pulled out two full waterskins. He handed them both to her.

She seized them in her hands, acting on pure animal instinct, and brought one to her lips. Three gulps she allowed herself, but then no more. Just because she had more water now didn't mean there was no reason to conserve it.

"You can drink more. In fact, I think you should," said Pahlo, looking her over. "There's more where that came from. Not tons, but more." He shook his pack. A distinct sloshing sound echoed inside.

"How much do you have?" she asked.

"Enough for both of us to stay hydrated for another couple days at least." He ran a hand through his long, dark hair. "I took a lot, perhaps more than I should've. I wanted to play it safe. I also refilled at the pool a while back. Oh, and I brought food rations of course. And other supplies."

Oleja mumbled a thank you. Relief took a heavy weight from her shoulders in an instant. Another ounce of energy filled her.

"I have some food left over from my supper," she said, gesturing to the bits of coyote meat. "It's not good, but it's warm. It won't keep as long as the rations, so, if you'd like it, it's yours." Immediately she felt foolish—she should save all of the resources she could for herself. Though until that moment she had been convinced of Pahlo's betrayal, she felt less sure of it now. Or maybe exhaustion restrained her arguments. Until he proved her wrong, she would stick to her convictions, but she still owed him for the water—a warm meal seemed like an even trade.

Pahlo took a bite of the meat. He screwed up his face as he chewed—and chewed, and chewed, and chewed. When finally he swallowed, he smiled to Oleja, though it lacked the genuineness that he usually exhibited.

"It's good."

"It's not."

"It's not," Pahlo agreed with an apologetic smile. "What kind of meat is it?"

"Coyote—one from the group that stole my jackrabbit."

"Ah." Pahlo nodded and took another bite. "Anyway… so here's what happened after you left," he said through a mouthful.

Oleja settled in and listened.

"So, you turned and jumped off the tower—which was super cool, by the way. When you deployed your glider and soared away, everyone was pretty amazed and surprised. Trayde cheered, so did Kella. After everyone settled down, the excitement died off pretty quickly and everyone got serious. I think Hylde started yelling at Casmia first. A big fight broke out. None of the others knew what Casmia had planned. It turns out that night when she went off—'she needed air' I think was her excuse—she rode off to find Honn and struck up the deal. When we climbed the tower, we all thought we were rushing to your aid to save you, but when Casmia told us to stand down everyone got confused, thinking she had a plan or something. Well, she did, but not a good one. Afterwards, everyone was furious. I thought Trayde and Hylde might actually kill her. I don't know how it all ended though, I left during the arguing. I slipped down the stairs and hurried back to the wagon. I almost took a horse, but I didn't—if they belonged to Casmia, I absolutely would've, but they're Trayde's, so it seemed rude. I did take all of the spare waterskins and a bunch of food and loaded up a scavenging bag. I took a tent and the sword I've been using and some other stuff too. And then I went off to find you."

Oleja watched him as he recounted the events following her abrupt departure. He showed no signs of lying. After a pause to finish off his meal, he continued.

"It was hard to find your trail at first, since you didn't leave one for several miles while you flew. I really hoped you stuck to a fairly straight path since I only had the direction to go on. I didn't find it until the next morning, though. Then I saw the mutant snake dead in the sand with one of your arrows beside it and I got worried. Your path turned due west and started winding around like you were fighting something, but it was just your trail in the sand as far as I could see. I found a bloody bandage too, but your trail kept going, so I took that as a good sign. I followed it to a pool, which I knew meant you had water—more good news. Then it took me through a valley where the temperatures got deathly hot. I found a spot there where it looked like you lay down in the sand, and a lot of bird tracks wound around it—vultures, I think. I worried about that too at first but there was no blood or a body or anything, and your trail kept going, so I did too. At one point I saw animal tracks that crossed yours. It was hard to stray from your path, but I decided to follow them in hopes of finding more food and perhaps another water source. I only found a carcass picked clean. That only made me more afraid that you had met a similar fate, so I hurried back. Your trail kept going, so I did too. And then I caught up with you here."

"I see."

Pahlo nodded enthusiastically. "I didn't expect to catch up with you so soon—I went kind of slowly, covering up my trail and yours as I went, and in some spots, you left *quite* the trail. I guess it's your leg, huh? Helped me catch up to you." He looked down at her leg where her bandage sat on clear display, but she paid no attention to that, she was more caught up in something else he said.

"Why were you covering our trails?" she asked. "Honn's surely dead, and I don't think the raiders will come after us. I'm useless to them now, and it sounds like Casmia lost a lot of her backing regardless. They probably won't care too much about the stuff you took either, it's just food and water and a bit of supplies; it's not like you walked off with their more valuable loot and personal belongings. They can replace them."

Pahlo's face darkened. "Honn is still alive, Oleja."

The dark news settled down around her, enveloping her. For days she'd considered him dead. How had he managed to survive?

"How can you be sure?" asked Oleja, her voice flat, steady.

"After I came down from the tower and collected stuff from the wagon, I saw him stumble out of the stairwell back on the ground. I never saw the raiders; I don't know what happened to them. Their arguments could've been raging on, giving Honn an opening to sneak past them, or he could've killed them, or Casmia could've let him go. Judging by the state of things when I left though, I doubt any of Casmia's orders held the same authority over the group. If one of them wanted to kill Honn, they would have done so regardless of what Casmia told them to. All I know is that Honn reached the ground, and I never saw the raiders."

Oleja groaned in frustration. Even when she could get past his armor, she couldn't kill him. He was still out there, hunting her, doing whatever it took to drag her back to the eclipser camp and—if luck favored her—throw her back into the canyon, but more likely only her execution waited for her. Back on his sled, his wound meant nothing—it couldn't delay him if he didn't walk on foot. All she could hope for now was that when he finally caught up with her, his injured leg would give her just enough of an advantage that she could come up with something.

Except she bore the same disadvantage. She looked down at her own bandaged shin. Even if Honn moved slowly, so would she. Right now, she could barely pull together the strength to fire an arrow—no doubt Honn could blow her head clean off her shoulders with a single shot from his crossbow in the same time she needed just to take a step or nock an arrow.

"Well, this is grim news," she said at last.

"I think I did a fine job of covering our trails at least," offered Pahlo.

"It won't matter," said Oleja. "He will find me eventually. And when he does, I'll have to face him. I'm not fast enough to evade him like this."

Pahlo bit his lip. "But are you strong enough to kill him?"

"I'll have to be," she said wearily. Pahlo nodded in solemn thought, but then perked up.

"I'll help." He jostled his sword where it hung, sheathed at his side.

"It's my fight," said Oleja with a shake of her head. "He will only kill you too."

Squaring his shoulders, Pahlo sat up straighter. "So be it. I will fight by your side to the death if it is what has to happen. I'd give anything for your cause. I have to save someone; it might as well be you."

"I'm not asking you to do that," said Oleja, her voice rising in intensity though she kept the volume low. She could no longer be sure who might overhear her out in the wilds. "I would never ask you to do that."

Pahlo's shoulders slumped, though the tension did not dissipate from his frame. Though he clearly fared much better during his trek through the desert so far, it still took its toll. Weariness hung heavy in his eyes and dragged his shoulders down to the earth. Sure, his veins contained no traces of rattlesnake venom, he was well hydrated and better fed, he had no infected wound—or wound at all, as far as she could see—and with his raider's robe still intact, it appeared he dodged the worst of the sun's heat as well, protecting him from the sickness or burns it inflicted upon Oleja. But had he slept? Worry was a burden just as heavy as any other.

"We will have to make hard decisions when the moment arises, it seems," said Pahlo, his voice hardly more than a whisper. "You can make yours, and I will make mine."

Oleja thought on that for a moment. A dark assertion, but he left her no room to argue with him.

"That sounds fair to me," she said. He nodded in agreement. They sat together in the dark for a while, illuminated only by the dying light of the low fire and the waking light of dawn. Clearly it was not the time to tell him she still wanted to go off alone.

But why? She was dying out there on her own. It was fair to say that his appearance saved her life. She could rebuke death and pull herself along by determination alone, but none of that mattered when dehydration and starvation kicked her to her knees, miles from the nearest drop of water in the middle of the desert. Pahlo wasn't trying to take over her plans, he was offering suggestions. He wasn't botching plots, he was saving her life. What reason did she have to send him away?

"I'm going to set up the tent," said Pahlo. "We can camp here for the first half of the day so that we don't have to walk in the heat, then figure out our next move and walk for the remainder of the day and into the night when it's cooler." He paused. "That is, if it's okay for me to join you again. I know it may seem like I betrayed you, but I promise I did not. I understand if you'd rather part."

Oleja looked up at him. Going in separate directions could be as easy as speaking a few words to him. The perfect opening lay before her, and she could do it free of guilt.

"I'll accept your company," she said, surprising even herself. Pahlo smiled.

"Great. I'll set up the tent, then." He hurried to do so.

Oleja looked out east, watching as the sun peeked over the horizon, a sliver of orange that bathed the sky in hues of pink and pale blue. Somewhere out there, Honn trailed her. The pursuit resumed, and it wouldn't be long before it ended—truly, this time.

One way or another, their chase was about to come to an end.

CHAPTER TWENTY

They ducked inside the tent as the sun rose, dragging the day's dose of heat along with it. Even beneath the canvas, the hot, dry air permeated the material alongside specks of the harsh sunlight. It deflected most of the heat and light, however, keeping the inside just cool and dark enough to not be miserable. Oleja was out cold as soon as she got her body halfway horizontal.

An hour into the sun's descent, the two of them were up again. They made a meal from their combined rations, though the quantity of their food supply fell short of the plentifulness Pahlo had alluded to. After they ate, they broke down the tent, packed up, and started on their walk —continuing Oleja's course northwest after she shared her aims with Pahlo.

Oleja now wore the last of her three bandages. Her wound looked no better—rather, quite the opposite. Putting pressure on her left leg brought sharp bouts of pain, but she ground her teeth and forced herself to endure it. She had to get out of the desert; she had to stay ahead of Honn for as long as she could. The afternoon sun offered her sweating and weariness, and coupled with the pain from her leg, her body shook, breaking down as she drew all of her energy to keep herself walking at a reasonable pace. It was no surprise that Pahlo noticed the toll the walk took on her.

"Do you need some support?" he asked, extending an arm. "I can help take some weight off your bad leg."

"I'm fine," grunted Oleja.

Pahlo hesitated before drawing back his arm. "Are you sure?"

"I got this far, didn't I? I can keep going."

He let his arm fall. "I believe that you *can*, it's just about how much energy you're going to expend in doing so."

"As much as I need to."

Pahlo stared at her for a long moment. "I mean this in this nicest of ways, but do you know what your problem is?"

Oleja's anger spiked, fueled by the pooling frustration that already sloshed about in her mind. She readied to round on him, tell him off and send him away like she should have done the night before, but he didn't give her a chance to speak before he continued.

"You let your determination get the better of you. Every challenge you face, no matter how daunting or impossible, you tell yourself you can beat it as long as you force yourself to endure enough suffering. But that's not how you overcome big obstacles. You do it with help."

"I—"

"You can't save our people if you die first."

Oleja's mouth snapped shut. She wanted to be angry at him for being so rude, but whether she didn't have the energy or whether something else stopped her, she couldn't fan the flames hot enough. Instead, his wording caught more of her interest.

"'Our people,'" she said.

"What?"

"You said 'our people.' You've been calling them my people."

Pahlo thought for a second, then shrugged. "I guess I have."

"Why the sudden change?"

"I don't know," Pahlo admitted. "I guess I've just started to see them as my people too—the people in the canyon, I mean. At first we regarded them as a different groups, but I think they're more connected than that. They might not have contact, but we are all united in our oppression beneath the earthborn. And… they'll be united under you, when you lead the uprising to liberate them all. I consider myself one of your people. And even though I don't know anyone else from down in the canyon, I'm determined to help them. I don't have to know them to know what they've been through, because in a lot of ways it's what I've been through too, and I can understand the pain and fear that's been laced through the generations. I want to help free them from that."

Oleja's foot hit a loose stone that slid under her weight and she stumbled, staggering to regain her balance. Pahlo caught her and pulled her back upright. She nodded a thanks.

"I'd never thought about it in those terms," said Oleja. "I intended to free the people aboveground too—killing the eclipsers would pretty much do that by default—but I always thought of them as two separate camps. That is, after I found out people lived up top."

"I always wanted to do something," said Pahlo. "I knew how much everyone suffered and how much better off we'd be if we had our freedom. But I never knew what to do. I don't think anyone would've followed me if I tried to lead a charge. Our numbers were too small anyway. And I never had the intellect to come up with anything more strategic. I don't know if I have what it takes to be a hero, and when we get back there, I don't know how much help I can be. Not like you—you are a hero, that's clear. You have what it takes to save our people. I just want to help however I can... and if I can."

Oleja looked at him. "You have what it takes. You can be a hero too."

As they walked in silence for a few minutes, Pahlo seemed to become restless, grappling with something in his mind. Tension filled the air—or perhaps it was just the tangible heat—until at last he spoke.

"Tell me, truthfully—why did you yell for me to wait at the gate lever?"

Oleja sucked in a sharp breath, then tried to mask the sound with a light cough when she realized Pahlo had likely heard it. Of course he wanted to know—her lie after his first inquiry was less than convincing. It wasn't believable then, and she could expect just the same now. Pahlo would have questioned her further at the time, certainly, but Honn's debut appearance saved her from being grilled about her motives.

Could she tell him the truth? It was a selfish one, one that resulted in her own failure as well as his and could very well have gotten him killed. Her need for heroic glory cost her the chance at freeing the village, which just made it more of an embarrassing truth to confess. But he wanted an answer, and she had to provide something better than claiming a false fear for his life like last time. She could either tell the truth or come up with something fast.

"Well, I said I saw the eclipsers coming and—"

"And you worried they might kill me," said Pahlo, cutting her off. "I know what you said before, but it didn't sound like the truth—or at least not the whole truth. What's the answer, honestly? I won't blame you if you doubted yourself or… or if you second guessed what you should do."

"It wasn't that," said Oleja, waving away the idea that she could have been unsure of herself. For him to think that was embarrassing, almost even more so than the truth.

"What then?"

"I…" Oleja's heartbeat quickened. Her voice quieted. "I wanted to be the one to do it."

Pahlo looked at her, shock striking him across the face first, followed up by disbelief, with something like anger bringing the sequence to a full-on beating.

"Oleja," he started, his voice level despite a power boiling audibly behind the words. "Why would you do that? What does it matter who pulls the lever so long as it happens? You recognize that I could have pulled it, right?"

"Yes, I recognize that," said Oleja, reinforcing her own voice as his challenge cemented her convictions. "And I didn't want you to."

"*Why?*"

"Because it had to be me! I had to pull the lever. It was my plan—I trained for it, escaped for it, fought for it. You just walked out of a nasty-smelling barn and ran after me. It was *my* chance to be a hero, you can go make your own after you've spent ten years of your life preparing for it!"

"That's not how it works!" shouted Pahlo, laughter bleeding into the edges of his words.

"Yes, it is," snapped Oleja. "I was meant to free them. I'm Oleja Raseari, a skyborn girl. I came from the sky and I was *meant* to bring my people back to it. I was meant to be the hero. *Me*. Not *you*!"

The anger on Pahlo's face simmered to frustration, but then dissipated slowly, draining out of him and getting left behind as they walked. Oleja's words hung in the air as Pahlo collected himself and then spoke again.

"This is exactly what I meant, Oleja. Me helping you doesn't make you any less of a hero."

"If you pulled the lever, you would have freed the village, no?" She stared him down. She was right and he knew it.

"Technically speaking, yes, I suppose one could say that, but only when looking at it so literally. You're still the one who escaped, and therefore the one who gave me the opening to pull the lever. Do you think I would've done it otherwise? Because I wouldn't have. If you had never flown out of the canyon, I'd still be shoveling shit and dreaming of the world outside the earthborn camp. Even if I'd tried to pull that lever on my own, I never could've reached it without you fighting off the earthborn."

"Exactly! I would have gone through all of that work—the escape, the flight, the fighting—only for you to end up pulling the lever and being the hero. You'd have stolen the victory without any of the work."

Pahlo shook his head, dark curls poking free from the hood of his robe. "It doesn't boil down to who pulls the lever and who doesn't. Being a hero isn't about pulling a lever, and if you still can't see that, you are so *incredibly* stubborn."

"Well, I am," she said flatly.

"Believe me, anyone who has spoken to you is well aware. But glory can be shared, Oleja. When you shoot an arrow, is the action all in your hand? With it, you draw back the arrow and then release it. Those actions are the most defining, yes, but you couldn't shoot with one hand alone. What about the other hand that holds the bow, or your eyes that take aim? Even your legs keep you upright and balanced so you can move around and take a clear shot. Or… or your glider. It's made from a lot of pieces working together. They each—"

"If you preach to me for another second," started Oleja, cutting him off, "I will leave you behind."

Pahlo cracked a wide grin. "Good luck with that," he said, gesturing to her injured leg. "But you take my point, then?"

"I tried to take it a hundred words ago, but you seemed unwilling to part with it until you'd talked it to death and beaten me over the head with it. You remind me of… Well, you remind me of an old friend." A tinge of a smile played at her lips.

"They sound very wise," Pahlo said, sarcasm pulling his grin wider.

"Maybe he is, but only in an insufferable way, and I'd advise you against ever feeding his ego by telling him such things. You two could waste away a week simply talking at one another."

"I hope to meet him once we have freed our people," said Pahlo.

"I will make sure the chance arises, then."

The pair reached a knee-height ledge in the rocky ground. Pahlo stepped down without issue and kept walking. When Oleja took her turn, she hit the ground hard with her bad leg and it buckled, pain shooting daggers up through her thigh. She staggered and sank to one knee, scraping the skin and freeing a few drops of red blood. A hiss of pain slipped through her teeth. She clenched her eyes shut and waited for the waves of suffering to subside.

When she opened her eyes again, she saw that Pahlo stood beside her, arm outstretched, waiting to help her back to her feet. She took his hand and hauled herself up, and then, after one weak, staggering step forward, she hooked her left arm across his shoulders, bracing herself so she could alleviate some of the strain from her bad leg. Together, they moved ahead.

"What do you mean when you say you're a 'skyborn'?" asked Pahlo. The question surprised Oleja at first, leading her to wonder when she used the term, but just as with her conversation with Kella, she realized after a moment that she'd let it slip without intending to use it.

"In my village, we sometimes have babies that come down from above. They just sort of appear at random. They're the only people who ever enter the village; everyone else is born there. A long time ago, the people believed they were born from the sky itself and that it made them special. People don't believe that so much anymore— at least most don't. I don't really know if I do, but..." she trailed off for a moment, biting off a chunk of her pride but hesitant to swallow. "I guess it just made me feel special or important. Gave me a reason to believe in myself—that I could do good or something. I don't know."

"Wait, they come down from above?" asked Pahlo,

completely disregarding the very personal feelings she shared with him. He was so irritating.

"Yes."

"Babies?"

"Yes, did you miss it the first time?"

"How old?"

Oleja shrugged—an odd gesture with her arm draped over Pahlo's shoulders. "Very young, usually a few days old. Why?"

"You don't come from the sky. You come from us—the slaves aboveground. Sometimes the earthborn take newborns from their mothers and they never see them again. We never knew what happened to them."

"How do you know they're the same babies?"

"Well, I don't," admitted Pahlo, "but it makes sense if you think about it. The work we do aboveground isn't too dangerous; everyone lives a natural lifespan, more or less. But the mines are more treacherous. You said yourself people die down there a lot. The earthborn want to keep the population stable down there. They probably don't want to send down adults—remember what Honn said? Something about breeding hope out of the people down there? They don't want news of the aboveground to filter down."

Oleja didn't know how to feel about all of this. Her mind reeled. Pahlo's theory made perfect sense and was likely the truth. Part of her always knew some mundane reality backed the stories. There had to be a logical explanation for the skyborn babies, and maintaining the population seemed as good as any. Babies weren't just born from the sky, hero fledglings in the making ready to take up arms against their oppressors. She *knew* this. She always had. But that didn't change the fact that some part of her—no matter how small or how deeply buried in the depths of the old abandoned mines—just wanted to cling to the idea that perhaps, just maybe, there was a slight chance that the blood running through her veins held something special, something more important than the gold and copper in the mines or the food that came down every day or the crystal-clear water running through the canyon. That maybe she was born into heroism, fated to burst forth from the rock and lead her people to victory and freedom. That she was special.

But she was just the girl who spent all her times fantasizing in the darkness of the underground caves, shirking off her duties in favor of her own ambitions.

"That makes sense," she said, more of a mumble than three distinct words.

"I'm just glad the earthborn don't eat them. Some people think that's where they're taken." Pahlo breathed a heavy sigh. "What a relief."

She supposed, if she looked at it that way, it did come as a relief that an eclipser hadn't eaten her as an infant. At least she could find some solace in that.

They walked on through the night until the dark cover of the night sky thinned and gave way to the light of dawn again. The sun had leapt fully into the sky by the time they made camp in a low range of rocky hills. Much to Oleja's dismay, they saw no sign of food or water from which to replenish their stash of rations, which grew thinner by the hour. Oleja highly suspected Pahlo of hyperbolizing in his assessment of the supplies he brought with him from the raiders' wagon, likely as a way to try to comfort Oleja and give her a shred of hope when she had none. It worked at the time, certainly, but now realizing that they worked with less than she thought almost made it worse altogether. If she had been aware of the extent of their supplies from the get-go, perhaps she'd have rationed it better. Now they'd need to make significant cuts the following day—and any day thereafter—until they found the means to restock. It felt like her life was a never-ending cycle of having too little, and she was sick of it. The mountains, with their promise of lush landscapes, abundant in water and wildlife to hunt, could not appear soon enough. If the prosperity she found there turned out to be another exaggeration, Oleja would be ready to rip her hair out.

Undressing her wound brought only grim news once again, and without another clean bandage, she doubted more positive news loomed in her near future. Pahlo offered a cut of his robe, but Oleja denied him—she saw no sense in letting him suffer the heat for the sake of her leg, which needed more than just a new strip of cloth anyway. She knew well the heat that came in after cutting apart the robes, and she would not expose him to it unless it became necessary. Besides, his robe was by no means clean, and they could not spare the water to wash a strip of it to use as a bandage, which made the whole idea moot.

She tied the old bandage back around her shin and

crawled into the tent. Sleep did not find her as easily as the day before, however—a lot churned inside her mind, and silencing it all to give herself a moment's peace created no small task. One thing above all kept returning to the forefront of her mind.

Glory can be shared.

CHAPTER TWENTY-ONE

B y the time they both awoke, the sun hung low in the
sky and dusk was rapidly sweeping across the land.
Just as the day before, they rose, ate, and packed their
things. Oleja didn't even bother checking on her wound
again. The pain she felt along with the swelling and redness
visible around the edges of the bandage were clear
indicators that she'd see nothing good underneath.

The situation with their rations brought no reassurance
either. Since their supply didn't miraculously replenish
while the two slept, their waking meal marked the first in a
decrease of portions. The cuts weren't too dire yet—not to
the extent that Oleja reduced her own intake while alone—
but she didn't want to see them reach that point. Still, their
water intake crept low enough that Oleja readied herself for
dehydration to set in soon once again—if she ever even
made it out of that pit during her short-lived period of false
abundance.

When they set off for another night's walk, Oleja once again put her arm around Pahlo's shoulders to steady herself. Her body seemed to be growing weaker—certainly not the progression she hoped for.

In their path lay a range of hills taller than any Oleja had yet encountered, mere silhouettes in the darkness of night. They earned the title only by a bit, but the height difference was enough to take note of—especially given how much difficulty she had walking across even ground, let alone the gentler, lower slopes they had so far bested. It felt like a cruel joke that she should come to them now. Although, when she thought about it, her end goal lay within a range of hills supposedly rising up with an enormity surpassing any of these hills with ease, so perhaps it was best to bite her tongue and save her complaints for later when she had bigger hills to climb— quite literally.

That was, of course, assuming they made it there at all.

They had to. She wouldn't accept failure, not after coming so far with the aim of finding refuge while working through her grander problems. She'd taken a gamble— heading for the mountains instead of back to her village— and she just hoped it was the right move. They couldn't die out there, never even returning to the village. They wouldn't. Regardless of Pahlo's comments, she had to remind herself: death was not an option. Determination needed to carry her just a little bit farther, and then she could decide how to progress from there when the time arose. *When*, not *if*. She was going to get out of the desert if it was the last thing she did. And she really preferred it not to be.

Before they reached the taller hills, the descent of the smaller range they camped atop lay before them. Typically, a descent allowed for a good easy walk before a more strenuous uphill climb, but not today. Not with her leg so swollen and infected. Every step down just added force to the impact, which sent fresh fractals of misery crackling through her leg. She winced each time, at first trying to hide them from Pahlo, but soon giving up on that ordeal as it only meant supporting more of her own weight with each step down, adding to the burning she suffered each time. The pain soon outweighed her pride. If Pahlo made any comment about her showing weakness again, she'd clock him in the jaw. Then he could share in the pain.

Reaching flat ground that leveled off for a bit provided a brief oasis of relief in the valley between the two ridges, except that oasis still came with its fair share of torment. All too soon they headed back upwards, and the climb proved to be nothing short of excruciating.

Oleja started to wonder if perhaps what she felt came from an aftereffect of the venom, or if truly the pain all stemmed from the infected wound. She expected it to hurt, but did so much agony truly come from just one wound? She had no way to know, and knowledge either way wouldn't ease her suffering. For the moment, she just had to ignore the throbbing aches as best she could and make it to the top of the ridge.

Climbing the slope became a slower process the higher

they went. Though her leg still slowed them most, other factors began pulling against them as well. Dehydration closed its grip around both of them, and hunger complained in their stomachs. Weariness settled in over the previous day's exhaustion. Pahlo never shrugged off Oleja's weight no matter how tired he became. A thanks sat patiently on Oleja's tongue, but she couldn't push it out. Perhaps after she was well rested and nourished, she'd speak it, but in the meantime, fighting herself on the matter just wasted energy. Too many other wants and needs clouded her vision.

When at last they crested the ridge, the sight before them made as good a shot of adrenaline as any. Below, a valley carved across the landscape, as sandy and dry as any of the others they'd seen. But beyond it, far in the distance, towered an immense wall of dark peaks. The low light shrouded many of the details but could not hide the enormity of the hills. They rose higher than the ridge they stood atop by ten times or more, and up close they promised to make the canyon wall look like a small step built for a child's stubby legs. Oleja breathed a slow breath. She could hardly grasp the idea of something being so large. Surely the tops of the mountains scraped the very sky above them.

Though darkness hung about the slopes, the upper pinnacles of the tallest peaks took on a light hue that reflected the minimal light cast by the moon. Oleja could form no explanation for what occurred there atop the mountains, save that the sky itself rested upon them in silver-white sheets, and if she climbed high enough, she too could touch it. No desire in her heart had ever drawn her with such force. She wanted to be at the top of the tallest peak.

Her leg throbbed, bringing her back down to the ground. Climbing a single-story staircase would make a laborious task in her current state—best to leave mountain climbing for another day.

The pair began their descent with renewed vigor, knowing now how close the mountains loomed. They could reach them the next day at their current pace. If they both walked with health and full bellies, reaching the mountains by dawn could have made a reasonable goal, but doing so required a degree of spryness that neither possessed at the moment. They'd have to settle for reaching them the next day, though excitement made them long for it to come sooner.

They agreed that a path downhill was more likely to bring them to a water source, and neither could deny their desire for such a meeting. Thoughts of water and their long-anticipated acquaintance with the mountains helped to quicken their feet, though Oleja's wounded leg expressed no great joy about this new pace. Perhaps it came from looking ahead to the high peaks, or her lack of nutrition, or some combination, but Oleja's mind grew dizzy as she stumbled her way down the slope of the ridge. A few times she called a pause to catch her breath and stop her head from spinning. Pahlo never protested, as he seemed to be experiencing a similar phase of delirium. They each took a few sips of water and ate a small handful of nuts from their food rations, then kept moving.

In their descent, they reached a crevice cut into the side of the hill. The lip ran parallel to the top of the ridge and continued both left and right as far as they could see. The opposite edge continued down the slope to the valley, and beyond it, the mountains, though the gap stretched nearly ten feet across to the other side. In depth, it went perhaps twenty or thirty feet, though which end of that range Oleja struggled to determine with her mind so clouded. Climbing down and back up demanded an incredibly draining undertaking from two hungry, dehydrated—and in Oleja's case, wounded—individuals. Not to mention time consuming; it could take them hours to complete the climb in their condition, if they could manage at all, and they couldn't forget that somewhere behind them, Honn still scoured the desert for their whereabouts.

Pahlo studied the crevice. "We could jump," he said after making his final assessment.

Oleja gestured to her leg with a questioning glare. Pahlo made a face to say he took the point.

"Plus, I don't think either of us is in the condition for jumping crevices right now. Even if we were in peak-condition, that's a big jump."

"You're right," said Pahlo, returning his focus to study it again. A moment passed, and then he pointed. "What if we jump to there instead?" he asked, indicating a ledge around six feet below the top of the crevice but on the side opposite from them. "Then we'll only have to climb up that bit instead of the whole thing."

Oleja sized up the gap. Still a big leap, but far more reasonable. The impact on her leg sounded like a nightmare, but she could handle it. She didn't have any other choice.

"I suppose that'll have to do," said Oleja.

"All right. I'll go first so I can help you across," said Pahlo.

Oleja scowled. "I'll be fine, I can manage it."

"That's okay," said Pahlo as if he hadn't even listened to her. "I'm still going first." He gave the gap another once over, moving up and down the ledge as he pinpointed the best point to jump from, and best place to jump to. After making up his mind and preparing himself, he took several steps back, and then darted forwards. He planted one foot firmly at the edge and leapt, sailing into the air, rushing towards the other side of the crevice.

Oleja was right—neither of them stood any chance of making the jump all the way to the other side. For a split second, she doubted that Pahlo would even make it to the ledge he aimed for. Her heart caught for a moment between rapid beats in her chest. But then Pahlo's feet hit the ledge and he pressed his chest to the stone wall, clinging to handholds as he found his balance and steadied himself on the new ground. He grinned up to Oleja.

"I made it!"

"I can see that. You wouldn't be speaking to me if you hadn't."

Pahlo glanced down to the bottom of the crevice. "You're right."

Oleja paced the edge, but she wobbled unsteadily on her feet. She sank down onto a boulder near the ledge.

"You coming across?" called Pahlo, standing on tiptoes and looking over his shoulder to see her past the edge of the crevice.

"Yeah, I am, just give me a second," she called back. Her head pounded. Dizziness swept coiling clouds around her. She needed water.

She allowed herself one sizable gulp—likely more than she should have, though with the mountains in sight it became hard to heed the knowledge that another day of walking remained before they reached the foothills, and who knew how much longer before they found a water source amongst the new terrain. The drink thinned the clouds just a bit. She wanted to take another, but reason stopped her and forced the waterskin back into her bag. She needed it for later.

Planting her feet firmly in the dirt, she rose. "Here I come," she called. Pahlo turned around, shifting so he faced back towards her. A wide spot of ledge sat just to his left. That was where she aimed to land.

All of her gear felt heavy where it hung from her body. Her glider on her back, quiver on top of that, bag pressed against her left hip. Even her bow, slung over her shoulder, and the knife at her hip, tiny as it was, seemed to weigh as much as a great boulder. Her left leg shook as phantoms of the pain to come spiked under her skin. It was now or never.

She dashed forward, the fastest she could recall moving in days. The ledge raced to meet her. Pain flared in her leg with every step, but she allowed herself to feed it only a wince and nothing more. The ledge got closer with each step. She prepared to jump.

Her right leg found purchase on the lip, though it was by her design that her good leg served as the one with which she jumped. She bounded off the edge, throwing all of her energy and strength into the muscles in her leg, pushing off with everything she had. She forced herself skyward, but she only seemed to push the earth down.

A *crack* rumbled through the air, followed a thunderous grating sound. The ground fell away just as she pushed off, absorbing all of her momentum and channeling it back down into the earth. She fell forward, momentum gone, plummeting for the bottom of the crevice.

By some stroke of luck, her fingers caught the very brink of the ledge just where she aimed. She sank her fingers deep into the craggy surface, clinging to it with all the force of her life—which was precisely what lay at stake. She swung forward and collided face-first with the rocky cliff below. Blood sprang into her mouth. Sand stung her eyes. The sky-shattering grating still echoed above.

"Oleja! Oleja get up!" screamed Pahlo, pure panic ringing in his voice. Oleja shook off the stunned haze and looked up.

The ledge she jumped from had cracked and broken free; an immense chunk three-times larger than her slid and started to lean outwards. It pivoted as it caught on a ledge on the opposite wall—its arcing course aimed directly for where she hung by her fingertips, doomed to strike her with the force of a hill collapsing down, crushing the life from her.

For a split second, the prospect didn't sound all that horrible. It was the death she'd always been destined to face—the fate shared by all of her people, that which all of them confronted the fear of daily. It had claimed the lives of half or more of the people throughout the history of the village, her parents included: being crushed beneath falling rock.

But then she snapped back into herself. She was Oleja Raseari, girl of the sky, and she was not going to be buried beneath some rubble.

She kicked for a foothold and found one beneath her left foot. Grunting in pain, she used it to haul herself up, grabbing the ledge with her full hand, then two, then a forearm. Adrenaline filled her as she scampered up the side of the crevice.

"Oleja!" Pahlo shouted again. A dark shadow passed over her head. She wasn't quick enough. Her eyes pressed shut as she readied for the impact.

A deafening *crunch* filled the air, a dozen cracking sounds like twigs snapping in a bonfire. Something dripped on her fingers. She looked up just as Pahlo howled in pain.

He stood over her, crouched low, precisely in the path of the crumbling boulder which now pinned him against the wall. He pushed back against it with his full force, holding the stone against the opposite wall and keeping it from falling any farther. The only thing standing between the stone and Oleja was Pahlo's body.

"Get up here… quickly," he croaked through ragged breaths. His face contorted in the truest display of pain she had ever seen upon any of her people as they toiled away, suffering in a million different ways with every passing day. She didn't need him to say it a second time. Hands slick, she clawed her way up.

The boulder scraped on the stone walls as it slid. Pahlo screamed again, his agony echoing in the still night air. Oleja was nearly at the top.

Pahlo's body crumpled as he lost consciousness. The boulder careened down, slamming against the ledge. A new *crack* sounded in the crevice, though this one brought with it a pain unlike any Oleja had ever felt.

Her left leg—the same that had endured so much torment already—was crushed beneath the falling chunk of rock. It snagged her leg and pulled. Her body lurched downwards, wrenching her fingers away from their holds on the stone face. Ringing filled her ears, as well as a distant scream that sounded much like it belonged to her. The boulder cast her body aside as it shifted and fell. Freefall stole all of the weight that had been holding her down.

The floor of the crevice returned it with a little extra just for good measure.

She landed on her back, the air leaving her lungs in one quick gust. The world shook as the boulder crashed down beside her. Cracks split the ground under the impact, breaking apart the earth in one enormous crash. The impact surely shook the ground from the old ruined towers to the mountains and perhaps all the way back to her village. The sound echoed for many long minutes afterwards as Oleja gasped for breaths of the thick air, filled with a haze of sand and dusty debris launched by the quaking tremors of the ground.

As soon as she could speak, she did.

"Pahlo?" she called, though her voice sounded far away. Her ears were still ringing.

She tested her limbs. Her fingers curled in one-by-one at her command, and her arms shifted and shook, scattering tiny bits of rubble. Her right leg gave the same results. Her left was less prompt. She looked down.

Below the kneecap, her leg bent at an angle it surely shouldn't have. Bone stuck out, pure white, a beacon of shining sunlight amidst a pool of blood as dark as the night around her. The shape of her leg was lost, crushed flat with shreds of skin clinging to the remains. The boulder had struck her and dragged it against the wall, grinding it to a pulp. She leaned her head back and clenched her jaw as the pain, delayed by the stunned confusion and adrenaline, finally exploded within her.

Only halfway through her scream did she remember she meant to look for Pahlo. Gritting her teeth, seizing as wave after wave of pain slammed against her, she shook the stars from her vision and looked to where the boulder rested.

Pahlo's body lay there. He looked nearly

unrecognizable, just the same as her leg, though no part of him had been spared from the blow. His legs hid completely out of sight, buried beneath the boulder. Smaller chunks of rubble scattered the ground around him. His chest held nowhere near the form it should, reduced to a flattened mess of shattered ribs and torn-up skin and fabric. An entire lake of blood surrounded him, deep crimson and seeping rapidly into the dirt.

No question concealed the truth from her eyes. Pahlo Dirin was dead.

CHAPTER TWENTY-TWO

Despite it all, the night felt almost tranquil. A warm summer air blanketed the world, and when Oleja looked up at the sky, visible as only a strip between the two ledges above her, she could almost imagine she lay on the ground back in the canyon—back in her village, enjoying a simple evening by the fire alone to sit and think and plan some fantasy wild beyond her capabilities.

She was in over her head.

A sob shook her body, the first of many. No tears came— she didn't have the water in her body to produce them. The jolting movements pained her. She didn't care enough to stop them. Every glance she stole to where Pahlo's body lay only renewed the force of her sobbing.

Stars twinkled above, unaware of the great tragedy unfolding below. Perhaps once she might have looked to their company as that of friend or kin—Oleja, skyborn. But the truth behind her skyborn heritage brought nothing but the knowledge that rather than being born of a village of dirty mining slaves, she came from a village of dirty cattle-tending slaves. No blessing of the sky and sun and moon and stars coursed through her veins, leading her to her fated hero's seat. She had found her fate—doomed to die at the bottom of a hole from one of countless forces she had no hope of overcoming, all of which would be all too happy to steal away her life—the life of the girl who always thought herself so high above them.

And those forces counted many in number indeed. For one thing, food and water still ran low, but that was hardly out of the norm nowadays. Lying at the bottom of a crevice carried little chance of finding more of either, and with what she had left, dehydration would probably kill her within a few days. At least if she died, she wouldn't need to worry about food. She could go longer without eating than without drinking water, so at least she knew hunger couldn't kill her.

She also faced the fact that a lot of her blood no longer resided inside her body where it belonged. Even if she had more bandages, no amount of cloth could fix her leg. She needed proper medical attention, the sort that came rarely in the middle of the desert. The closest thing she could come by was a vulture, who would happily take a good look at her leg for her, no doubt. Blood loss could kill her—perhaps faster than dehydration, even. She couldn't say how much blood she'd lost so far, only that it was "some," and that "some" is more than "none," which is the proper amount of blood to lose.

Adding to the pile, and certainly not the least of her problems, was Honn. Though he had made no appearance since the tower, he lurked out there somewhere, and he could only be so far behind. Her present situation made any option of countering his advance fairly impossible. With her leg—broken, to understate matters—she could neither stand and fight him in one final showdown nor continue in her flight.

Her flight—her coward's flight. Why hadn't she fought him while she stood at least a sliver of a chance? She knew the answer, of course: fear. Her own fear had kept her on the run. No prospect of victory sided with her now. Now the question was only a matter of how quickly he planned to end her or drag her away.

Though the mountains were now in view—at least, they were before she landed herself at the bottom of the crevice —they had seemed so dauntingly far when her leg still functioned, albeit painfully. Now her only choice was to crawl or drag herself across the ground. Death would catch her before she ever reached the first whiff of a slope, let alone the peaks she wanted so badly to summit.

No—she had no chance of getting food or water, no chance of bandaging her leg and getting herself back on her path to the mountains, and no chance of besting Honn. This was her end, right there, at the bottom of the crevice. She looked over at Pahlo again and her throat seized. A fresh wave of sobs gripped her, though whether they were for him or for herself—or both—she couldn't tell. A sinking hopelessness weighed upon her, trying to pull her down into the earth, deep underground, and she hated it. She failed.

The peaks of the sobs fell away into another valley of shaky breathing and she pulled herself into a sitting position. Everything ached. Bruises would paint her skin if they got the chance to bloom before her body went cold. Scrapes crisscrossed her limbs in a web of red, but they felt like a gentle caress compared to the roaring pain creeping up from her twisted and mutilated leg. The muscles of her thigh still shifted at her whim, but it became immediately clear that she should never attempt it again. She clenched her fists and sunk her teeth into her lip, which dripped more blood onto her tongue. Great; releasing more blood from her veins was exactly what she needed to do.

When the sweeping pain of her folly dissipated, she took a few steadying breaths, shrugged off her belongings, and then, ever so slowly, began to push herself across the uneven rocky ground to Pahlo. He lay on the stone with eyes closed. Blood speckled his face, seeping from gashes on his cheek and forehead and spattered there by the impact of the boulder when it landed on top of him. Despite the blood and the paleness of his skin, his expression almost looked peaceful. She had to look away for a moment as she fought to maintain her composure. Steeling herself, she returned her gaze, and then hauled herself closer.

His body lay half-buried under the rubble, pinned beneath so much weight that, even if she wished to, she wouldn't be able to free him, as the boulder was simply too large. She looked upon his face one final time. Blood and dirt caked his long dark brown curls. Grains of sand glittered in his eyelashes. His lips parted just a sliver, but no breath passed between them, nor would it ever again. The image of him lying there rooted itself deep into her mind with a strength that she doubted her ability to pry out no matter how long she lived—which wasn't looking to be too much longer.

"You will be remembered as a hero as long as I draw breath," she said, and then with a heave she shifted a stone up and onto him. Repeating the process until no part of him remained visible, she buried him as best she could.

She leaned back against the crevice wall, heavy breaths making her chest rise and fall. Gratitude washed over her for the fact that she still drew breath, no matter how much longer it lasted. Because of Pahlo, she was alive. If not for him, she would be the one buried beneath that boulder, never to rise again. The gratitude took a step aside as guilt emerged to join it.

Alongside the guilt surrounding Pahlo's death, Oleja blamed herself for a million other things. How many times had she thought to abandon him and go off on her own? It had been the first item on her agenda the moment she saw him, and found a home among her most recent thoughts of him as well, giving her cause for debate after he caught up to her following her flight from the tower. He only ever wanted to help, and she only ever wanted to leave him behind. All because she thought she was better off working by herself. Alone, she'd be crushed beneath the rubble, and there wouldn't even be anyone around to see her final moments or know her fate. She continued to draw breath not just because Pahlo had taken the force of the boulder and sacrificed himself for her, but because he had been with her at all. He was right—she needed other people there to help her. She just wished it hadn't taken his death to make her believe it. Ude would be so disappointed. He always tried to tell her the same, but she never listened to him either. Stubbornness ran too deep within her.

One truth among all others settled like a sharp stone in her heart. One she could hardly bear to admit.

She had never cared for Pahlo in anywhere near the capacity he cared for her. He followed her from the eclipser camp, helping her throughout her journey because he so desperately wanted to see her succeed in her ambitions. He tracked her down after her flight from the tower, hardly sleeping in an effort to catch up with her, bearing more weight than he needed in order to deliver to her the rations to stave off her slowly encroaching death. Not once did he stop and give up on her or her quest to save their people. Even when it came to the point of throwing his life on the line to protect hers, he did it without hesitation. He did exactly what he told her he intended to, and what she told him not to, but she had argued against his interference thinking of her own pride, not of his wellbeing. Everything he did for her, she took for granted, and returned the favor with wishes to leave him behind. Now that he was dead, she could not claim to have cared deeply for him. She did not deserve to be the one crying beside his grave. She could not call herself his friend. Sure, she never wished an ill fate upon him, but neither had she cared overmuch for his success. She stole his moment of glory and heroism out from under him right from the start, and she could never return it to him, especially now.

If anything, she cried because he did not deserve the fate he received, and that was all. And now she pitied herself more than she did him. She couldn't even bring herself to wish that it *was* her beneath that pile of rubble. She didn't, and it only made her angrier at herself. Soon her turn would arrive, and no one would be there with her as she died. Just as she deserved.

She leaned her head against the rough stone and tilted her gaze skyward. A tiny wisp of a cloud drifted across the patch of sky visible between the two edges of the crevice—a sight all too familiar. Not only her first, but soon it would be her last as well. At least in between she got to see the rest of the sky, if only for a short time. How long ago did she leave the village? It felt like ages. With her head still swimming, she gave up hope of figuring it out.

Perhaps Ude sat back there in the village, looking up at the same sight as her, the same sky above his head. He thought her dead—at least if he bore some wisdom, and he liked to believe he did. Though death hadn't found her the day she escaped, she'd meet it soon. She may as well have died that day in his mind—he'd never know anything different. Maybe if she had listened to him in the first place, she could've pulled off her plan the first time and never landed herself in this mess. Now her record contained: failing, fleeing like a coward, and dying in a ditch. Even after failing, Tor had stood tall and faced the consequences of that failure. Oleja only ran. Some hero she turned out to be.

Though she tried to avoid it due to the pain and nausea it brought on, she took a moment to look over her leg again. The break was about six inches below her knee, clear by the fact that at that point it bent grotesquely off to one side despite the clear lack of a joint there when last she checked. Skin hung in shreds, ground away from the boulder pinning it between the wall and itself while it slid. Sand clung to the exposed, blood-dampened flesh, and in some places sharp pebbles found a new home imbedded in the soft tissue. Her boot still protected her foot, but removing it would—in the best-case scenario—cause her to black out, and in the worst, pull the entire foot off with it. As a result, she had no way to know the state of her lower shin or foot, but given her inability to feel anything in the region besides excruciating pain, she guessed it looked no better than the rest of the leg. A trail of blood ran from where she landed after her fall to where she sat now beside Pahlo's grave. Looking at her leg—bent at such an angle and leaking so much blood—made her lightheaded. Pain came in bursts. She felt the blood drain from her face—probably off to escape out her leg, which promised to do no one any favors, least of all the blood, destined to pool uselessly on the ground if it did so. She looked away once more. If she searched for some beacon of hope, her mangled leg made a bad place to look. It provided nothing but a reminder of her impending death.

Once again, and with the same level of slowness, she shifted her position and dragged herself back over to her things. Rummaging in her bag, smearing the contents with the blood that coated her hands—hers or Pahlo's she didn't know—she withdrew her waterskin and took a small sip. Why she continued to ration it, she couldn't say. Part of her wanted to just down the last of it in a few big gulps and enjoy that one final moment of bliss where moisture coated her mouth and her tongue did not feel like a great slab of sand. Perhaps it was because she had one last choice she could make: whether to let dehydration kill her or wait for Honn to arrive and do it himself. Unless blood loss came in to challenge those two, it was one or the other, and since she knew neither how much blood had vacated her body in favor of the ground nor how much she could lose before it became lethal, she focused on the other two for the moment. If those made up her final options, she chose Honn. Having him arrive at the edge of the crevice only to see her lifeless corpse half-cooked under the sun would be embarrassing at the very least. Killed slowly in a ditch by the forces of nature—no, she much preferred to meet her demise on the wrong end of a blade. Or a crossbow bolt. She wouldn't be *that* picky.

It just seemed more honorable that way. The last shred of heroism she could attain. Besides, she didn't even know whether or not dehydration would kill her before Honn reached her, so even if there was no choice truly, at least this way she felt as though she made some decision. The freedom to choose her end mattered most, whether hollow or not. If for no other freedoms, she escaped the eclipser's rule for the ability to decide her cause of death—a consolation prize for all of her effort that died right alongside her.

She looked up at the night sky. There was nothing left to do but wait for Honn to come and kill her.

All the distance she traveled meant nothing in the end. Just as always, she sat imprisoned at the bottom of a hole, fully at the mercy of the eclipsers, and there was not a single thing she could do about it.

CHAPTER TWENTY-THREE

When Honn arrived, she'd either meet an immediate death or a delayed death. In the case of a delayed death, the delay would only be as long as it took to get back to the village and eclipser camp. Not much of a way to spend her final days—bound, dragged along behind an eclipser hunter—but she had been through worse. If he wanted her alive, at least he'd provide food and water.

She could not say which option she hoped for. A quick death might be nice, or at least less demeaning. Easier for Honn too—if he toted around her corpse, he wouldn't be able to hear every last nasty thing she had to say about him, which she'd be all too happy to share given the chance, nor would he have to worry about keeping her alive long enough for the return journey. A corpse had very few needs, and food and water never found rank among them.

But if he kept her alive, giving her the sustenance she

needed, she retained her hold on the slim possibility that she could find a way to best him and slip free after using him to bring her back to health—or as close to health as she could get in a short time. Even if fortune continued to keep its distance, perhaps she would still be taken before the leader of the camp before her execution, giving her the opportunity to share some of her grievances with them.

She tried to push the hopeful thoughts of escape from her mind. They did her no favors. Even if an opening presented itself, she was in no shape to take it. This marked the end of the line for her, and soon Honn would arrive to seal it.

The ledge of the crevice loomed above her, still as the night. She imagined Honn coming up to it and looking down to see her lying there in pain and defeat. Chances looked high that such a sight could be one of the last she ever saw—him, standing there above her.

How comical would it be if, in his approach, the lip of the crevice gave way beneath him just as it had her? He'd plummet down, landing atop her, killing them both. What a twist of fate.

Wait.

She couldn't stand and fight Honn in a duel—not in her prime, and definitely not now—but she could lead him into a trap using herself as the bait. No honor came from such a plot, but the time for honor had passed. It was time to survive.

If she weakened the ledge, she could send him hurtling down into the crevice. It would kill him if luck favored her, or leave him heavily injured even if it didn't, but either ending made him an easier adversary than a fully-healthy eclipser soldier in armor she couldn't penetrate wielding weapons she had no hope of deflecting. Sure, it wasn't a full plan, but it gave her something she could do—a fight she could put up in her final moments. It wouldn't get her out of the desert or fix her leg, but it was better than giving up. Anything was better than sitting there and waiting to die.

She studied the crevice wall. About a foot below the top cut a receding gash in the stone that ran parallel with the top ledge and continued down the length of the crevice in both directions—no more than a foot deep, but its presence had put her where she lay now. The hollow looked natural, some product of ages of erosion. It would have to be bigger. No one spot guaranteed collapse as far as she could tell— and though Honn weighed more than her, this was no time for guesses and gambles. If she planned to act, she had to do it right.

First, she needed a pickaxe. Carving the hollow deeper into the cliff face required the right tool for the job. But the nearest pickaxe that she knew of lay hundreds of miles away back in her village, and of course she hadn't bothered to bring one with her. She hardly brought water, let alone the deadweight of her old mining tools. Something else would have to do. She sifted through her bag.

Plenty of small scrap clinked around inside—she never found herself with a shortage of that—but nothing large enough to form the head of a pick. She dug deeper until her hand reached the bottom of the bag. Her fingers brushed something long and heavy, larger than anything else inside. She pulled it free.

A bent pickaxe head balanced in her palm. For a split second she wondered why in the world she let such a thing weigh her down. Plenty of odd scraps found a home in her bag, but this certainly took the role for most useless. Then it clicked. *Palila.* The young girl from her village, the one whose father needed a new pick and who she gave her own to in exchange for this broken one. At the time, it seemed like a fairly silly gesture—she planned to free the village within just over twenty-four hours, making the pickaxe unnecessary, but she couldn't voice that at the time. She kept the banged-up pickaxe head to maintain the image, and then forgot it in her bag. Even when she and Kella dumped the contents out and picked through them, she regarded it passively, sweeping it back into her bag without a second thought alongside all of the other, equally-useless bits of discarded metal. If she had remembered, she likely would have tossed the pick head aside—it sat heavy at the bottom of the bag, adding a good deal of extra weight she didn't need to carry. Thank the sky she never did. Now, it served as a crucial piece of her plan. She just had to deal with the damage it sustained. Desperation cannot be picky.

None of that changed that the head was without a handle, however. Nowhere around would she find discarded bits of wood, and certainly her bag couldn't hold anything so long. Something else had to stand in for the time being.

Stone wouldn't work. To forge one from her metal

scraps, she required a fire, which in turn demanded wood—not to mention time. An arrow shaft was too thin. She looked over her things.

Her eyes fell reluctantly on her glider. The second of its kind, so recently completed. With a sigh, she extended one wing. A glider couldn't kill Honn, but the pickaxe might. She didn't have any other choices.

One limb fell away with a few quick motions of her fingers, dismantling the frame and severing the cloth. When she finished, she held one wooden stick, perfect to serve as a handle. She removed the second half of the limb too and set both pieces on the ground beside her.

Assembling a new pick was easy enough. The new handle fit into the slot on the head with only a small amount of reshaping, and then she bound it tightly with twine—certainly not something ready to stand up to years of wear in the mines, but enough to get her through the night's task. As best she could, she bent the head back into shape, though little progress showed in the shape of the heavy iron. Its purpose was to be smashed repeatedly against rocks; if she expected to alter it by doing the reverse, she was sorely mistaken. It would have to do as it was. After crafting a makeshift harness for the tool out of some rope from her bag, she slung it and the second wooden stick across her back, then looked up to the cliff rising above her.

The face didn't run entirely vertical, which provided some relief, and it made more of an extremely steep slope if she had to label it. The bonus it afforded to her next task was slight, but still something.

From her bag, she took what remained of her raider robe. Not even bothering to cut it, she wrapped the garment gingerly around her leg and tied it off tightly using the sleeves. Though it remained dirty and filled with sand, she could do nothing to change that. She shed no worry on the matter. A million other things were snapping at their leashes trying to kill her; what difference did another bout of infection make?

Rising to her right leg and leaning her palms against the wall cast doubt into her mind. Already, her left leg howled, making her sway. Dizziness still wriggled its way into her mind in fits. Before her rose a cliff nearly thirty feet in height, and only one of her legs remained in functional condition. What made her think she had any chance of reaching the top? She cast a glance back at Pahlo's grave. His words rushed back to her.

Do you know what your problem is? You let your determination get the better of you. Every challenge you face, no matter how daunting or impossible, you tell yourself you can beat it as long as you force yourself to endure enough suffering. But that's not how you overcome big obstacles. You do it with help.

No one was around to help her now, not even the sky in her veins. She would do this the way she always had. One last time, she had to let her determination grab her by the scruff of her neck and drag her through as much as she could take, because nothing else fought on her side. Maybe determination had led her too far, but now it would carry her just a little bit further.

She was Oleja Raseari, and if nothing else, she had determination. And that was enough.

She grabbed the rockface in both hands and pulled herself up. Her arms shook. Her muscles ached. Pain and dizziness clouded her vision. She didn't care. She could take it.

Her right foot found purchase on the rock and then she moved her hands one at a time to new handholds. Over and over she shifted her holds, her left leg dangling below her, a burden far heavier than the weight of it alone. She gritted her teeth and kept moving. She would have time to feel the pain later, but not now.

When she threw her first arm over the top and hauled her chest up onto the ground, the relief crashed over her and made her feel as if she soared around on her glider once more. She took several minutes to lie there, face-down on the hard stone ground, catching her breath and waiting for the pain to subside.

Before she weakened the ledge, she needed to make sure she could guarantee which spot at the crevice's edge Honn would approach. That meant covering up their trail and creating a new one, one obvious enough to lead Honn exactly where Oleja wanted him. Covering up their trail from before was easy enough, minus the fact that she couldn't walk and had to drag herself across the ground wherever she went. Her bandaged leg only accumulated more sand that clung to the once-white fabric now saturated thick with blood, no longer retaining its original color besides in slivers around the edges and in places more thickly layered. Dragging her body across the path provided as good a way as any to erase the footprints in the sand, so long as she stayed smart about it and never applied so much pressure that her crawling became obvious in the loose patches of earth.

Once through with that, she met up with the new end of their trail up the hill. She could not walk upright—not with two legs and a typical gait, and especially not with the four that marked the trail up until that point. More crawling and dragging was the best she could do. At the very least, Honn would be confused seeing the trail change so drastically. Curiosity made as good a bait as any.

She dragged herself through the sand all the way up to the lip of the crevice, making sure to leave as clear a path as she could. Then came the hard part.

Spotting a small ledge just down the face of the crevice side, Oleja eased herself over, right leg first, until she stood upon it. Seven or eight inches below ground level, the rock face gave way to open air. The hollow below dug inwards just over a foot. A good start, but not enough to pitch Honn into the abyss below, and nowhere near sufficient to get his sled too if she wanted such an outcome. She did, of course —fighting off eight coyotes in the wake of their master's death sounded little better than fighting the eclipser himself. If she could kill all nine birds with one stone, she might just stand a chance. A chance for what, she couldn't say. With her leg broken, leaving the desert seemed like a distant fantasy, but hope lived in her mind again, and it promised not be so easily evicted this time.

Swinging the pickaxe while balancing on one foot, perched atop a tiny ledge thirty feet up, proved to be no easy task. The first few swings came slow and awkward, breaking away only chips of the rock which skittered away and clattered on the stone below. As the hollow widened, leverage became easier to find, as she could lean farther in. When she could climb inside, the true speed of her work took off. Through her exhaustion, she forced herself to keep moving, keep swinging, burrowing deeper. Even after her arms grew numb and dull, she kept working. Fortunately, the stone was soft and crumbled easily—not like the hard stone of the mines back in the village—so the bend in the pick head did little to slow her as the stone chipped away beneath its strikes regardless. Hours passed. Oleja's limbs and eyelids grew heavier. Dust and rubble clung to her clothes and skin, damp with blood and the few small beads of sticky sweat that appeared on her brow. She supposed the fact that any sweat at all dripped from her skin came as a good sign.

Crawling back out of her hollow, she drew the second wooden stick from the sling on her back and propped it under the opening. It wouldn't hold much weight, but it served as a safeguard to keep the ground from collapsing prematurely. Using her bow, she could shoot it and knock it aside from a position on the ground.

She cast the pickaxe down to the bottom of the crevice. It struck the stone with a loud *clang*. Bearing its weight during her descent meant wasting her energy, and she was finished with it anyhow. With everything set, she scaled back to the floor of the crevice—easier by a slim margin, but still very nearly as painful as the ascent. Back on the ground, she had never been so happy to be at the bottom of a hole in her life.

She drank from her waterskin, the last few drops trickling out onto her tongue. Another sip or two filled her canteen. She looked to Pahlo's grave. A sad resolve washed over her. She would want him to do it if their roles were reversed.

When she buried him, she never expected to be reacquainted with hope again before her death. Taking his water and food rations didn't matter then. Now, it did. She had a shot at living to see another day, and when that day came, she needed to have all of her options on the table. Perhaps she couldn't change her fate and she would die in that hole regardless, but a chance hung in her future, and she intended to make the most of it.

"I'm sorry. I am so sorry," she muttered as she shifted away the stones placed atop him by her own hands. She tried not to look at his body as she uncovered it; something about it felt wrong. With her arms so shaky and numb from hours of labor, moving the stones took an immense amount of effort. Even with that part of the task completed, his body still lay on his back, pinning his pack beneath him. She sighed and took a deep, steadying breath.

"I am really, *really* sorry," she said, and then as carefully as she could, she lifted his shoulder. All warmth had vacated his body, and his skin no longer felt like skin. A softness remained, but a sickly one. It sent chills through her. Using her knife, she cut the straps of his pack and slid it from beneath him as quickly as she could, then let him fall back to the ground, gently, to be at rest—and hopefully for good this time. Summoning her strength again, she heaped the stones back over his body to form a large mound. Breathing heavily, she returned to her things and dropped to the ground.

One of Pahlo's waterskins burst in the fall, but the other remained intact. Water sloshed around inside. She took the food from Pahlo's bag as well and added his other supplies to her own. The tent poles were reduced to splintered dowels, no longer fit for further use, so she ditched the tent in its entirety. If she hoped to go anywhere—and she still knew not how far she could even manage to drag her failing body—travelling light would be a necessity.

She made a quick meal and swallowed it down in haste, in equal parts due to her groaning hunger and her fears of being unready when Honn arrived. The meal marked the most she'd eaten in days, and her stomach expressed its gratitude as a brief and slight reprieve from its unceasing grumbling and moaning. Any ounce of strength she could amass made her better prepared. She hoped no fight would unfold and that her plan worked as intended, but if it came to a fight, she was prepared to go out in a blazing fountain of blood—both Honn's and her own.

With everything else set and her things collected and packed, she moved to sit by Pahlo's grave down the crevice a dozen or so feet. Being beneath the collapse would be just as deadly for her as Honn, and she needed a better shooting angle besides. She settled in and placed her bow across her thighs.

As she unlatched the cover of her quiver to draw an arrow, a thousand tiny splinters cascaded out and scattered across the ground, followed by snapped arrow shafts, bits of fletching, and arrowheads. One single arrow, still intact, fell into her lap.

So be it. She only needed one shot anyway.

CHAPTER TWENTY-FOUR

The hours ticked by in long, drawn out fits of restlessness. Sitting still didn't come easily to her; the time spent waiting for Honn was the longest she had sat doing nothing in memory, and the flares of pain in her leg didn't make it easier to sit and focus. Her attention wandered and hands fidgeted. She itched to pull her tinkering bag closer and set to work making something to pass the time, but she didn't dare. Her mind needed to be focused and sharp. When Honn arrived, she had one shot. She couldn't afford to be caught off guard.

The hard stone ground quickly became the least comfortable place to sit. Each time she shifted, she somehow invited more sharp pebbles to wedge themselves underneath her. She entertained herself by collecting them and bouncing them off the far wall where they struck the stone with a high-pitched *tick* before coming to land on the ground amidst another shorter sequence of clicking sounds.

Eventually, this turned into a game of seeing how close she could get them to a designated spot she shifted each time she found success, though the rules of the game were fairly fluid, with the only real objective being to keep herself engaged.

Deep into the night she continued to wait. The sky grew a shade lighter after a time, though hardly enough to notice if she hadn't been looking to everything around her in search of stimulation. Then, between the clicking sounds of her thrown stones finding new homes, a rumbling, scraping sound emerged. Quiet at first, it steadily rose in volume. Her heart beat faster in tandem with the rising sounds of metal sliding on stone, of dozens of padded feet on the ground, of barking and gnashing teeth. Oleja nocked her arrow quickly but kept her bow laid across her knees, her hands ready to raise it in an instant. Only one shot—both literally and figuratively. If she didn't pull it off, she would be quickly acquainted with death. One shot. She could do it.

Two snouts appeared on the ledge first, but nothing more. The attached coyotes stood just to the side of the weakest point of the ledge. They tugged at their harnesses but could not budge. Drips of saliva hung from their jaws and swung like pendulums as they threw their weight against the sled's brake system, trying to get a look down into the crevice to where they could no doubt smell her. She doubted her odor was anything pleasant, but that probably only made her all the easier to sense. Rows of cruel teeth lined their mouths, glistening in the moonlight. Either one of the beasts looked happy to rip her to shreds given the chance. With luck, neither of them, nor any of the others, would ever get one.

Footsteps echoed above the barking and guttural snarling, metal on stone, the sound of Honn drawing nearer. His gait sounded uneven—his wound still affected him. If this moment marked her end, Oleja would go to the grave relishing in the knowledge that the wound she inflicted on the hunter still slowed his pace. She had dealt back to him a small fraction of the pain his kind had put her people through.

He still owed her a great debt.

Armor glimmered in the low light—the first part of him to come into view. He held one of his swords in his hand, relaxed at his side. Visor up, the pale skin of his face lay exposed. His eyes roved the darkness, searching for movement. The toes of his boots came to rest just at the edge of the drop, directly above the weakened ledge.

First, he scanned the bottom of the crevice immediately below him—a good guess, given the trail Oleja left, which indicated a wounded creature dragging itself to the edge. A fair analysis, and true of course, but while he likely expected to find her broken body crumpled dead on the ground, he was sorely mistaken. Because she was very much alive. And she was ready to end this.

He scanned to the left and right next. Hardly a moment passed before he spotted her, but Oleja's intentions were never to hide from him there at the bottom. When their eyes met, he grinned. She could tell his focus fell on her leg.

"Looks like someone took a bit of a hard fall," he said, his voice low and coursing with menace. "Where's the other one? I know he found you again after your stunt back at the city ruins." His eyes flicked to the mound of rocks behind Oleja, then up to something on the cliff face above her. He seemed to put the pieces together as amusement sparked brighter in his eyes. "Looks like he took the fall even harder."

Oleja's knuckles turned white on her bow. She breathed a heavy exhale through her nose. He had no right to speak of Pahlo in such a way. His presence pushed them to go so fast, casting caution aside as they tried to outrun him. Honn carried the fault for Pahlo's death. Now death would come to him in repayment.

Thoughts of Ude flashed in her mind as she readied to raise her bow: the old man shaking his head at her on the last day she practiced with her bow. *You cannot let your anger doom you.*

Honn still looked down at her. For only a second, she closed her eyes, releasing the anger crackling in her heart and letting it melt away as best she could. One steady breath filled her lungs, and then curled back into the dry desert air through parted lips. She opened her eyes.

"You have suffered so greatly out here in this wilderness," said Honn. "Wouldn't it have been so much easier to take my offer the day you fled? A quick trip back to my people and yours. I offered you a mercy then, greater than you could have known." His eyes narrowed; his lips pressed into a thin line. "I will not show it now."

"And neither will I."

Oleja raised her bow. Honn smirked, already raising a hand for his visor. Oleja fired.

Thunk. The arrow pierced the wooden stilt beneath the ledge, batting it aside and sending both sailing to the crevice floor. Honn got only a moment's confusion before the ground beneath him buckled and gave way.

Coyotes yelped. Honn shouted. A thundering rumble ripped through the still air, stone sliding on stone. Honn pitched forward, releasing his sword as he swung out both arms, grabbing for something, anything, to save him from plummeting to the bottom. But they came up empty, finding only open air.

When he landed head-first at the bottom, a cacophony of metal crashing down split the very earth beneath Oleja. It shredded her ears and made stars dance in her vision. Honn's sword clattered on the rocks beside him.

The chunk of the ledge that broke free came hurtling down next, crashing against the crevice walls as it fell. The two lead coyotes slipped, their claws skittering on the stone as they lost all footing and fell. Their harnesses pulled taut, and as the ground continued to give way, the next two in line slid forward to meet their companions. They yipped and howled in pain. The four dangling over the edge tugged on the straps and the rest of the team and sled lurched forward with a snap, careening over the edge, joining in the collapse. Other debris crumbled away, tearing free from the stone around it and crashing down in a massive avalanche that spread up and down the length of the crevice with each new stone that joined in the downfall of Honn. Even as he stirred, the largest chunk of the rubble struck him, crushing him beneath its weight, handing him the same demise that Pahlo met mere hours earlier.

The rocks kept coming. Oleja pulled her legs away just as a stone twice the size of her head crashed into the ground where they had been moments prior. She rolled onto her stomach and crawled in a panic away from the avalanche, closer to Pahlo's grave. Pebbles and rocks as large as her fists pelted her back and legs, sending stinging bursts of pain through her broken leg whenever one struck it. When crawling proved fruitless, she pulled her legs in and folded her hands over her head, covering her neck and skull. More stone rained down on her as she lay there, eyes pressed shut. Images of the countless cave-in victims from her village flooded her mind—neighbors, acquaintances, old smiths who gave her some of the only semi-official training she ever received, and of course, her parents. There were others too—people she never even knew the names of but whose faces simply vanished from the crowds in the days following a cave-in, never to emerge from the mines again. Trembles wracked her body. Of all the ways for death to catch her, she hated none more than the thought of being buried alive. It ranked last, sitting at the absolute bottom of the list. She refused to let it happen.

Ignoring the pain in her leg as she dragged it behind her, she kept crawling.

The roaring sounds of stone collapsing slowed and stopped. The noises came from far off, barely audible above the thunderous ringing in her ears. Cautiously, she opened one eye, then the other. Dust filled the air, and the dry, earthy smell of sand lingered. Her eyes stung as she blinked away the airborne debris.

Behind her, a massive mound of stone rubble rose up, a mountain compared to the one under which Pahlo rested. Honn's sled and coyotes rested atop it in a tangled heap. Honn was nowhere in sight.

Nothing moved.

Oleja rolled onto her back again and leaned her head against the ground. She let out a loud sigh of triumphant relief—or rather, she imagined it was loud. The ringing swallowed up all sound. Air filled her lungs in short, deep gulps as she fought through the haze to get clean air. She took a shaky breath. Honn was dead. It was over. But she still sat in the middle of the desert with a broken leg. If she could make it to the mountains, to the civilization the raiders spoke of, she stood a chance. To get there, she had another whole valley to cross, and then an unknown stretch of mountains. Dawn approached; the blue sky, bearing fewer stars now than before, made clear indication of that, though without a view of the horizon she could only guess at exactly how long she had until the sun appeared. When it rose, it would bring with it another day of heat. Time closed in on her window for escape.

Oleja gathered her things. She still had her glider—crippled as it was—her bag, and her quiver, now empty. She had her bow too, wherever it landed. In her haste to cover herself to guard against falling rocks, she dropped it. She looked around.

One limb poking out from beneath a few stones and a hill of sand helped her locate it, but when she gave it a tug only half came free in her hand. She reeled in the string, which pulled along with it the second half. Broken in her hands, she looked down at the weapon with an air of sadness. Sure, she was out of arrows, and without ammunition the bow was useless, but she had carved that bow by hand. Years she spent fine-tuning it, whittling it away and experimenting with the length of the string until she held her perfect weapon, reliable enough to shoot an eclipser through the eye without a second thought. It was the bow at her side when she started her journey. Now, the sun set on its run.

She unhooked the string and coiled it around her fingers, tucking it safely into a pocket in her bag. The limbs she left beside Pahlo's grave, joined by her quiver. Then, burdened by her gear, she struggled to her feet and leaned her weight against the side of the crevice. A long climb, made longer now by the added weight she carried, but she had no other choice.

Before, it had been a race against Honn that propelled her to the top. Now, she raced against the sun. And the sun was an awful lot harder to kill.

CHAPTER TWENTY-FIVE

Oleja collapsed on the ground, breathing hard, her lungs burning but still a mere pinch compared to the pain shooting up out of her leg. She pulled herself across the ground, away from the ledge, fearing that it may give way beneath her, especially after everything she had put the surrounding terrain through so far that evening. Two cave-ins, both caused by her—one accidental and one manufactured. She did not need to make it three.

Ringing filled her ears. Loud and high pitched, it swallowed up all other sounds in the dying night. She threw off her bag and glider and rolled onto her back to stare up at the sky. The stars faded as the sky turned to a deep blue. The rocky ground beneath her felt cool to the touch as it pressed against her exposed skin, still red and raw from her sunburn. The cool temperatures would soon flee under the light of the sun, and she'd be pushed to the limit once more—this time lacking the ability to walk. A fun day lay ahead of her. That was, if she made it through the day at all. Her chances still looked somewhat up in the air.

She cast a glance back across the crevice. A massive chunk was missing from the other side like a giant bite taken out of the ground, chewed up, and spit into the abyss below. The crater expanded beyond the bounds of her expectations. Fantastic work on her part, truly; Honn would have needed a great stroke of luck to avoid the collapse.

Quite abruptly, Oleja realized that this was her first time on the far side of the gap—the side she and Pahlo tried to quicken their route over to. Hours and hours had passed since they first approached, yet only now did she set foot on the other side. Well, not set foot exactly; she had yet to stand and didn't plan on doing so with any great haste. She'd be lucky if she managed to get to her feet and keep her balance on one leg at all. And that was before trying to cross the valley in such a manner. Hopping on one leg for the remainder of the distance sounded less dignified than crawling, though neither struck her as particularly heroic.

Slowly, her breathing returned to a normal pace, and the ringing in her ears began to fade. The clarity brought with it no genius ideas of how to reach the mountains, but it did bring something else to her attention. More curious than anything, the drowning noise faded into a different sound: an irregular, high whine. Even as the ringing dissolved into nothing, the new sound persisted. Pushing through the aches of her body, Oleja sat up and listened. It sounded again, filtering up from the bottom of the crevice. She froze.

Cautiously, making no sound, she moved closer to the edge. At the lip, she looked down.

A haze still hung in the air, blurring the bottom behind a veil of sand. Rubble layered the crevice floor. Honn's sled rested atop it all, dented and broken in places but otherwise mostly intact. The coyotes lay in a heap, their harnesses keeping them tangled together in a mess of straps and limbs.

All except one.

One coyote stood apart from the rest, pieces of its harness still attached to it but otherwise free from the wreckage. It whined as it pawed at the other coyotes and nudged them with its nose. Their heads and limbs lolled to the side as the lone survivor pushed them about, trying to wake them. Blood spattered thick across the stones made it clear the animal would not soon find success, but it kept trying. From one, to the next, to the next, cycling through the lot until it came back to the first and tried again in another round, it worked to wake its companions. Oleja watched it until a fresh bout of pain clutched her leg and she hissed through clenched teeth. The coyote looked up. The pair locked eyes.

Oleja scuttled backwards, dragging herself across the rough ground. She went for her bow before remembering its fate, then drew her knife from her belt instead. The bow would have served her well—she could kill the thing without having to get anywhere near it, risking a strike from its sharp teeth or claws. If it took her other leg out of commission, she would be thoroughly doomed—if she wasn't already. Lacking alternatives made brandishing the small blade an easy choice.

Fleeing made a poor option, of course. Doing so before only kept her at a short lead over Honn on his sled, but against a lone coyote it became an impossible feat. Even running full speed, unhindered by injury, she knew a coyote could beat her in a race. Crawling across the ground, leaving a trail of blood in her wake—the coyote could walk and still catch her without exerting itself at all. It had to be a fight.

But first the coyote needed to get out of the crevice. How good were coyotes at climbing? The cliff face on this side wasn't completely vertical either, which might aid the animal if it truly wanted to come after her. Whether coyotes could climb or not was not a question she had the time or means to find the answer to. She'd see the answer in quite apparent terms before long, one way or the other. Fearing to look back over the edge and risk coming face-to-face with the beast, she opted to remain at a distance and wait.

If the cave-in had killed Honn and all of his coyotes, she'd have taken care of the whole collection of stuff trying to kill her in one sweeping blow. Killing Honn and having to fight the coyotes would have been disastrous, but fighting one? She could do that. It was only one, and she had a knife. One alone certainly gave her better odds than fighting two or five or all eight. Even in her state—her delirious, weakened, unable-to-stand state—killing one coyote was a manageable feat.

Foolishness had made her think she could be lucky

enough to kill Honn and all eight coyotes at once. She should have planned better for a fight after the dust settled. She still got lucky, with only one survivor. Her heart pounded. She felt silly. Worry gripped her over a fight with a coyote smaller than her; she had brought eclipsers to their graves with swift shots from her bow, beings that towered over her. What made this coyote so deadly?

She didn't have her bow anymore, nor could she fight much more efficiently than brandishing a knife from where she lay on the ground. The creature itself might have been smaller, but it had every other tactical advantage. Minus the knife.

A scratching sound came from the crevice. Oleja tensed and gripped her knife tighter. A moment later, two paws grabbed at the cliff's edge. Two ears followed, then an orange snout, and then the rest of the animal, though it climbed awkwardly. It scrambled for footing, and when finally it stood by the edge of the drop, it shook some of the sand from its coat and then trained its attention on Oleja. Brown eyes stalked her. Its black nose bobbed in the air as it caught her scent. It hunkered low, brushing the lighter beige fur of its belly across the ground. Baring its fangs, it let out a low growl, and then slowly began to advance on her.

Oleja backed up, knocking against her bag and glider. She let the copper-colored blade glint in the waning moonlight. The knife caught the advancing beast's eye but did not deter it. The coyote kept coming.

Oleja sized it up. This coyote was male, and bigger than any of the wild ones she'd seen, as all of Honn's were—bred and trained to pull a sled and, if she was just unlucky enough, kill. Despite this, it crept forward on thin, bony legs, and as it moved, she thought for a moment she could see the faint shape of its ribs just beneath the skin and pelt. Though not as emaciated as the coyote that stole her jackrabbit, this one certainly could not be deemed healthy or well-fed. A wave of short-lived relief crashed over her. Killing the animal became at least marginally easier if it was anywhere near as starved as her. When she finished clinging to that small boon, she refocused on the approaching fight.

The coyote growled again; a low, rumbling sound broken up by quick huffs. Oleja held her knife out at arm's length, still hoping the coyote would suddenly gain some keener awareness of the properties of blades and shy away. It showed no such breakthrough. Or maybe it, too, had sized *her* up and determined it could win. They'd just have to see who triumphed in the end.

Unless she offered it a peace.

The thought came from nowhere. It sounded like something Ude would say to her, or perhaps Pahlo. The moment's confusion made her falter and she lowered the knife an inch. The coyote barked, a shrill call that sounded almost painful and echoed back off the hilltops. Oleja made up her mind in a second. She kept her eyes trained on the beast as she reached back and felt around in her bag. She tore off a piece of the salted meat from her rations. After a quick prayer that she did not make the dumbest mistake of her life, wasting her meager supply of food on a creature that already had its eyes on its next meal, she tossed the scrap to the animal. It came to rest near the coyote's front paws.

The coyote flinched as it watched Oleja throw something in its direction, but then it bowed its head and sniffed at the meat, never breaking eye contact with Oleja. The food disappeared in seconds, chewed once by sharp fangs and then swallowed in a single gulp. The coyote continued to advance, though even slower now. Oleja's stomach lurched. Fight it was.

But when the coyote came within a few feet of her, it hunkered lower and then lay down on the ground. It rested its head between its paws, nose pointed towards her, eyes glued to her bag. The situation became clear after a moment, in which Oleja risked a quick glance backwards to be sure it didn't focus on some new threat approaching. Fortunately, only her bag lay behind her—one more fight she could indeed win should the need arise, so long as victory didn't hinge on her lifting it again.

Food served as one of her most precious belongings, but Oleja weighed her options and deemed it a worthy cause. If she could stave off the coyote with another bit of meat, it certainly resulted in a better outcome than the beast pouncing and killing her. She ripped off another small chunk and leaned forward to toss it gently in the direction of the coyote. This one landed another several inches in front of the animal's snout. Rather than stand and take the few steps, the coyote wriggled through the sand until it reached the treat, and then gobbled it up just as quickly as the last.

It lay there for a moment and watched her, then took another few cautious steps in her direction. It whined, looking to the bag and then back to her. Oleja shifted to the side to hide her bag from view. Spectacular—in trying to deter an attack, she only provoked it to fight her for her food.

But the coyote did not. Instead, it came up next to her and settled back down on the ground, though it never moved its eyes from her. Oleja squirmed in discomfort. She wanted to keep the thing from being hostile, yes, but she didn't know how close she wanted it to her. It could still jump on her in an instant and sink its teeth into her throat. She kept her knife in her hand, though she laid it on her thigh, no longer using it for failed attempts at intimidation.

The coyote poked its nose against her right leg. Cold and wet, it dampened the fine layer of dusty sand that coated her, and when it drew back its snout the film of dirt stuck to it. It nuzzled her again, and then licked her a few times. Oleja almost shot to her feet as her heart thundered and shivers raced through her body. What was it doing, tasting her? Trying to determine whether or not she'd make a good meal after all?

No hostility shone through its actions. Either it

possessed a fantastic talent for masking its intentions, or it truly didn't intend to eat her. In her exhaustion, Oleja wanted to believe the latter.

Its scratchy tongue stung her sunburn, but pushing the animal away seemed a good way to anger it and get bitten.

"Sorry, I can't spare any more of my food. I'm going to need it... I hope," she said aloud, though she didn't quite know why. Delirium, perhaps. The coyote looked up at her, and then laid its head back down.

Deeming it safe enough, Oleja turned her head and looked out across the valley below to where the mountains waited as great black silhouettes in the darkness. Too far to crawl. Unless she could fashion some sort of crutch, she stood no chance of walking. And her surroundings offered no good crutch-constructing materials—even her glider didn't have wooden pieces long enough for that. What a sick joke to have come so far in the wrong direction seeking refuge only to die when at last the end came in sight. In about an hour, when the sun rose, the heat would only make the situation worse. According to her food and water rations, she had about a day left before things got critical— only enough time to cross the valley in full health, and that seemed fairly impossible. She couldn't just heal her leg in an hour.

Her eyes drifted back to the crevice. She could make it her final resting place—the bottom, just next to Pahlo. Giving up promised to be less painful than trying, and failing, to drag her weakened body across the last leg of desert, suffering from her broken leg, starving, dehydrated, and burnt to a crisp under the hot sun. Out there, she'd become food for something—vultures, coyotes, or maybe some worse beast. Once again, her options were not over how she wanted to live, but how she preferred to die. No matter how far she went from the eclipser camp—from being a prisoner in a hole—no matter how much freedom she seemed to find, none of it changed her situation in the end. She never truly became free of anything, she just found new ways she could choose to die, and not one of them made a hero's death. Not one was worthy to claim the life of a skyborn.

But she wasn't skyborn. Or, she was, but it didn't mean anything. Even skyborn children came about with no particular rarity. Whatever high she had been clinging to all her life, it was all a farce. She was no less ordinary than any other, and she'd meet as ordinary a death as any of her people who got buried namelessly in crowds deep beneath the ground where they should never have been to begin with.

She couldn't go anywhere. Once she died, the coyote at her side would probably just eat her and then trot happily away to go live a truly free life unburdened by Honn or the other eclipsers. No broken leg could keep it back, and with its stomach full from feasting on her corpse, it could make it across the valley with no problem. It could do all the things she couldn't.

Oleja froze. Her racing thoughts slammed to a halt. That was it.

The coyote could cross the desert—no wounds held it

back, and with some food and water, it could make the trip that she couldn't. Hitched to a sled, it might just be able to pull Oleja to safety.

But one problem remained: she barely had enough food left to fill one stomach, let alone two. Giving the coyote what it needed to fuel a trek across the valley meant leaving nothing for herself. She'd be taking a blind gamble. The plan meant making her entire life dependent on the coyote's ability to cross the valley, dragging her to the mountains no matter her state of health as she went without food or water for the entirety of the day. It promised no heroism, only the curse of faith and dependency. She hated the plan. But it just might be her only chance.

If she ate her food and drank her water, it didn't change the fact that she couldn't move on her own. No rations could heal her leg, only the time she didn't have. The coyote, on the other hand... all it needed were those rations. But could it pull her on its own? And how did she plan to get the sled out of the crevice? Holes and flaws riddled the plan, not the least of which was that if even one aspect of it failed, she would have given all of her food and water over to an animal that then had to do her bidding to keep her from dying when it, alone, could survive fine. What kept it from running off with a full belly just as soon as she had no more food to give it?

Once again, her choice lay between two paths that likely ended in death; one allowed her to die on a full stomach, while the other sent her to the grave on an empty one. Neither was pleasant, but with a deep breath, she cast her thoughts to Ude, and then to Pahlo. She knew exactly what advice they'd both spout at her. A slightly higher likelihood of survival waited down one of the two paths. She just had to let herself be saved.

It wasn't time to be the hero. It was time to live.

CHAPTER TWENTY-SIX

Shifting away from the coyote made nothing short of a terrifying experience. She prayed the animal wouldn't attack as she half-crawled, half-pulled herself away, putting her weakened state on full display—an easy target for sure, save for the knife she wielded. The coyote didn't move from where it lay, curled up, eyes shut, presumably asleep. Moving made Oleja realize the extent of the heaviness in her limbs and how fiercely she longed for sleep. But now was not the time for it. She grabbed a coil of rope from her bag, one she took from Pahlo's things, and went to the crevice's edge. She dropped the rope over the side. It landed in a heap amongst the rubble. Burdened only by her knife and the clothes on her back, she began her descent.

In all honesty, she was fed up with climbing up and down the crevice walls. Falling down once had been plenty, and having to climb back out afterwards was more than enough. But then climbing back down, and then back up, and now down again—and soon back up—drew on energy she didn't even know she possessed. As soon as the opportunity presented itself, she planned to sleep for a full day straight. With Honn no longer at large, sleep could come to her unbound by worries at last, no longer plagued by fears of waking to find an eclipser dragging her away. So long as the sleep she found at the end of her path wasn't the endless slumber of death, the work would be worth it.

At the bottom, she took a moment to breathe, but beyond that brief pause she wasted no more time. She scooped up the coil of rope and went to the sled. Before, she hadn't cared for the shape of the vehicle after its tumble into the pit, but now she looked it over more critically. Fortunately, the frame seemed more or less intact, minus a dent in one of the two runners. Honn's belongings lay strewn about, with many of them buried alongside their owner. Oleja took a moment to look for food or water but found nothing. The time and energy she'd expend searching through the rubble and excavating the rocks in search of whatever supply he carried would likely be counteracted by the limited amount she found—if she found any at all and if she verified it both edible and safe for humans. Determining that the eclipser carried nothing useful to her—save perhaps the crossbow, which now lay entombed below at least a ton of stone—she drew her knife and cut the bag from the sled in an effort to lighten it. The less weight she had to pull up out of the crevice, the better.

She tied one end of the rope around the frontmost bar of

the sled, and then tied the other around her waist. Then, knife in hand, she moved to the harnesses.

Sticky blood spattered the leather straps. She tried not to look at the heap of carnage. Where one coyote's body ended and the next one began was often hard to tell, as blood-soaked fur seemed a constant across it all. A quick survey confirmed none of the others clung to even the faintest spark of life. It seemed the lone survivor found luck beyond likelihood. And, just maybe, so did she.

With a few quick strokes, she cut through the leather straps that still bound the corpses to the sled, though she left one harness intact and joined to the body of the vehicle. The remaining harness still contained the broken body of a coyote, and so began a gruesome task. The limbs of the creature moved relatively freely, appearing to be dislocated or broken in places. Getting the head out of the tangle of straps proved trickier, but she managed after some prodding. Soon, the coyote carcass fell away and the harness came free, leaving the sled no longer weighed down by the carnage of her own making. Fresh blood stained her hands even darker red than before. She wiped them clean as best she could and then returned to the crevice wall.

One last climb, that was all she had to do. Two climbs down to the bottom and three to the top seemed absurd in her condition, but she had come too far down the path to turn back now.

Sand clung to her blood-coated fingers and made her grip slick on the stone. A few times she slipped when searching for handholds but caught herself each time. She fell into a rhythm: right hand, left hand, right leg. Right hand, left hand, right leg. The rope dangling behind her grew heavier the higher she got as it uncoiled and rose into the air behind her. When she threw herself over the top and lay panting on the ground, the relief helped instill a new surge of hope in her, but it slipped away quickly as her thoughts turned to the next step of her plan, the part that truly put her dwindling energy to the test.

A few tugs on the rope proved more useful for pulling her body closer to the edge than for pulling the sled up into the air. A second attempt made it rock back and forth and budge an inch or two. The metal grated on the stone and shrieked as it shifted, but it never lifted off the ground, only settled back into position after a moment. Oleja, on the other hand, breathed heavily as she looked down at the sled in frustration.

An outcropping of stone jutted up from the ground just behind her. She pushed herself over to it and wound around behind, the rope growing taut around her waist but allowing the movement with just enough give. On the other side of the stone, she lay back and braced her right leg against the side. And then she pulled.

Shrieks split the air, this time accompanied by a chorus of cracking and shifting as she felt the sled move across the crevice closer to the wall. Another yank and it seemed to lift off the ground, hitting the wall with a *clang*. Stars danced in her eyes. Her head spun. Oleja loosened her grip and the sled hit the bottom once more. This was useless. She was too weak to pull the sled out.

Options swarmed her mind, none of them good. She could take apart the sled and haul it up in manageable chunks, but that required a trip climbing down and back up for each piece, which she felt equally too weak for. Aside from carrying the individual pieces, she could use more rope to tie up each and then bring all of the other ends up, pulling them to the top one by one. But she didn't have more rope, and that plan still required another trip down into the crevice, which also pushed beyond her limits. She could construct her own sled up at the top, but of what materials? Or she could get the coyote to help her pull—but she barely even had faith in it to refrain from eating her; it seemed unlikely that the coyote wanted to help her drag the sled from the crevice—a sled it had spent a good deal of time bound to, probably against its will. And just because she wanted it to do something didn't mean she could get it to. Even when it came time to direct it towards the mountains, she just hoped it knew what to do. She didn't know the first thing about tending to animals; that was Pahlo's skill.

She had one option—the one she already sat in the middle stages of: pull the whole sled up to the top as she initially planned. It was that or die in the desert.

She took one deep breath, two, three, and then pulled together all the strength within her. The sled lifted off the ground again as she grabbed the rope hand-over-hand, reeling it in. She had to get it to the top. Her determination had never known limits, and she couldn't start boxing it up now.

She pulled with her right hand, then her left hand.

She was Oleja Raseari, skyborn.

Right hand, left hand.

So maybe her birth wasn't a badge of fated heroism. Maybe the sky didn't make her special.

Right hand, left hand.

But she was still Oleja, skyborn daughter of Rasea and Uwei.

Right, left.

And she got to decide what that meant.

Right, left.

And she had made up her mind.

Right, left.

She knew what it meant.

Right, left.

It meant she was the hero of her people.

She was going to get out of the desert. She was going to save them.

Right, left.

With one final surge of strength she pulled the rope and the sled landed on the ground with a crash like the sky splitting apart. The coyote perked its ears up. Oleja flopped onto the ground and threw her arms out to her sides. Her lungs burned. Her arms ached. She felt like her body fell slowly through deep water. But she had a sled now.

Stars blinked out one by one. From her place on the ground, Oleja watched them go. She gave herself a moment's rest, but then pushed herself back up. There was still work to be done.

She dragged the sled another few feet away from the edge—much easier now that its runners sat on the ground and she wasn't trying to lift the full weight of it up through the air. When it came to rest where she wanted it, she grabbed her bag and got to work. The single coyote on its own couldn't pull the sled meant to be drawn by eight even with all of Honn's supplies removed and with a lighter, starved human on board in place of an eclipser in full metal armor. The sled needed to be as light as possible—the lighter she could make it, the faster and farther the coyote could go. Everything but the barest essentials had to be stripped away.

She took off the metal bar Honn held while riding first. The avalanche bent it out of shape and snapped one side off, making it easy to finish the job. Next, she tore apart the braking system. Stopping found no place in her plan—only going, as fast as possible, until they reached the mountains. The whole platform at the front for loading gear and other items went next. Canvas, wood, and metal fell away as she severed tethers with her knife, bashed away bars with rocks, and unhooked various fasteners with her tools. Every discarded piece of scrap got tossed into a heap off to the side, and soon the parts removed towered in a mass larger than what remained. Oleja took that as a good sign but kept working.

Last to go were the boards that formed the platform on which the driver stood. Removing all of them left her with nowhere to ride, so she pried up every other instead, creating a precarious, gap-filled floor on which one wrong move promised to pitch her off the sled entirely. When she finished, only the bare bones of a sled sat before her. A quick job of bending the dented runner back into shape through a complex and precise method involving her fist and a big rock completed the job, and then the sled was ready to go.

From her bag she pulled a bit of the salted meat. Immediately, the coyote perked up and came trotting over. She dropped the treat to the ground and then, after a moment of hesitation, took the coyote's broken harness in her hands and slid her knife through a few of the straps. It fell away and the coyote shook off the rest. Thankfully, it seemed grateful, and given that it could have reacted one of two ways to Oleja putting a knife near its body, she regarded it with equal gratitude. With another bit of meat in her hand, she led the coyote around to the harness at the front of the sled. When they neared it, the animal shied away. Oleja bit her lip.

"Come on... please? This is the only way I'm getting out of here," she said, her voice hoarse. The coyote didn't seem to comprehend. Oleja tossed it the meat and then grabbed another piece.

Cautiously, the coyote approached. Oleja let it eat as she made quick and gentle work of fastening the harness to its body. She scooped up her things and took a seat on what remained of the driver's platform.

The need to travel as light as possible meant making a

few hard decisions. Her bag she had to keep. It had been with her through far too much already, and tinkering was the only thing she knew to use in order to keep her hands busy while she sat to think. If she ran into a problem, something in the bag could come in handy. It stayed with her.

She sighed as she turned her attention to her glider. It had already lost the ability to function after she dismantled one limb to serve as a pickaxe and stilt. Without the limb, the rest became useless, and though she could repair it easily, it just added more dead weight in the meantime. After a moment of pause, she laid it on the ground. Only her bag with her tools and materials, her food and water rations, and her knife remained on her person. With her gear set, she turned her attention to the coyote hitched to the front of the sled. It looked back at her with curious eyes.

In her bag, she closed her hand around the bundle that contained all of her remaining food. As soon as she gave it to the coyote, it'd be gone, scarfed down in seconds, and she'd be left with nothing. If this plan failed, that failure left her without food or water. She had to be sure of what she wanted to do before she enacted the last step, because after she did, there was no going back.

It would work. And even if it didn't, it was her only shot. She couldn't get out of the desert alone. To survive, she needed help, even if that help came from this coyote— little more than a wild animal and dead-set on killing her not long ago. Living meant putting her trust in it to get her out of the desert in once piece.

Slowly, with reluctance still stalling her hand, she withdrew the bundle. She unfolded the corners until the cloth fell away, revealing the last of her food. The coyote perked up and panted, its tongue lolling about as saliva dripped from its maw.

"Here you go," she said, setting the bundle down in front of it. "Don't let me down. Get us both out of here."

In moments the coyote gobbled down the food in its entirety. She held out her canteen next and emptied it into the animal's mouth. She took a sip from her last semi-full waterskin—Pahlo's—and then gave the coyote some from there as well. A few gulps remained. She stowed the waterskin back in her bag.

"Uh, that way," she said, pointing ahead to the mountains. The sled lurched forward as the coyote started off at a run. Oleja almost toppled from the platform but managed to hold on as they took off down the hill. Thankfully, the coyote got the message, because she didn't know how else to direct it. Maybe eclipsers could all speak coyote.

No, that was a stupid thought. Delirium gripped her tighter and tighter as the hours went by. She curled up on the platform, tucking her braid over her neck and under her chin to keep it from getting caught on anything below the sled as it sped across the ground. Bumping over obstacles hurt her injured leg. Pain swirled like white rapids around her, pulling her down. She glanced at the sky. Dark blue gave way to streaks of pale gold as the sun neared the horizon, though it had yet to arrive and bring about the new day. Oleja's eyes drifted shut. She was on her way to the mountains. There, she could finally rest, and after she recovered, she could make a plan to go back to her village and save her people.

Consciousness visited Oleja in ripples throughout the ride. One moment she looked ahead at the expanse of sand and in the next she dreamt, though never deeply. Fits of rest found her and restored some strength to her limbs, but it was sapped just as quickly by the heat of the sun as it rose and cast the earth into fiery heat. The sled rattled on, bouncing and shaking across rocky patches and gliding smoothly in the sand. A few times Oleja awoke in a start fueled by fears that she was falling off the sled, but each time she awoke to find herself still firmly atop the platform, curled around her bag as she hugged it close to her chest. During one such awakening, she bolted awake to see the sand passing by slowly beneath her. She rolled over through flares of pain and looked to the coyote.

It trod through the sand, kicking up waves as its paws padded across the loose earth. Its tongue hung low from its jaw. Huffs filled the hot, still air as the animal panted heavily in the day's heat. A quick glance skyward told Oleja the hour lingered around midday. Despite the heat and the burden it hauled, the coyote kept going.

The mountains loomed nearer, and features of the slopes presented themselves—trees tinged with green and silver-brown cliff faces.

Oleja grabbed her waterskin and leaned forwards on the sled. The coyote slowed and stopped, and when it turned its head back, she helped it gulp down the remainder of the water. Her own mouth felt as dry as the sand around her; her tongue stuck to the roof of her mouth. But she saved nothing for herself, letting the coyote finish off every last drop. With the water gone, the coyote took off at a run once more, picking up speed as the drink brought fresh energy to its limbs. Oleja dropped the empty waterskin back into her bag and curled up as they raced across the sand.

"Thank you," she muttered aloud to the animal. It needed a name, something heroic. It felt too early to call it "Pahlo," given how fresh his death was. She didn't want to name it Ude either, since the old man still lived.

"I'll call you Tor," she said, though the words hardly seemed to come from her mouth. It felt like her tongue had jumped free and lay somewhere in the sand far behind her. "It's the name of an old hero from my village," she added.

And then sleep took her once more.

CHAPTER TWENTY-SEVEN

A cloud cradled her, or so it seemed; the waking world came upon her lazily and in fragments. She couldn't remember ever being so comfortable in her life. Cold air kissed her skin. Oleja shifted and stretched out her arms as she awoke. Blinking once, then twice, the world came into focus.

Silky blankets swaddled her, and she realized after a moment that she lay in a bed—the finest bed she had ever slept upon. Nothing like the scratchy cotton blankets, canvas cots, or straw mattresses from her village, these blankets were smooth and light, crisp white in color unmarred by stains of dirt and blood and worse things. Heavily-padded plush made up the mattress beneath her. She sank an inch into its surface.

Stone walls surrounded her—five, all etched with curving designs. The stone was grey and cut into polished blocks rimmed with expertly-applied mortar. The room looked as if part of it intended to form a square, with the wall opposite her and those to either side complying in the design while the fourth and fifth walls deviated from that shape and bulged outwards, turning what would be the fourth wall into a pointed addition. Her bed rested within the intersection. The headboard fit perfectly into the corner, making the bed longer in the middle than on either side. Windows looked out to her left and right, free of glass panes or bars or wooden latticework. Sunlight shone in— not harsh and deadly like the desert sun, but warm and pleasant, an aspect of it she had never felt before. Wind entered through the windows as well, floating in one and out the other, a gentle breeze that carried aromas entirely unfamiliar to her. They smelled almost earthy, but less dry. Glancing out to the world beyond, she guessed it was the smell of trees, though strange ones. One large trunk stood a short distance away, laden with thick fur of dark green and taller than any scraggly, prickly tree she saw in the desert. Alongside the smells, the wind brought in a chill that made her shiver.

Her black hair cascaded down the pillows—long, clean, untangled, and freed from her typical braid. She almost never let her hair down.

Movement in the corner of the room caught her eye and she turned. Tor—the coyote—lay curled up atop a round pillow on the floor. His head rose high above his shoulders, ears standing tall, his whole body alert. When he saw her turn to look at him, he jumped up and crossed the floor in a single bound, leaping onto the bed and colliding with her side. Oleja uttered a muted "oof," but it was drowned out by the excited yips from Tor as he licked her face. She tried to push him off, but weakness still burdened her limbs and she struggled to move his determined and bouncing form off of her. After a moment she gave up, though the licking remained off-putting. It seemed good-natured, so she allowed it.

Footsteps came from somewhere outside and Oleja looked up. Through a door in the corner opposite where Tor had been sleeping, a young woman entered. Her skin was pale, just like some of the raiders, but even more shocking was the halo of fire-red hair atop her head. It framed her face in curls, detracting from her other features, though Oleja did notice a smattering of spots across her face adorning a small, upturned nose.

"Oh, lovely, you're awake!" said the woman. "I heard the dog barking and I hoped to see as much. My name is Maloia, I've been seeing to you for the past few days since your arrival. What is your name, dear?"

"I'm Oleja. Oleja Raseari," she responded. Her voice was hoarse, and the words came out in more of a sandy growl than anything. She coughed. Maloia hurried over and picked up a cup of water from a table at her bedside. Cold water graced her lips, contained in the clearest cup of glass Oleja had ever seen. She gulped down the whole cup before handing it back to Maloia, empty.

"Oleja. That's a very pretty name. You must be from the south."

"West, mostly," said Oleja. "Where am I, exactly?"

Maloia smiled. "You're in Ahwan, dear."

"What is 'Ahwan'?"

Maloia gave her a curious look. "It's the city."

"What's a city?"

Brushing her hand across the blankets to smooth them, Maloia sat down. "No worries, dear, we did suspect you might have had some head trauma when you arrived. You will be better soon enough, though."

Oleja didn't know how best to explain the reality of the situation to this woman, so she bit her tongue and let it go; she'd get her answers later. If she had to guess, it seemed she'd made it to the civilization in the mountains—a "city" if she used the term right. Honn used it once as well, referencing the ruins with the towers. Relief filled her to the brim; tension melted off of her in an instant. She was alive. She made it.

She laid her head back against the soft pillows. Tor nuzzled her arm and curled up beside her.

"A few days, you said?" asked Oleja.

"Yes," answered Maloia with a nod. "You were discovered by a band of scouts near our border, pulled on a sled by your coyote, though you were unconscious and badly wounded. We have your sled, of course, though it looks to have seen better days. We gave the dog a bath, too. Does he have a name?"

"Tor."

Maloia smiled and reached across Oleja to scratch Tor behind the ears. "You're lucky to have a companion so loyal. Anyways, yes, you have been here for a few days now. We made sure you've been getting food and water and medical care, though until now you've been unresponsive. Quite the toll you've been through."

"You could say that," said Oleja dryly.

Maloia patted her arm. "Well, if you need anything at all, I will be around to fetch it for you. Let me start by getting you some more water… and you'd probably like some food too, yes? You haven't eaten anything solid in days." She picked up the cup and started towards the door.

"Thank you," said Oleja, sitting up in her bed, "but that's all right, I can get things on my own." She moved to stand.

"Oh! Hold on, one moment," said Maloia. She put the cup down on a shelf by the door and grabbed something from the corner. When she turned back around, she held two crutches in her hands.

Oleja waved her off. "I don't need those, I'm fine."

Maloia gave her a puzzled look, but her expression quickly shifted to one of hesitation, like words sat upon her tongue and she only had to speak them, yet hadn't.

"Um… well, I don't know if you will find that to be the case," Maloia said, selecting her words slowly. She advanced with the crutches.

Oleja threw her legs over the edge of the bed. The cobbled stone floor was cold under her foot.

Her right foot.

She pulled the blanket aside. Her knees hugged the edge of the mattress, but just below her left knee her leg stopped. The entirety of her calf was gone. White bandages shrouded the base of what remained, no more than two inches past her kneecap. They wound up to her thigh where a knot tied the ends of the wrappings off neatly. No blood stained the bandages—they looked fresh.

She flexed her knee a few times. Sore, but functional. The feeling was an odd one—moving her knee as if she lifted her leg into the air was now a jarringly easy movement, like the feeling in one's shoulders after shrugging off a heavy burden. Except that burden was her leg, and she needed it to walk. She needed it to return to her village and save her people.

Nothing would hold her back. Not now. Not even this.

Tor crawled over and laid his snout across her thigh. Oleja glanced around the room. Her tinkering bag lay on the floor just beside Tor's bed. She looked up to where Maloia stood hesitantly with the crutches.

"Actually, if you're grabbing things..." started Oleja, gesturing to the corner. Maloia followed her gaze. "Could you get my bag?"

It seemed she had more work to do than she thought.

ABOUT THE AUTHOR

Cameron Bolling is an author and college student living in New Hampshire. He can be found in the woods, or not at all.

For more information visit cameronbolling.com

Made in the USA
San Bernardino,
CA